"Kiss me," she pleaded. "Kiss me the way you did that first night."

Kitty's mouth sought his. Again she felt Max waver, holding himself back. But she wrapped her arms around his neck and kissed him hungrily until she felt him respond. Until his lips opened and his tongue darted in to taste the sweetness of her mouth.

"Don't you feel it?" she murmured. "This force that's drawing us together? Perhaps you don't remember. But surely you can feel its power. As if it's telling us this was meant to be."

She could feel him fight to hold himself aloof, even as his body responded to the touch of her mouth against his. He pushed her back, looking down into her face.

"You *are* dangerous," he growled.

"But if it wasn't dangerous," she whispered, "it wouldn't be any fun. . . ."

My One and Only

Katherine O'Neal

BANTAM BOOKS

NEW YORK TORONTO LONDON SYDNEY AUCKLAND

MY ONE AND ONLY

A Bantam Book / January 2000

ISBN 0-553-58121-X

Published simultaneously in the United States and Canada

Bantam Books are published by Bantam Books, a division of Random
House, Inc. Its trademark, consisting of the words "Bantam Books" and
the portrayal of a rooster, is Registered in U.S. Patent and Trademark
Office and in other countries. Marca Registrada. Bantam Books, 1540
Broadway, New York, New York 10036.

PRINTED IN THE UNITED STATES OF AMERICA

OPM 10 9 8 7 6 5 4 3 2 1

For
Ramsey and Victoria

I have loved you through each long season,
Through the span of each day, each meter of the
night, that I have wasted, alone.
In darkness I have lain awake
Filling the hours with the sound of your voice, the
image of your body, until desire lives within me.
Mere memory of you awakens my flesh, brings
singing to limbs that are numb without you.
I am impoverished without you.
Thus into the darkness I call: Where have you
gone, houri of my heart?
Why have you gone from him who could teach the
sun of burning?
Who is more constant than is dawn to day?
I hear no beloved voice answer and I, too well,
know how much I am alone.

ANONYMOUS

PROLOGUE

A rough hand, clamped against her mouth, muffled
Kitty's scream. She bolted awake, her eyes dart-
ing in alarm, frantically seeking to orient herself
in the darkness. Her heart beating a staccato rhythm,
she tried to wrench herself free, but the hand tightened
against her mouth.

"It's me, Baji," a soft voice said. "Don't be afraid."

Her terror subsided and she relaxed into his arms.
Cameron! He was only thirteen to her eleven years, yet
his confidence, his assurance, his undaunting bravery,
had sustained her though this ordeal.

She reached up and removed his hand from her
mouth. "I'm not afraid."

"Something's happened," he whispered urgently. "A

rider's come with news from the outside. Try not to wake the others."

Clustered around them were the slumbering bodies of ten other children, all younger. Together they were the victims of the most despicable kidnapping in the three-hundred-year history of the British Raj in India. Kitty and Cameron picked their way through the curled, prone figures tangled in their blankets on the ground, hearing nothing but the soft cadence of their breathing.

The night was warm, the sky cloudless and filled with stars. The air carried with it the distinct flowery aroma of the hill country of South Rajasthan. Land of kings. Land of the Rajputs, India's fiercest and most noble warriors, a people who'd never willingly accepted foreign rule. Who'd never submitted to the Mughals and who, even now, were simmering in rebellion against the British overlords and their maharaja puppets. A people so proud that throughout history their code of chivalry had demanded *jauhar*—mass ritual suicide—rather than bow to an alien master.

Crouching low, Kitty and Cameron found their way to a promontory overlooking their captors' campfire. Below them, facing each other across the fire, were two men the children knew well: the bandit chieftain, Haghan Mukti, and his lieutenant, Ngar Mahabar. Both men sat erect and proud, both sported bushy, soup-strainer mustaches, trademark of the Rajput warrior. Their hushed voices carried softly in the night, barely audible to the eavesdroppers. They spoke in Rajasthani, which the children—born and raised in this land—understood almost as well as they did English.

"The British resident refuses to negotiate," Ngar

told his leader. "He will not even see us until the children are returned."

"Then the children die."

Kitty clutched Cameron's hand with a small gasp, but he merely put his finger to his lips in a gesture that demanded silence.

"Die most foully," Haghan continued in a fierce growl. "We will show the sahibs that we mean business."

Ngar leaned across the fire. "I beg you to reconsider this," he hissed. "This is not an act that's worthy of our people. It will mobilize the might of the British Empire and bring down upon us the wrath of the entire world."

Haghan leapt to his feet. "The officials of this mighty British Empire have systematically looted Rajasthan for the past decade!" he snarled, pacing angrily before the fire. The flames flicked across his face, etching his features in fury so the scar along his cheek seemed to take on a fearsome life of its own. "We've made one appeal after another to Calcutta, where the viceroy refuses our right to even make a grievance." He jabbed an accusatory finger at his compatriot. "This was your idea. You said taking the children would force them to negotiate. We have been sitting idle for three months and they have not budged an inch. Stubborn British curs. This is on *your* head. *You* miscalculated."

"Still," said Ngar, rising in his leader's wake, "they're good children. It is not their fault that—"

"Many good children will die before India is free."

"The miscalculation is mine. Take my life. Let the children go."

"You're too valuable to me. They're not. Besides which, killing the children will force them to acknowledge us. But I will make one more attempt. The viceroy himself must agree to meet me and hear our grievances in three days' time or I swear before Shiva that I will make good on my promise: twelve small heads staked to poles on the Grand Trunk Road."

Three months had passed since the band of Rajput horsemen had swept into the schoolyard at Jaipur, snatching a dozen British children in the midst of play. Kitty heard the screams an instant before she felt herself lifted and flung onto the front of a galloping horse. The next thing she knew, they were clattering through the streets of town toward the desert beyond, the panicked screeches of the teachers ringing in her ears as they ran after them in vain. For hours they rode, flying across the desert sands like a marauding horde, stopping for nothing, not rest, not water, not food. Until they reached this remote hideout in the rugged foothills of Mount Abu.

Kitty had been as terrified as all the rest. But she'd found solace in Cameron Flemming, son of the British resident. Two years her senior, he'd been a shadowy figure in the schoolyard—a tall, dark boy who'd kept to himself. As she'd lain awake that first night, shivering on her pallet beneath a vast and menacing sky, Cameron had braved the wrath of the guards to creep to her and whisper, "I need your help. We have to keep the little ones calm." He'd laid out a plan that had given her a sense of purpose, and kept her sane. He had a gift that he shared with them all—that of turning terror into excitement, of molding uncertainty into endless possibility. He gave them hope. And astonishingly, he made their grim ordeal seem like an escapade from Kipling or *The Thousand and One Nights*. He took a frightened band of children and infused them with a sense of self-reliance and sometimes, through the sorcery of his imagination, even fun.

As the two eldest, Kitty and Cameron had become, in effect, the guardians of the family of young captives; comforting the children at night, demanding a goat to provide milk for the youngest of the brood, bolstering spirits with games and stories. Telling them in hushed voices that they were the Swiss Family Robinson, ship-wrecked on a Pacific island, living a life of storybook adventure, until their inevitable rescue.

Out of this, a rare and intimate friendship was born. Like two souls thrust into the drama and danger of war, Cameron and Kitty quickly discovered a special bond that linked them on a level that wouldn't have been possible had it developed in normal circumstances. They became a team—Kitty the candle and Cameron the flame. They began to think as one. Often, Cameron would finish her sentence or Kitty would nod in understanding before the words had left his lips. At night, lying beside him beneath the stars, Kitty felt her heart beat to the rhythm of Cameron's breath. Had she been older, the word "love" might have sprung to her mind. As it was, all she knew was that in a strange way, she'd never felt so complete.

This odd contentment, however, was marred by her realization that the leader of their captors, Haghan, was growing increasingly frustrated and violent. Every time he left the camp, no doubt to push his demands, he always returned in a rage. Often he would slap the children for no apparent reason, or kick them if they wandered into his path. One day he seemed to reach his limit. In a fury, he stormed through the startled camp, bellowing, "Enough! I will show them I mean business." He suddenly grabbed Kitty, who was closest, and carried her down to the river. Dangling her upside down by the ankles, he suspended her over a grotto teeming with crocodiles. As they snapped their vicious jaws, straining for her, the man dipped her low, almost within reach, dunking her again and again, tormenting the beasts in a sneering tone. "Here's a tasty British morsel for you."

Kitty was so petrified, she couldn't even bring herself to scream. She heard the smaller children call, "Cameron! Cameron!" Below her, the gnashing teeth were now only inches from her face.

As Haghan raised her up high for a final dunk, a force came from out of nowhere and knocked them both to the ground. Cameron had thrown himself into Haghan, pummeling him with his fists as Kitty scampered away. But he was only a boy. Haghan recovered swiftly and proceeded to release all his pent-up frustration by thrashing Cameron senseless. But his fury had been vented and Cameron's unselfish act had saved Kitty's life.

That night, as she was watching over Cameron as he slept, Ngar, the chieftain's more kindly second in command, squatted beside her beneath the shadow of the towering promontory wall.

"He shouldn't have done that," Kitty objected in a bitter tone. "It wasn't fair."

Ngar regarded her thoughtfully. "Were you frightened?"

She'd been more frightened even than during the
initial kidnapping. But she glared at him, too proud to
admit it.

"Listen well, little one. You may think of yourself as
being British, but it is well known that your grandmother was Rajputana. She was one of our most noble
princesses."

Kitty was aware of her Anglo-Indian heritage. Her
grandfather, the famed General Skinner, had married
four Rajputana princesses. One of their daughters, Sita,
had in turn married Kitty's father, Reginald Fontaine,
and had died giving birth to her. But that heritage
seemed remote to her. She'd been raised by her English
father, who rarely spoke of his half-Indian wife.

Kitty's Indian blood didn't show in her dark auburn
hair, green eyes, or fair skin. It was the shape of the eyes
that told the tale, the aura of otherworldliness about
her, the pride of her carriage even at a tender age.
Rajputs were known across India for their pride and
their regal bearing.

Ngar spoke softly now, his words intended for her
ears alone. "Much time will pass, I'm afraid, before this
situation is resolved. Therefore I will fill it by acquaint-
ing you with a part of that heritage that will be most
valuable to you. If you listen, and learn well, you will
never have cause to be afraid again."

In the weeks that followed, during the numerous
absences of the ever-watchful Haghan, Ngar spent
hours each day instructing her in what he called the
ancient Rajput secrets of survival. It wasn't long before

Cameron, fascinated by what she was learning, asked if he could join in. Kitty began to relish the time the three of them spent together. Once Ngar felt they'd learned the basics, he taught them what his own Rajput master had taught him: the sacred art of stealth. How to blend into the landscape so that not even an animal could detect their presence. How to scale the most precarious heights without a tinge of dizziness or fear. How to seemingly disappear into thin air, leaving no trace.

"A true Rajput master can do things not even the greatest yogis can. Things that seem to defy the laws of nature. Move objects by the force of will. Cloud superstitious minds so that they see what he wants them to. Scale great heights with the ease and agility of a cat. Skills that seem miraculous but can be learned with infinite practice and patience."

Kitty and Cameron were apt pupils. Gradually, it dawned on Cameron that there might be a further purpose behind the lessons. That even though Ngar's loyalty to Haghan wouldn't allow him to voice it, he was providing them with the means of escape.

"Baji, look," Cameron whispered one day, using his special nickname for her, as they were ladling out the children's food. "In front of us, the landscape is rolling hills on three sides. Easily guarded. But look behind us." She craned her neck to see the sheer rock cliff that rose nearly two hundred feet above them. "If we could get the children up that cliff without being noticed, we could escape. I heard one of the guards say that it's only half a day's trek to the main railway line to Baroda. Once there, we could flag down a train. We can do it, Baji. Together, you and I can do anything."

To any other eleven-year-old girl, it would seem an impossible task, dragging ten small children up a cliff that would pose a challenge to the most seasoned mountaineer. But Kitty's faith in Cameron was unflagging. He'd comforted, cheered, protected her, while keeping the other children from despair. And he excelled under Ngar's tutelage as if he, himself, were a Rajput warrior in the making. When Cameron said they could do anything together, she believed him.

Over the next three nights, he'd sneaked out of the sleeping camp to explore the terrain, to find the best path up the wall of rock, while Kitty stood guard with a warning signal at the ready. On the fourth night, she joined him on the climb. He took her hand and said, excitedly, "Come, Baji, come fly with me."

Together they scaled the outer face of the rock, climbing higher and higher as the world of their captivity grew smaller beneath them. Alone with Cameron, high above the petty struggle for existence, Kitty found a world that no one else could touch. Where they soared like eagles rising to the stars, feeling the power and glory of absolute freedom.

"You see, we can do it," Cameron crowed into the night. Then he quieted and stood with his arms outstretched, looking all around. "Do you feel it, Baji? Up here we're part of the sky."

Now, looking down on the determined face of Haghan as he paced like a demon before the flames, Cameron whispered, "Tomorrow night."

A sudden misgiving gripped Kitty. "But your father's the resident. Surely he'll appeal to the viceroy. Surely they won't let us die here—"

"We can't count on that. We can't count on anything but ourselves."

She swallowed hard, trying to quell the flutter of uneasiness inside. But Cameron knew. Cameron always knew. He turned to her and asked, "Afraid?"

"I know we have to do it. And when we were high on top of the world, I knew we could. But now . . ." She thought again of their triumphant climb, when all of Ngar's teachings had come together in the one glorious act of reaching the summit. "No," she amended. "As long as you're with me, I know there's nothing to fear."

He touched her face with his hand. "My brave little Baji." And then he leaned over and gave her mouth a kiss. Just a sweet, innocent kiss. But it thrilled her beyond measure, and would burn in her heart forever.

That night, lying in her blanket on the hard ground, she touched her lips with wonder. And she knew in that moment that, young as she was, she loved him. She would always love him.

The next day, they quietly briefed the children, telling them they were going home that night, warning them to secrecy and caution. Around noon, Ngar sought them out. A troubled look puckered the lines of his face.

"Things do not look good, my young friends. Were I you, I should pray for a miracle. Or"—he gave his pupils a brief piercing glance—"perhaps your wits will be of more use than prayer."

The moon was nearly full that night, which served

their purposes well. As usual, the children took to their pallets at dusk, but only the youngest slept. Kitty could feel Cameron's energy as he lay beside her, carefully planning every movement. Finally, when the guards had settled into lethargy, Cameron rose on his haunches. "Okay, it's time."

Silently, they roused the other children. "Stay close together," Cameron instructed. "Put your hand on the belt of the one before you. Whatever you do, don't look back. Kitty will go first. I'll bring up the rear." He turned to Kitty. "Ready, Baji?" He looked to her, in that moment, standing in the moonlight, not like a young boy of thirteen, but like a hero from some Greek myth. In his eyes she saw caution and alertness, certainly. But behind it all there was a twinkle of excitement, a private message to her alone that tonight they were embarking on a grand adventure. For the first time she understood that his jauntiness wasn't just an act to keep the children amused. He really *did* find a thrill in danger. And she realized with a shock that she felt it, too.

Suddenly the crack of a rifle shot split the still night air.

They wheeled about, hearts pounding. But it wasn't aimed at them. It came from down below.

More shots. The sentries were firing at something . . . There was the thunder of galloping horses . . . a gurgling cry . . .

The camp was under attack!

Kitty looked at Cameron. She could see her own stark, if irrational, disappointment mirrored in his eyes. The British forces had apparently followed yesterday's messenger and were mounting a rescue effort. Their grand adventure wouldn't happen after all.

Too bad, his eyes seemed to tell her. *It would have been great fun.*

The retort of gunfire and the screams of dying men moved closer. Cameron called, "Take cover, everyone, wherever you can. Lie flat on the ground and don't lift your heads for anything."

Little Sarah, the youngest of the group, stared up at him with tears shimmering in her eyes. "I'm scared, Camwon. I want to go home."

Cameron crouched down before her and spoke to her in a gentle, soothing voice. "We'll go home soon, sweet. But first, let's play the game one more time. Let's hide from the pirates. Can you do that, honey?"

But Sarah stuck out her lower lip. "No!" she cried. "That's my daddy down there. I'm going to my daddy."

With that she broke from them and began to run down the hillside. Swearing beneath his breath, Cameron tore off after her. By now shadowy figures on horseback were swarming into the clearing, firing at the rebels who were scattering in their midst. Kitty watched, her heart in her throat, as Sarah scampered into the open space below, fully illuminated by the bright, silvery light of the moon. A perfect target.

But Cameron followed close on her heels and scooped her up in his arms. Kitty felt a rush of relief. With Cameron, Sarah would be safe. But as she watched, Cameron turned and froze in his tracks like a deer caught in a lantern's glare. Slowly, he eased down and placed Sarah's feet on the ground, shooing her to safety. Then he straightened once again with the same mechanical wariness of someone who realizes he's in the sights of a rifle. A shot rang out and the impact of the bullet knocked Cameron backward.

Horrified, Kitty saw him fall to the ground. The crimson of his blood filling his chest clashed with the dreamy white glow of the India moon. She raced for him, down the hill, into the light of the moon. Dropping to her knees, feeling the crunch of sand beneath them, she fell on him. "Cameron, Cameron . . ." His name constricted in her throat. He lay so still beneath her. Putting her hand to his chest, she felt the sticky wetness of his blood. But no breath moved that mangled chest. She tugged on him, but there was no life in his body. His eyes were empty and glassy.

From somewhere behind her, she heard a ragged sob. "My son!" Turning, she saw, as in a dream, the face of Cameron's father moving toward her.

The resident dropped to his knees beside her. "It can't be," he gasped.

Another voice said, "Sir, we must move. They're mounting a counterattack. They have twice as many men as we expected. We must get the children now and go."

"My son—" the resident cried.

The soldier bent down to feel for Cameron's pulse. "He's gone, sir. We'll have to leave him. There's no time."

"No," Kitty cried. She threw herself on Cameron and clung to his body. "I won't leave him. I won't!"

But she was dragged away. She felt firm hands hoisting her onto a horse, felt the soldier mount behind her, the horse lurch and gallop off into the night. Gunfire rang in her ears along with her own screams. She fought the soldier's grip, wanting desperately to go back, to remain at Cameron's side. But the soldier held her fast. She looked back, straining to see despite her tears and the whipping of her hair in her face. To see the lonely patch of moonlight where Cameron's abandoned body lay. To watch helplessly as it grew smaller and smaller, just a beam, then a glimmer, then a hint of light, until at last it disappeared.

*J*t was a perfect night for a prowl. Dark, moonless, chilly enough to keep people off the street, but not so cold to numb her fingers. Kitty effortlessly scaled the outside wall of Timsley House using the cracks between the bricks as foot and fingerholds. Dressed in form-fitting black, with a dusky kerchief covering her hair, a mask concealing the upper portion of her face, she blended into her surroundings like a phantom. Far below, sentries walked their beat, blissfully unaware.

This job had required more careful planning than the others. Lord Timsley was a vigilant man. His house was guarded at all hours of the day and night. When asked, he explained that—as His Majesty's deputy foreign minister—he had to take special precautions in case of an intrusion by some foreign enemy of the Crown. But Kitty suspected there was more to it. She hoped that behind his closely guarded walls, he had hidden the Blood of India—the prize she'd come to collect.

Reaching the top floor, she swung her leg over the balcony rail then silently dropped into the enclosure. There she made her way to the French doors that she'd examined weeks earlier, while a guest at Lord Timsley's ball. A few quick motions with a pick and she heard the lock click free. With a swift glance about to make certain she was still undetected, she entered the mansion.

Once again she experienced the same peculiar thrill that always seized her at such moments. The excitement of being alone in a place where she didn't belong. She could feel the tingle of the hairs at the nape of her neck, feel the odd awareness of her own body, of each lithe movement.

It was the same sensation she felt when flying her aeroplane. "Kitty Fontaine, Queen of the Skies," the newspapers called her. She almost laughed. What would the adoring crowds think if they could see her now? Kitty Fontaine, cat burglar.

She crossed the room. The master bedroom was just on the other side of the door. One small sound, one careless move, and Lord Timsley would surely awaken.

She'd already determined where he kept the safe. Easing aside the portrait of Timsley's dour, bearded father, she put her ear to the combination lock and turned it with nimble fingers, feeling more than listening for the tumblers to fall into place. In seconds, the small metal door swung open.

She lit the candle that she'd carried in her pocket and placed it inside the safe where its telltale glow would be contained. Then she began to rifle through the contents. Stacks of papers. Stocks and bonds. Cash laid out in neat piles. These she shifted aside, reaching for the velvet boxes that lay beyond. With swift expertise, she opened and discarded one after the other. A diamond necklace. An emerald bracelet. A complete set of Kashmir sapphires. Flawless all, but not what she sought. Rings, baubles, pearls. But no ruby. No Blood of India.

"Working at night, you meet the most interesting people."

The voice, deep, masculine, mysterious, startled her. She wheeled around, her heart lurching. But the man who stood before her wasn't Lord Timsley. The man was, in fact, an eerie mirror image of herself.

Like her, he was dressed in black, the soft material, chosen for ease of movement, emphasizing every line and contour of a hard-as-granite frame. A kerchief was tied about his head, covering his hair, his nose, the whole top half of his face, while providing slits for eyes that seemed to burn through the mask with an intensity that sent her erratic heart rushing to her throat. All she could see of his face was a strong, clean-shaven jaw and a bold, sensual mouth.

"You!" she gasped.

Light flickered in those dark eyes before he stepped back and gave her a mocking bow.

She knew who he was, of course. For months, this audacious cat burglar had defied gravity to enter the sacred inner domains of London's wealthy, foiled all alarm systems, and confounded and humiliated Scotland Yard by his seemingly miraculous feats of robbery

and his ghostlike ability to disappear into thin air.
While the gentlemen of Mayfair wanted the scoundrel
brought to heel, the women had turned him into a
romantic idol and figure of fantasy. Several times during his midnight forays into ladies' bedrooms, he'd
been rumored to awaken them with a kiss and a few
seductively whispered words before vanishing, leaving
them strangely thrilled to have their jewels lifted and
their fancies titillated by such a dashing rascal. Con-
foundingly, these purloined valuables were returned,
miraculously showing up in the pocket or handbag of
the victim in the midst of a crowded party. This phe-
nomenon had led to many a fluttered fainting spell as
the women realized that this rogue had been close
enough to them to so intimately replace the items without detection. Lady Humphrey, the grande dame of
Mayfair society, upon hearing a comment about this
"blasted cat," sniffed with her most imperious air and
proclaimed, "Darling, that man is no cat. He's a *tiger*!"
Hence the nickname, which Fleet Street quickly took
up. *Lloyd's Weekly News,* a Sunday paper dedicated to
violence and crime, had devoted countless columns to
his daring hijinks. Knowing her own burglaries, if discovered, would be blamed on this notorious Tiger,
Kitty had used him as a cover for her own private quest.

Oh, yes. She knew who he was.

He straightened and for an instant looked directly
into her eyes. She felt a current, like a shimmer of
electricity, skim through her. In that moment, there
passed between them an unspoken understanding, a
singular recognition. They were the best of the best. No
one else could break into this highly guarded sanctum.

Mutual admiration tinged the air. Yet there was something more, something unfathomable.

Suddenly Kitty realized the spot she was in. Was this meeting a bizarre accident? Or had he tracked her here?

Warily, they took each other's measure. He said, sardonically, in that soft conjurer's voice, "So this is the cat who's been dogging my tail."

The veiled sarcasm aided her in recovering her wits. Despite her trepidation, she assumed a confident, even bantering tone.

"And this," she replied, "is the infamous Tiger. Let's see, tall, dark . . ." She ran her eyes over the length of him. "Handsome?"

She reached up to remove his mask, but with a lightning-quick move, he grabbed her hand.

"Tut-tut," he murmured.

"Ah," breathed Kitty, "the *ever elusive* Tiger."

"And you . . . my impostor."

She sniffed. "Hardly an impostor."

"But then," he mused, walking a thoughtful circle, examining her with a sharp, curious glare, "what is a cat but a minuscule version of a tiger?"

Kitty drew herself up in indignation. "I'd match my skills against yours any day."

"*That,*" he drawled, "might prove an interesting challenge."

As he moved closer, his breath against her cheek, Kitty felt a flicker of arousal. And in that moment, she knew what it was that was hanging, like a promise, in the air. An uncanny sense that they were the same breed. A recognition of self.

"How did you know about me?" she asked.

He shrugged, drawing the material of his shirt

tightly across the muscular expanse of his chest. "I received credit for a few jobs I knew I hadn't pulled. Jobs in which the safe was left in disorder, yet nothing was taken. So that brings up a most intriguing question: just what are you looking for?"

"How impertinent of you to ask," she said, dodging his question. "Don't forget what they say about curiosity killing the cat."

"But cats have nine lives," he purred. "And *my* curiosity hasn't even begun to be satisfied. Let's see what you look like beneath your"—his eyes swept her body with an insolent glare—"mask."

His fingers touched her face. Virile hands, confident of their authority, neither asking permission nor begging apology. Slowly, hypnotically, he slipped them up her cheeks to slide beneath the mask, causing her to shiver. Ordinarily, she could have darted free. Yet she found herself gripped by an odd languor. His voice, his eyes, the invasion of his hands, had rendered her immobile, as if he'd cast a sorcerer's spell. She felt utterly in his power, curious as to how far he might take this game. What did it matter if he discovered her identity? He could hardly turn her in without implicating himself. So she stood motionless before him, closing her eyes, feeling the erratic rhythm of her breath, as he leisurely lifted the covering from her face. She felt his gaze on her, compelling her to open her eyes. When she did, she thought she detected in his shadowed gaze a look of surprise.

"What do I look like?" she taunted softly.

"Dangerous," he told her. "Like a siren meant to tempt men's souls."

A rush of unexpected pleasure swept through her. He

spoke as if these unguarded words had been ripped from some inner recess he was loath to reveal.

"I'm more dangerous than you know."

"Are you?" His eyes flicked over her. "And what have you taken that should be mine?" His arm clamped itself about her back, pinning her close. "What secrets do you have hidden in your siren's body?"

His hand wandered down her face to her collarbone. Then she felt his palm against her breast. She jerked in rebellion, but his arm, powerfully muscled, merely tightened its grip on her back.

"Take your hands off me or I'll scream," she ground out through clenched teeth.

"And risk your own capture?" he mocked in a seductive tone. "I think not. What are you hiding from me?" His hand began its search, examining her outthrust breast with businesslike efficiency. But as it closed upon the soft flesh, it lingered, the thumb rotating wickedly around her nipple, which hardened beneath his touch. She shuddered with reckless longing, even as she fought to pull away.

"There's nothing here worth taking," she gasped.

"Nothing?"

He held her captive. As he clamped her against him, his hand was free to wander where it would, kneading her lush breasts, her tiny waist, reaching behind to cup a rounded buttock, then to slip like a thief between her legs. As his fingers toyed with her, lust rendered her insensible. Her breath scorched her throat, sounding tumultuous in her ears. Sweet longing gripped her, making her burn with a fever she'd never known. His hand, lusciously invasive, made her wet between her thighs.

"I'd wondered what you were like," he rasped, his voice mesmerizing, making her feel drunk with the potent arousal of his words. "What kind of woman are you? A woman who defies the perils of the night. And did you have to be this beautiful?"

"*How* beautiful?" she asked, even now, as she melted like molten lava, grasping at weapons she could use.

"Like a curse. Like temptation so sweet it hurts."

She felt his breath on her cheek. He came closer and closer still, bringing his lips to within a breath of hers, holding them there so she could feel the pull of his mouth. She felt herself sway forward, and as she did, their lips met. A shock jolted her.

"Do you do this to all men?" he asked against her lips.

"Do what?"

He lifted his head and studied her face for a brief span. She felt so drawn to him that she held her breath, waiting, suspended, for . . . she didn't even know what. It was as if time stood still and she waited beneath his gaze for some flash of truth.

"Make them want you even when they tell themselves it's folly? Make them forget everything because the lure of your goddamned body is like sweet poison?"

"I don't know what you mean."

He gripped her face in his hands and searched her eyes. "No," he muttered. "I don't suppose you would."

She didn't understand. She only knew that she wanted him to kiss her again. Wanted to experience again the sensation of floating blissfully like a flower tossed into the river. She lifted her lips, offering helpless invitation. He answered her call, crushing her to him with fierce, seductive power, until she felt herself melting into his kiss, into the folds of arms like steel that gathered her trembling body up as a treasure to be branded and possessed. Yet as she reached for him, as her hands found his sculpted chest, he hardened the kiss, grinding his lips into hers with a passion that mystifyingly felt like anger—or contempt.

With his lips hovering over hers, he growled, "So you thought you could have your fun and blame it on me."

She was trembling beneath his onslaught. But she challenged, tartly, "What if I did?"

"And what if I don't like it?" he snarled.

"Careful," she warned, with a throaty laugh. "Those who play with cats must expect to be scratched."

Once again he studied her face. "Then scratch me," he told her, "if you dare."

His lips crushed hers once again. She felt his hands everywhere, caressing her with a possession that no other man had ever dared. What splendor, to be so swept away. The danger, the thrill, the unvoiced awareness that detection was but a heartbeat away . . . She was drowning in the ecstasy of it all.

But then, all at once, she remembered who she was. Why she was here. And, in a startling flash, that she was engaged to be married. That she'd forgotten everything because this man—known, she realized shamefully, as a rogue who could turn women to putty in his hands—had played havoc with her body and her mind.

Appalled at her behavior, she thrust herself away. In her daze and her struggle to regain her senses, she stumbled back and bumped into the door that led to the bedroom.

As one, the burglars froze.

They heard a cry. "Who's there?" Kitty turned toward the bedroom door. She had to get out. Now.

Whirling around, she discovered that she was alone. The Tiger had disappeared without a trace.

She ran to the balcony but could see no sign of him. He'd simply vanished. But there was no time to ponder the mystery of his disappearance. She heard the bedroom door open and hurriedly leapt over the balcony to make her own escape before Lord Timsley could sound the alarm.

2

Kitty raced through Mayfair, taking a series of back alleys, careful not to be seen. Despite the cool March night, her body felt as hot as a raging furnace. But it wasn't just her flight from danger that had her churning inside. She was jumbled by her unprecedented reaction to the Tiger.

She lived in a modern age in which Edwardian women were testing their wings as never before, speaking openly of new sexual liberties once forbidden them, flaunting their new quests for freedom with bold talk. Some even smoked in public, an act of defiance that seemed, to the older Victorian holdouts, like a slap in the face to the notion of prim and modest womanhood. Kitty was more daring than all of them, yet sex was a completely alien concept to her. She'd never felt the stirrings of desire, even for her fiancé. Yet what had happened? She'd allowed this man's rude seduction to completely distract her.

At last she reached her destination, a gracious town house on Curzon Street. As she'd done so many times before, she passed the mews and went to rap softly on the back door. It was opened immediately by her fiancé, Charles Flemming, a man of twenty-four, the younger brother of Cameron, the boy who'd so tragically died before her eyes fourteen years before.

"Thank God you're safe," he whispered as she ushered past him. "Come, Father's waiting in the library."

Charles's presence comforted her, even as it stirred feelings of guilt. He led her through the house to a room off the main hall. As he opened the door for her, the light from its fireplace spilled out onto the polished wood floor, an age-worn symbol of welcome. Standing before it was Sir Harold Flemming, long the British resident of Jaipur, now retired to London and knighted for meritorious service to the Crown.

In the five years since his retirement, Kitty had virtually become his surrogate daughter. The love they shared for his martyred son, Cameron, was a bond that held them tight. Earlier this year, when he'd expressed his wish that she and his other son, Charles, marry, Kitty had agreed. Charles was in love with her, she knew. She'd vowed to make him a good and loyal wife, if only to repay him and his father for their kindness and devotion to her.

Sir Harold turned from the fire with a relieved smile and extended his hands to her. She crossed the room and took them affectionately in her own. In his late fifties, he still stood erect and tall, as if the years of officiating at formal functions had left their mark.

"Your hands are cold," he told her. "Come warm them before the fire."

"Thank you, but I'm quite hot—from running." She reached up and pulled the kerchief from her head. As she did, her auburn curls cascaded down to drape across her shoulders. She ran a hand through the tangles and tucked the black kerchief into the pocket of her form-fitting pants.

"Were you pursued, then?" Sir Harold asked.

"Nearly. Timsley awoke, but I was able to escape before he could rouse the guards."

"And the ruby?"

"Not there, I'm afraid."

"Damn," said Charles.

Kitty turned to look at him. He was tall, like his father, with sand-colored hair and mustache, and pale blue eyes. Soft features, a gentle chin, a face virtually the opposite of his older brother.

"I was sure Timsley had it," Sir Harold was saying. "It made such sense. He had just the right India connections." Shaking his head, he added, "This is a grave disappointment. And a potentially costly one. If we don't find that ruby soon, we're going to allow the only chance we have of saving your father's life to slip from our fingers."

Three months ago, a scandal had erupted that suddenly altered the course of Kitty's life. The Colonial Office had uncovered conclusive evidence linking her father, Colonel Reginald Fontaine, with a long-term conspiracy by which the province of Rajasthan had been plundered during his tenure there. The conspirators had amassed an untold fortune and had frequently resorted to murder to protect their scheme from discovery by the Raj authorities. Under normal circumstances, they might have tried to hush it up and let the colonel off with a reprimand. But news of the crime had leaked out and the Indian princes were demanding retribution. England's hold on the country was becoming increasingly tenuous. Cooperation with the native rulers of the princely states was imperative to the continued success of the Raj. So to keep the peace, the culprits had been given the maximum sentence. Court-martialed and convicted, Kitty's father was now incarcerated in the British prison in the Andaman Islands of the Bay of Bengal, where he awaited execution. Held incommunicado in a maximum-security cell, without visiting or letter privileges.

During the difficult months of this ordeal, as Kitty made numerous appeals to the viceroy in Calcutta, she found only one ally: Sir Harold, who was as convinced of her father's innocence as she was. When all their efforts on Colonel Fontaine's behalf failed, it was Sir Harold who came up with their last desperate chance of freeing her unjustly convicted father. He'd secretly contacted Miguel Soro, the notorious pirate scourge of the Indian Ocean, who'd agreed to use his forces to storm the Andaman Islands and free the colonel in exchange for one thing: the notorious Blood of India—a hundred-karat ruby that was stolen from the Lahore Museum during the Mutiny of 1857. No trace of the stone had turned up since then, but Soro was convinced that it had fallen into the collection of some English aristocrat.

When the dimensions of their plight became clear,

Kitty came up with a brilliant plan. Fleet Street's fascination with the series of Mayfair jewel robberies already had her thinking about the ways and means of cat burglary. It occurred to her that she, herself, had once possessed similar skills. If she could draw on her memories of the Rajput art of stealth she'd learned as a child, and use what she remembered to glean through the jewel collections of aristocratic London, perhaps she could find that ruby. If so, she could take the trauma of her past and channel it into a worthy cause. Sir Harold, of course, argued against the idea. Perhaps there was another way. But Kitty insisted there was no other way. They couldn't buy the ruby: Sir Harold's recent financial reversals had left him in strained circumstances; and even if they could afford it, the owner couldn't acknowledge his possession since it was technically stolen property. So, Kitty reasoned, why not steal what had already been stolen?

"The ruby wasn't there," she told them now. "But you'll never guess who *was*." The two men turned to her expectantly. "The Tiger."

"Please tell me you're joking," Charles said, his shock causing his voice to tremble.

"Not at all. He sneaked up on me as I was rifling the safe. And then, when Timsley awoke, he disappeared again into thin air. As advertised."

"Blast it all!" Sir Harold cried. "What did he say?"

Kitty blushed faintly and turned toward the fire. "Nothing really. Some rubbish about my dogging his tail. Called me an impostor."

"Bloody cheek," Charles swore. "Did he take any liberties? The rogue!"

She recalled the feel of his lips on hers, his hands

everywhere, kissing her, possessing her, in a way Charles would never dream of doing, engaged or not. Her heart skipped a beat, annoying her. So silly. Why had she responded to him that way, when she'd never responded to a man before? Perhaps that blatant seduction had been his way of keeping her off balance. If so, it had worked all too well.

"I can handle myself, thank you," she said. But had she?

"Did he take anything?" Sir Harold asked.

"Not that I noticed."

"I wonder," he mused with a frown, "if it's possible the blackguard could be looking for the same thing we are?"

Kitty turned and looked at his somber face as the color drained from hers. "He couldn't be!"

"He robs women of their jewels, only to return them in the most flamboyant way. Why else return the gems? Because he hasn't found what he was looking for."

"But why *this* ruby?" Kitty asked. "I know why we want it, but why should he—"

"Because it's the ultimate prize," Sir Harold snapped, realizing the threat this realization engendered. "He must be a professional jewel thief. Someone who knows the great gems of the world. Most likely from the Continent. Did he have an accent?"

"Not exactly, but the inflection wasn't wholly English, either. Now that I think of it, he may have taken pains to disguise his voice." That soft, seductive whisper. "He spoke like one who might have learned English in another country."

"He's no doubt heard the rumors that the ruby is in London. He returns the gems he's stolen at parties, balls, public gatherings. Obviously, he can't be masked during these events, so he must be an invited guest. Someone with a pedigree that wouldn't be questioned. He *was* a man?" he belatedly thought to ask.

"Yes," murmured Kitty. "He was most definitely a man."

"I want you to stay away from him," Charles ordered.

Kitty looked at him in surprise. It was the first time he'd ever sounded like a jealous suitor.

"It . . . it could be dangerous," he added, a bit more sheepishly. "I don't want you near him."

"You're sweet to worry, Charles, but I hardly sought him out, did I? And I haven't the faintest notion who he is—although there *did* seem to be something vaguely familiar about him."

"You must have come across him at one of the parties," Sir Harold said thoughtfully. "For all we know, we might have entertained him here. Charles is correct, of course, that he's dangerous. But not correct that you should stay away from him."

"Father!" Charles gasped.

"I believe this Tiger is after the same thing we are. That makes him a threat to us. As it is, we know nothing about him. But if we could discover his identity, we could at least neutralize his advantage over us."

"And perhaps," Kitty added, "I could determine if we really are after the same prize."

"Would you know him, do you think, if you saw him again? Without his disguise?"

"I'm not sure. Perhaps."

"There's a diplomatic ball tomorrow night at the French Embassy. If he is a member of European society, he's likely to be there."

"Yes," Kitty agreed, "I could see if I can pick him out of the crowd."

Excitement seized her. The Tiger may have had the upper hand tonight, but tomorrow night, she'd be in control. He'd surprised her in the act; now she would surprise him. Suddenly, she couldn't wait.

"I don't know that I approve of this," Charles informed them. "I don't like putting Kitty in danger."

"I don't like it any better than you," Sir Harold agreed. "But there seems to be no other way. If I could find the ruby myself, I would. But I don't have Kitty's skills."

"If there were any other way, I too would take it," Kitty assured them. "But as it is, what better use of those skills than to use them to get my father safely out of India?"

"Then it's settled," Sir Harold proclaimed. "We shall lay a trap. Tomorrow night, we go tiger hunting."

Charles escorted her home. She'd changed at his house, as she always did, back into an evening gown, leaving her cat-burglar attire behind. They walked the four blocks to Berkeley Square, where her aunt and uncle lived in a three-story row house.

"Would you like to come in?" she asked at the door.

"No, thank you," he declined. "It's late. And we've both had too much excitement for one night."

He didn't know the half of it.

"Charles, do you think I'm beautiful?"

"Of course," he answered matter-of-factly.

"Beautiful enough to . . . tempt men's souls?"

He squinted at her uncertainly. "I suppose so."

It wasn't exactly the romantic response she'd sought. "Kiss me, Charles."

She suddenly reached up and kissed him with a force that clearly surprised him, wanting to blot out the memory of that other man, hoping to find the same thrill in the arms of her fiancé. He responded in kind, drawing her into his arms and deepening the kiss. His moan of pleasure told her this was the most passionate moment of his life. But for her, the kiss was tepid, his lips too thin, too closed, too guarded. Nothing like the Tiger's blinding mastery.

"You've never kissed me like that before," he gasped.

His sweet sense of wonder made her feel wretched. She'd sought to prove to herself that there was nothing extraordinary in her reaction to the Tiger's arrogant overtures. That it was the novelty of induced passion that had made her respond so shamelessly, and not the man. But sadly, Charles's kiss had left her feeling restless and dissatisfied.

She tried to mask her disappointment with a teasing tone. "We *are* engaged, after all."

"So we are," he proclaimed, puffing up at the unexpected prospect of the intimate life they'd soon share. "So we are."

Emboldened now, he pulled her close. But she was suddenly weary. Putting a restraining hand to his chest, she demurred. "As you said, it's late."

Once inside, her sense of relief at being left alone unsettled her further. She'd never felt this way about Charles before. The tenderness he'd elicited in her had, in one night, turned to dread.

"There you are!" she heard her aunt Mathilda cry,

coming into the front entry. "How was the play, my dear?"

She was in her forties, still attractive with a sweet, girlish face, her light curls arranged neatly atop her head. The younger and only sister of Reginald Fontaine, she'd risen above her merchant family's station by marrying David, Baron Huxley, two decades her senior.

"I believe Mr. Maugham has himself another hit," Kitty lied, choosing a safe assumption.

"Kitty, dear, I don't mean to harp, but—"

"Auntie, please, not again. I've really had enough for one night."

Uncle David joined them, holding a copy of the *Daily Mail*. He looked like a typical country gentleman with his tweeds and pipe, his bald head perpetually tanned from nearly half a century of grouse hunting in the moors of Dorset. "Your aunt is merely expressing her concern for your well-being."

After the trauma of the kidnapping and Cameron's death, Kitty's father had decided to send her back to England to live with his sister and her husband—to keep her safe, and because she'd wanted nothing more than to escape India and its awful memories. The couple, devoted to each other but childless, had agreed to take her in. They'd been exceedingly kind to her, but lately the scandal involving her father had taken a heavy toll.

"Yes, I'm concerned," Mathilda said. "It's not proper, at a time like this, for you to be seen at such a frivolous public gathering."

Of course Kitty hadn't been to the play. But the idea that she should be hiding infuriated her. "This is exactly the time when I should be seen in public," she retorted. "It's time to fight, not shrink into the wood-work."

"And just how does your being seen at the theater night after night constitute a fight for your cause?" David inquired.

She wondered if it wouldn't be easier to just tell them the truth. "I should think you'd have learned to trust me by now. Do you remember when I first came here? How I was shunned and ridiculed? How that stupid girl scribbled the word 'wog' on my desk when I told her about my Indian grandmother? You wanted to take me out of that school, but I wouldn't give them the satisfaction. I found the girl and I slapped her face in front of everyone. No one ever called me a wog again."

"That's true, my dear," said Mathilda, "but surely you realize this is a completely different situation."

"And the flying. Remember the fuss last year when I wanted to learn to fly? How you said it wasn't proper for a well-bred young Englishwoman to take up a pursuit too dangerous even for a man? How you said I'd be ridiculed for it? You were wrong, Auntie. Nothing has garnered me more respect than my accomplishments in aviation. They may whisper about me, but by God they come in droves to see me when I take to the air. It's one of the reasons I can hold my head up through this injustice. I've earned the right."

"The *Times* called your last exhibition a disgrace," David reminded her. "They contend that it mocks the English spirit for a woman to fly in an aeroplane. I hardly call that respect."

"That's one stuffy editorial writer. These are modern

times, and every other paper in London has applauded me."

"That's all well and good, dear," Mathilda soothed. "But surely you can see that at a time like this, when a dark cloud is hovering over your family name, when your father, my own dear brother, is—" She choked on the words, unable to continue.

Kitty took her aunt's hands in her own. Gently, she said, "Auntie, they say I'm mocking the English spirit, but you know that isn't so. Cameron and his father taught me a great deal about what the English spirit is all about. When I came back from India, I was so confused. I didn't know if I was Indian or English. I didn't know where I belonged. But then I thought of Cameron, of his courage and fortitude, of his standing up for what he knew to be right, even giving his life for it. He represented all that was good and noble about that English spirit. And I thought if I just tried hard enough, I could live up to that ideal."

"My dear," said her aunt with tears in her eyes, "you don't have to prove you're English. It hurts me so that you think you must."

"But I do," Kitty insisted. "If I'm ever to put the past completely behind me, I must. You don't know what it's like, Auntie, to wonder who you are. To feel there's nowhere that's truly home. To remember, when some silly newspaper says I fly in the face of the English spirit, what it was like to see that horrid word scrawled for all to see. If I can accomplish something for England with my flying, if I can prove my father innocent and bring him home, then I'll have proved to myself and to England that this is where I belong. Sir Harold understands. I just wish you could, as well."

"I understand," conceded her uncle, "that you want to put your past in India behind you. It's only right that you should. But I do wonder if you're going about it in the proper fashion."

"I'm going about it in the only way I know how. I have to believe that it will all come right in the end."

She kissed each of them then went upstairs to her room and changed into her nightclothes, feeling heavy with fatigue. Once in bed, she huddled beneath her covers, trying to find comfort in the familiar items of her room. The pink and white flowered wallpaper her aunt had put in when Kitty had come to live here at the age of eleven. The pristine white shutters. The flying trophies, the newspaper clippings stuck into the sides of her mirror, the pictures of her posing with her plane—a cratelike assembly of wood and canvas, but the most modern of flying machines. All the mementos of the life she'd made for herself since coming to England. Her safe English world.

I belong to England now, she told herself for the millionth time. *India can never touch me again.*

But she knew the fallacy of her words, and knew how much there was yet to prove. India kept coming back to haunt her like a curse. Just when she thought she had finally exorcised it from her life, it had snared her father in its trap. The few times he'd come to England to visit her, she'd begged him to retire and leave for good. But Reginald loved India and couldn't imagine himself anywhere else. He'd asked her to join him there, but she couldn't do it. India, with its awful memories, was the one terror and confusion of her life. Nothing but ill had come of her time there. Seeking a definitive identity, she'd turned her back on her Indian heritage and had chosen England instead. She simply couldn't go back.

Without realizing it, Kitty fell asleep. Suddenly she was being dangled upside down by her feet. Below, she could see the gaping jaws of a crocodile—the crooked, yellow teeth, snapping within inches of her face. Terror paralyzed her. She tried to scream but no sound escaped her parched throat.

She felt the grip on her ankles slip. She dropped into the river, her body enveloped by the warm, murky water. Fighting for the surface, she found herself face-to-face with the crocodile once again. But this time the clacking teeth found their mark, clamping down on her arm. Panicked, she tried to wrench her arm free.

Then she saw him diving in to save her. He wrestled the beast free, battling with it round and round. She heard herself call his name. "Cameron, no!" And as she watched in horror, the flailing mass of limbs and leathery tail dipped into the water and disappeared. She dove into the depths, trying desperately to find them, to pull Cameron free. But when she was finally forced to the surface, her lungs burning, she saw the brave boy floating facedown. She lunged for him, turning him over frantically, to find him staring glassy-eyed, his blood staining the water all around.

Clutching his lifeless body, she screamed.

She awoke in a sweat. Tears streamed down her face. The pain, the sense of loss, were so real that she felt shattered anew.

It was an old dream, one that had haunted her for years after the kidnapping. Yet she hadn't dreamt it in some time.

It took several moments before she realized she was awake. Safe in her own room. Safe in England.

3

The French Embassy was ablaze with electric chandeliers. An orchestra provided waltz music; while a sumptuous buffet offered exotic tidbits for refreshment—ortolans, truffles, pâté de foie gras, and quail among the marzipan and fresh fruits and punch. When Kitty arrived with Sir Harold and Charles, the ball was already in full swing.

As their presence was announced, much of the British contingent came forth to greet them. Sir Harold and Charles were welcomed warmly. But the guests' reaction to Kitty was more awkward. While her family scandal might, in other circumstances, cause them to shun her, it was common knowledge that her father had been a victim of bureaucracy, brought on by the pressure of the Indian princes. This garnered her a certain sympathy, while her glamorous aerial exploits made her an object of fascination to them.

"Ah, our Queen of the Skies," Lady Quimby, wife of the head of the Foreign Office, exclaimed. "Tell us, dear, what new distance record do you intend to set at your exhibition next Sunday—three miles? Five miles?"

In October 1908, Kitty had been on hand to watch Samuel "Papa" Cody, the American adventurer, make the first heavier-than-air flight in Britain. Captivated, she'd charmed the forty-six-year-old Cody into taking her up in his biplane, where she'd experienced, for the first time, the exhilaration of flight. Those five minutes proved a revelation to her, stoking the love of heights she'd acquired at the hands of Ngar, her Rajput tutor. In the air, high above the world, she felt that she'd discovered her true calling. Afterward, she convinced the flamboyant pilot to give her lessons. And became addicted. She journeyed to the Voisin factory in France and convinced Monsieur Voisin himself to give her one of his newest aeroplanes, since the novelty and publicity value of Europe's first woman pilot was bound to increase sales. Under Cody's tutelage she'd become an expert pilot. As such she'd found herself one of the darlings of Edwardian society, England's hope amidst a field of Frenchmen who were all vying to be the first to achieve the goal that Fleet Street had declared the foremost challenge of the infant science of aviation: a nonstop crossing of the English Channel.

"I don't believe five miles is out of the question," she said now. "But come Sunday and see."

"You may be certain that I will, my dear. We

wouldn't miss it for the world. Although why you do it, I shall never know."

"I'll take you up sometime. You may see the attraction for yourself."

"Me?" Lady Quimby gasped. "In a flying machine? Why, my Henry would have conniptions, I'm sure."

She turned to a nearby group of friends, exclaiming, "Did you hear that? Miss Fontaine wants to take *me* up in a flying machine. Imagine!"

"But my dear, you should do it," one of her friends urged. "Imagine the luster you should carry ever after!"

As the conversation continued, Kitty studied the faces of the men around her. Any one of them might be the prey she was after. She caught Sir Harold's eye. He took Charles's arm and led him toward a group of friends across the hall, leaving Kitty to her own devices. A fiancé in tow would, after all, be an encumbrance.

The Englishmen she dismissed. Her instincts told her Sir Harold was correct in his assumption that the Tiger was foreign. If he'd been a local, why hadn't he begun his spree earlier? He was most likely someone who'd only recently arrived. That narrowed the possibilities, but not significantly. There was a large European community in London, with visitors coming and going from every country imaginable all the time. With all the embassies, there were dozens of ambassadors, not to mention their enormous staffs. Looking about at the proliferation of formally attired gentlemen escorting ladies resplendent in multicolored gowns, and dripping with the finest gems, she began to feel overwhelmed.

She turned to Lady Quimby.

"There are so many people here. Perhaps you could introduce me around?"

"I should be delighted," Lady Quimby said, surveilling the room expertly. "Yes, I know most everyone. You're in excellent hands, my girl. Follow me."

With an efficacy worthy of war maneuvers, Lady Quimby made the rounds of the room, seeking out the sort of people she thought might interest the younger woman. Some Kitty dismissed at once and cut the conversation short. She knew her prey was tall and handsomely built. The short, the portly, she ignored. She hadn't seen his hair, but she sensed that he was dark. What she'd seen of his coloring—dark, intense eyes—didn't speak to his having fair hair. Soon the list of possibilities dwindled, and the task began to seem manageable after all. If, indeed, the rogue was here at all!

Eventually her search narrowed to three likely candidates. The first was Prince Dimitri, the visiting cousin of the czar's ambassador. He was in his early thirties, tall, dark, and suave, athletically built. She accepted his invitation to dance.

"I am surprised we haven't met before this," he said, leading her expertly about the dance floor. "I've heard a great deal about you."

"Then you have the advantage," she told him with a smile. "Now you must tell me all about yourself."

"Everything?" he asked.

"Everything you think it fit for me to hear."

The last was a test, to see if he would grab the bait. The Tiger, she was certain, would jump at the chance for some spicy banter. But the prince was a disappointment. It became obvious from his discourse that he lived high, but had little money of his own. He implied that he lived mostly off the charity of rich relations. If he were the thief, he'd likely be keeping some of the gems for himself, to boost his own coffers. She studied his eyes as he spoke. They were dull, lazy. Not tiger eyes at all.

The next prospect was Señor Braga, the new chargé d'affaires from Spain. He too was tall and dark, not quite handsome, but with manners so impeccable that his charm acquired a beauty all its own. He spoke with a melodious Castilian fluidity that offered promise. But it became evident, as they waltzed, that he was far too extroverted, too eager to boast. Braga the Braggart they called him. Wrong, all wrong.

That left the American ambassador.

Physically, he fit the criteria. He'd come to London just before the first spate of robberies. His name was Rufus Collier and he had an easy, boyish manner that served him well as a diplomat. Yet as he squired her around the dance floor, she discovered an impediment to adventure. The American had a wife and child in New York whom he was planning to transport at the earliest opportunity. Besides which, his eyes were too ingenuous. There was nothing to thrill her in that flat, mid-Atlantic voice.

She was beginning to lose hope. She wandered about the hall by herself, slyly eavesdropping on snatches of conversation. As usual, the talk was all about the growing threat of Germany and the specter of the dissolution of the British Empire—especially in India. "England without its empire," she overheard more than once, "wouldn't be the England we love."

When all at once a man's voice filled her consciousness like a faintly remembered song. As she drew closer, she realized that he spoke with an Italian accent, the vowels soft and rounded, melodiously drawn out. Yet there was something about the tenor of that voice that made her tingle inside. It wasn't quite the voice she'd heard at Timsley's and yet . . . something about it seemed to touch her very soul.

She followed the sound until at last she came upon the source. She looked up to see a man surrounded by a group of women who were breathlessly hanging on to every word of his story about some exotic journey. He was tall, dark, devastatingly handsome, but in a hard, biting sort of way. His grin, while captivating the ladies, seemed faintly derisive, more of a wolfish smirk than a smile. He was looking down into the face of a particularly eager young lady, but all at once he lifted his gaze. As her eyes zoomed in on his, Kitty saw in them a drowsy intensity that mesmerized her.

Who was he? Why had she not seen him before? Why had Lady Quimby not thought to introduce her? So many questions. And most of all: *Was he the man she sought?*

"Having a pleasant time, dear?"

She started, finding Lady Quimby once again at her side.

"Lady Quimby, who is that man?"

The woman glanced toward the corner where the Italian was holding court. "Why, my dear, that's Count Aveli, of course."

"Count Aveli?" She'd heard of him. Something about having taken society by storm. A matter that, until now, had been of little interest to her.

"Max Aveli," Lady Quimby clarified.

"Why didn't you introduce us?" she mused aloud.

"I assumed you already knew him. Everyone does, don't you know. Certainly all the marriageable young ladies and their mothers. But then, you're engaged to Charles, so . . ."

"How long has he been in town?"

"Oh, a few months, I should think. He's a man of some mystery. I knew his father years ago. Lovely old gent. But I hadn't heard he'd had a son. He had a wife and three daughters, but they were killed in a train crash— Where was it now? Somewhere exotic, I think. In any case, this count has a bit of a reputation as a playboy. There was some talk of an affair with Lady Windemere. Everyone was expecting a duel, although Lord Windemere, from what one hears, declined on the grounds that dueling is against the law. No one knows for sure if the story is true or not, but it gives the count a rather dashing air, nonetheless. Handsome devil, isn't he?"

"Hmmm?"

"Well, come along, if you like. I shall introduce you."

She marched off, leaving Kitty staring behind her.

"Off with you girls," Lady Quimby admonished, shooing them away. "You've taken up enough of Count Aveli's attentions for the time being." The ladies, sporting pretty pouts, nonetheless bowed to the older woman's authority, each pausing to cast inviting glances at the count. Lady Quimby glanced back to see that she'd left Kitty behind. "Come, dear, meet Count Aveli. My lord, may I introduce Miss Kitty Fontaine."

Kitty came forth and the count gave her a courteous bow. "It's indeed a pleasure to meet England's illustrious Queen of the Skies."

"Oh, you've heard of her, then. In that case, my duties are performed. Do keep Miss Fontaine company, won't you? She seems a bit at loose ends."

With that she fluttered off in a swirl of French perfume.

"Subtle, these English," the count said, turning to Kitty.

"She means well, I suppose. I'd expressed interest in you." Those eyes . . . that voice . . . yes, there was something there.

"I'm flattered."

"That surprises me. From what I hear, you don't lack for attention. Oh, look. It seems we're about to be joined by Lord Windemere."

Count Aveli followed her gaze and spotted an elderly gentleman heading across the dance floor toward them. As she watched his face carefully, he gave a wry smile.

"The ever-so-publicly *cuckolded* Lord Windemere," she added when he didn't reply. "Or am I misinformed?"

"Signore Windemere's imagination exceeds his courage, I'm afraid. He had ample opportunity for retribution of his imagined slights, yet he chose to hide behind the skirts of the law."

"Then you *didn't* woo his wife?"

He raised a brow. "Woo her? Not with the intention of—how was it you so charmingly put it?—cuckolding him, certainly."

"With what intention, then?"

"You're a trifle blunt, signorina."

"And you, my lord, are a trifle evasive."

"It's a moot point, I assure you. The gentleman in question feels slighted all the same. He ducked a duel, yet still he persists in throwing visual daggers my way at every party and ball. He's obviously planning some revenge."

"It seems, Count Aveli, that you flirt with danger as well as women."

He looked her straight in the eyes. "Ah, well . . ." he said with an air of modesty. "If it wasn't dangerous, it wouldn't be any fun."

Something froze inside Kitty.

"Aveli, I'd like a word with you," said Lord Windemere as he joined them.

"Signore Windemere," she heard Aveli say, "how good of you to stop by. I'd love to stay and chat, as you English so quaintly put it, but I've just this moment promised this waltz to Miss Fontaine. You will excuse us, *si?*"

He took Kitty's arm and led her onto the dance floor. She felt him grasp her hand in his, felt his arm go around her back. She followed his steps automatically, as if she were in a trance. As if frozen in time. As if a ghost had just passed over her grave.

"What did you just say?" she asked him.

He gave her a quizzical look. "You tell me."

"Something about . . . the fun of danger."

"You disagree?"

His Italian accent was flawless. He was looking at her dispassionately, as if she were, indeed, just a woman he'd met at a ball. But there was something lurking in the back of those deceptively drowsy eyes. Was she imagining it?

She had to pull herself together. "I've been known to seek a thrill or two."

"As the peril-chasing aviatrix, no doubt."

She studied him closely. Was he mocking her?

"A daring young woman who flies an aeroplane, thrilling audiences with her death-defying feats. You, Signorina Fontaine, are the talk of the town."

"Oh? I thought it was you who were the talk of the town."

He shrugged, affecting modesty. "I've been known to turn a head or two."

"As Count Aveli you mean. Actually, I was speaking of your *nocturnal* conquests."

There was something so familiar about the way he was holding her. Her skin beneath his hand seemed to sizzle. They were dancing slowly, yet her breath was rapid.

"Conquests?" He laughed. "I fear you've been listening to the idle gossip of mothers with marriageable daughters. Or needlessly jealous husbands, perhaps."

"Actually, I was referring to your conquests of a feline nature."

"*Mi dispiace, signorina. Non capisco.* The language barrier, perhaps."

She cocked her head, noticing the gleam of mischief in his eyes. "There's something so familiar about you."

He chuckled. "Perhaps we met in another life."

"Do you deny meeting me before?"

"I never deny the accusations of beautiful women. However fanciful."

"How Machiavellian of you."

"But let's see, since you insist. Where might we have met? Paris? Milan? Budapest? Istanbul, perhaps, in the fall. I've traveled extensively."

"Or perhaps we met only last night. In the dark."

"Like two cats in an alley, perhaps?"

There was something sexual about the way he said it. A shiver rippled through her.

"You may drop the act, Machiavelli."

"You're quick, I'll give you that. However, it's Max Aveli." But he said it with a delighted grin, as if she'd just complimented him.

"Count Aveli. Or should I call you Tiger?"

His eyes lit up in amusement. "You sound quite certain of your conclusion."

"Call it instinct."

"A woman's instinct?"

"The instinct of one who recognizes a fellow thrill-seeker."

He dropped the look of enjoyment and peered at her. Long enough to make her squirm.

"Or is it," he asked, pulling her closer, "that you recall what it feels like to be held in my arms?"

His voice had changed completely. Gone was the Italian accent. In its place was the soft, seductive purr she'd heard at Timsley's.

She jerked back. "It *was* you!"

"I see no point in denying it. You'd have found me out sooner or later. What with your . . . womanly instincts."

She felt completely flustered. "Who are you?" she whispered, staring into his eyes.

"Who I am is of no importance. What I want is at issue here."

"What *do* you want?"

"No doubt the same thing you want. A certain ruby, perhaps."

She missed a step, destroying the rhythm of the waltz. "How do you know that's what I want?"

He guided her back into the waltz. "I wouldn't be much of a tiger if I couldn't sniff out the competition, now, would I?"

"You're very sure of yourself."

"I've had to be."

"There are many jewels in London. Why this *particular* gem?"

"I could ask you the same question."

"Red's my favorite color."

"Mine, as well. The color of fire, of passion. Qualities I seek in a stone—and a woman."

What was it about him that touched her on such a deep level? That made her churn inside?

"I'm afraid I'm going to have to deny you both."

He swept her with an insolent glance. She was beautiful, there was no denying that. And daring. Aviatrix by day, cat burglar by night. A woman after his own heart. He was more attracted to her than he'd like—to the soft feel of her in his arms, to the spicy banter that showed her keen mind. But her loyalties made her dangerous. She was too damned clever for her own good—or for his. He wasn't about to let her get the upper hand.

In a deceptively mild tone, he said, "You're welcome to try."

She flushed beneath his heated gaze. Changing tactics, she said, "I have no intention of turning you in. But you must also know that I need this particular stone, for private and completely altruistic reasons."

"I don't give to charity."

"Then I'll do it for you."

Suddenly he dropped the teasing banter and tightened his grip, jerking her to him so her breath left her lungs in a startled gasp. "You're invading my jungle, little cat," he growled. "If you think you can best me, by all means do your worst. But be warned: I'm faster, more clever, and better connected to the lonely ladies of this dreary city than you can ever hope to be. But in the spirit of healthy competition, we'll make a game of it, shall we? Lady Windemere, in a moment of weakness, let it slip that her good friend Lady Philipson has a rather impressive ruby among her collection of loose gems. It seems her boor of a husband illegally relieved it from some Burmese general. But the poor dear has her crosses to bear. The boorish husband insists that they retire for the evening at the beastly hour of twelve o'clock. Which means by midnight, on the nights when there are no balls to attend, they're both snoring away. Now that I've dangled this mouse in front of you, let's see which cat can get it first."

"How do I know you're telling the truth?"

"You don't. Oh, did I mention that the same boorish husband has taken precautions against the theft of his precious gems?"

She was digesting this piece of information when she felt his hand convulse against hers. "It seems you've been missed," he said in a strained voice.

"I beg your pardon?"

He jerked his chin, loosening his hold on her as he did. "We're about to be broken in on. By your fiancé, no less."

Kitty followed his gaze to find Charles making his way through the swirling dancers toward them. When she glanced back at the count, she detected an odd sadness in his eyes. It startled and confused her all the more. Was it possible that hearing of her engagement could have saddened the man? He was drawn to her, there was no doubt about that. But was it conceivable that he cared more than he was willing to admit?

It shocked her to realize how pleased she was by this thought. But before she could think what to say, he abruptly let her go. Before Charles could reach them, he was gone.

4

The engine of the Voisin biplane sputtered and died. Kitty felt the plane dip and then she was soaring through open, endless sky. A bird aloft in silent, blue space.

The prudent thing would be to restart the engine at once. But she couldn't resist the blissful silence of gliding through the air, freed from the noisy motor. She wrenched off her cap and goggles and let her hair fly free, feeling the crisp rush of air on her face. All around her were verdant fields, looming up toward her now as the plane began its fall. From here, high above, the boundaries were indistinct, the separate farms mingling together into one unity, one whole. The beauty of it, as always, took her breath away.

She loved the feel of falling. Swooping through the sky like a hawk rushing its prey. Free from everything—the responsibilities and obligations, the worries and defeats. Alone with herself, the only danger that of not restarting the engine in time. Of crashing to the ground in flames. Even that was a thrill. The possibility of failure. They said she had a death wish, all those spectators who came to watch her aerial feats. The sport of aviation was too new, too dangerous, for any sane person, let alone a woman. Let them think what they would. They didn't know. They couldn't even guess.

Cameron would love this, she thought. *Do you feel it, Baji? Up here we're part of the sky.*

Cameron. She always thought of him when she flew. When she'd flown for the first time, when she'd truly become a part of the sky, she'd felt him with her, felt his spirit soar with hers.

The plane lurched and gathered speed, racing to its meeting with the earth. The countryside loomed closer now. The farms were clear, one divided from the other. She could smell the sea. Settling her goggles back in place, she flicked the switch that would start the engine again. Nothing. Nothing but silence and the rushing air. She tried again. Again the controls failed.

The ground seemed now to be charging toward her. She tried again, quickly. With a slight sputter, the engine engaged, roaring to life. A gentle pressure on the throttle checked its descent, and once again she was rising, higher, higher, into the vast blue sky. Collapsing back into her seat, she allowed herself a sigh before turning the plane and heading for the grassy plain that served as an airfield.

"You scared the hell out of me," her mechanic,

Lawrey, scolded her when she'd pulled to a stop on the grassy field. "You keep pulling stunts like that and I'll be an old man before my time."

He was a big Yorkshireman who'd given up flying around the same time that Kitty had taken it up, following a crash in which he'd suffered compound fractures in both legs. Walking was still painful for him. He'd lost his nerve in the crash and as a result tended to goad Kitty for her recklessness in the air.

"I had everything under control the whole time," she assured him. But she hadn't, really. And he knew it.

"You're going to have to take this business more seriously if you intend to fly the Channel and collect that five hundred pounds the *Daily Mail* is offering. Right now, a half-dozen Frenchies are over there training night and day, determined to do it before the summer is out. And who have we got? A woman up there enjoying the scenery. Flying loops, for Crissake. Loops won't give you distance. To fly the Channel you need distance. You can't waste an ounce of fuel."

His words sobered her like a slap in the face. "You're right, of course. I *have* been distracted lately. It seems that I'm being pulled in so many directions at the moment."

He sighed. "I know you have problems on your mind, but when you're in the sky, you can't allow yourself to think of anything except the task at hand. If you succeed, no one will even remember your family troubles. And besides, England's honor depends on you."

"You needn't worry. I'm well aware of what's at stake."

He peered at her, unrelenting. "As far as I know, you don't even have your future husband's permission for a

Channel try. He told me he'd lie down on the runway before he'd allow it."

The mention of Charles made her realize she hadn't thought of him once that day. "He'll relent in time," she assured him, before moving on.

When her train arrived at Euston Station, she decided to walk the mile or so to Mayfair. She felt more shaken by Lawrey's warning than she'd wanted to admit. Lately, it seemed she was being torn in so many directions. Her father's plight, the search for the ruby, the lure of the Channel flight . . . and on top of it all, the new and unexpected threat of Max Aveli. . . . This demon who had firmly planted himself in the path of everything she sought—freedom for her father, and a contented married life with Charles.

Lawrey was right. She had to stay focused on one thing at a time. And right now, that had to be the challenge of beating Aveli to Lady Philipson's ruby.

After the ball, she'd told Sir Harold about the rogue's cheeky proposal. Sir Harold didn't like it, but agreed that there was no way they could ignore it. As he was a particular friend of the Philipsons', he could help her with some information on their security system and finding out the couple's social itinerary. Aveli, no doubt, already had much of this information. But Sir Harold was confident that he could match it, and—given the Philipsons' busy social schedule—that they could strike soon, perhaps as soon as that night.

As dusk began to infuse its gentle purple glow, she slowly made her way through the crowded streets, relishing the sense of anonymity the gathering darkness lent her, and enjoying the clatter and hustle of a city that constantly seemed to be reinventing itself before her eyes.

Truly, the London of 1909 was a city in bewildering transition, a city that lived and breathed in an uneasy interlude between the staid old Victorian era and the garish, fast-paced, exciting new world of the twentieth century. The old sensibility still had a firm grip on the manners and morals of daily life, but the modern new world was rushing in with the speed of a bullet. Aeroplanes, gramophones, and moving pictures had seized the popular imagination. Motorcars, motorbuses, and electric trams had all but replaced horse-drawn carriages, creating cleaner streets but more traffic and accidents. Lured by manufacturing jobs, more and more families were moving into the city, turning the green fields and gardens of the surrounding countryside into one vast tract of paved streets and seemingly endless rows of functional grey buildings. From Highgate to Hammersmith, the legions of the poor filled the streets of London, creating a constant pressure for dramatic new social reform, which, in turn, threatened the aristocracy and perversely spurred it to more excess, profligacy, and ostentation.

She passed a newsstand on Oxford Street displaying the *Times, Express,* and *Daily Mail*. As usual, their headlines screamed the growing threat of a war with Germany and more rumors that the king might be seriously ill—events that could well put a symbolic end to this waning first decade of the century that was already being called the Edwardian era.

Upon her return home, she found a letter waiting for her on the hall table. It was from India. Her father? No. The handwriting told her it was from her friend Victoria.

She took it to her room, feeling cheered by the prospect of reconnecting to her closest girlhood friend. When she'd come to England and found herself shunned for her mixed blood, it was Victoria who befriended her and helped give her the courage to stand up to the other children's cruelty. Victoria knew something about censure. Her mother was a domineering and properly formal woman whose sole purpose in life seemed to stem from her attempts to crush her daughter's rebellious spirit and turn her into her own vision of a proper young lady. From the first, Kitty and Victoria recognized in each other a similar thirst for adventure and desire to leave the painful past behind.

Victoria was fascinated by Kitty's early years in India. So much so that four years ago, when she met Mortimer Hingham, a rising star in the Indian colonial service, she promptly married him—effectively escaping her mother's criticism and realizing her dream of going to India in one impulsive move. Kitty hadn't heard from Victoria for ages.

She ripped open the letter eagerly, only to find more bad news.

Darling Kitty,

I realize you haven't heard from me in some time, but you have never been out of my thoughts. Particularly during these trying times. I'm so very sorry about your father, dear. I want you to know that I took it upon myself to appeal directly to the viceroy regarding his case. I have resisted writing all this time, hoping that when I did, I could bring you better news. Unfortunately, all my attempts have failed. The viceroy's office has officially set the date of execution for the twelfth of May.

Kitty darling, I know the pain these words must cause you. There is nothing I can say that will lessen your burden. But I must tell you this. I too have been through a period of anguish such as I would wish on no one. I thought the pain would never end. I thought my life was over. Everything I came to India to find seemed beyond my grasp. And then, Kitty, a miracle happened that has transformed my life so completely that I marvel that I was ever capable of such despair. I've realized only recently that I've found the one thing I desired most. I've found my soul mate, Kitty. You can't imagine the joy this discovery has brought. It seems that India was, indeed, the adventure I thought it would be.

I only tell you this because, knowing of your own feelings for your dear, lost Cameron, I feel certain you will understand. And perhaps to bring you some measure of comfort and hope during this difficult time. It seems the old cliché is true. Just when you think things are the darkest, you really do find that silver lining.

In the meantime, if there's anything at all that I might do to help, please call on me.

> *Your loving friend,*
> *Victoria*

Kitty sat quietly on her bed for some time, holding the letter. Victoria was right. The news of her father had devastated her. The twelfth of May! Would they ever find the ruby in time?

The remainder of Victoria's letter seemed to float to the surface of her mind. She was, of course, gratified to hear of her friend's happiness. But what did it all mean?

It was almost as if she'd written in code. Or perhaps she'd meant just what she'd said, that she'd finally found contentment in her married life. Kitty remembered Mortimer. She wouldn't have thought him capable of turning the head of such a free and loving spirit as Victoria. But people were capable of change. Perhaps she'd found the man of her dreams in him, after all.

Maybe that's what Victoria had meant to impart: the hope that, given time, Kitty could learn to feel the same about Charles.

Still, the words "soul mate" echoed in her mind, unsettling her. Whispers of India . . .

Sir Harold paced before the fireplace in his study as Kitty changed behind a screen.

"The Philipsons will be out for the evening, playing bridge," he told her. "It's not ideal, as Lord Philipson insists they leave by eleven so they'll be home well before midnight. That gives you a limited amount of time. Fortunately, this is the servants' night off, so the house will be empty. But you'll still have to contend with the dogs."

"Dogs?"

"Even before the threat of our friend the Tiger, Lord Philipson was overly apprehensive about robberies. The house is surrounded by a tall wrought-iron fence. You can scale it easily enough, but he has a pack of vicious hounds that roam freely, trained to attack. So vicious, even the servants are afraid of them. This will present your greatest challenge."

She felt a flutter of nervousness. She could easily have

bypassed the dogs as a child. But did she remember enough of her training to do so now?

The Philipson mansion was completely dark, as if to flaunt the fact that it was deserted. A perfect invitation if one didn't know about the predators lurking within the gate. Kitty rounded the property several times in preparation. The dogs were obviously well trained. If they were on the grounds they gave no indication in the hushed night.

Before entering, she tested the direction of the chill breeze. As she did, she tried to recall Ngar's words that long-ago day in Rajasthan. Something about animals judging your presence by your smell . . . your motion . . . your fear. She'd have to stay downwind of them, so they couldn't pick up her scent.

The breeze was coming from the southwest. Cautiously, Kitty made her way to the northeast corner of the imposing wrought-iron fence. All was quiet. Steeling herself, she carefully scaled the enclosure and dropped quietly to the ground below. There she waited again. No sound.

She used the rhythm of the breeze to move toward the house. Since there was no one home, she could enter from the ground floor and go upstairs in comfort.

All at once, the dogs began to bark. They appeared as if from nowhere, charging as a pack—huge mastiffs, half a dozen of them—toward the front gate, where they snapped and lunged at the iron bars. A man was passing by on the sidewalk. He veered from the crazed pack, cursing them, as Kitty blessed her luck, snapped the lock of the back door, and slipped inside.

She knew the floor plan of the house from Sir Harold's description. Once, at a bridge game, Lord Philipson had complained of the cost of installing a safe in his bedroom floor. Moving stealthily through the dark house, she ascended the two flights of stairs and found the bedroom door.

Inside, she felt more than saw the layout of the room. The canopied bed along the far wall, the windows at the side. The safe was hidden in the floorboards, beneath a small Persian rug. Silently she crept toward it. But when she reached the spot, she found the carpet had been moved and the trapdoor was standing on end. The safe was open.

A light flicked on. She whirled around, escape already foremost in her mind. The light was coming from a small Tiffany lamp perched on a dainty table. And sitting in the chair at its side, calmly sipping a brandy, was the Tiger in all his midnight glory.

He was slouched back in the chair, legs stretched out before him, brandy snifter in one hand. His mask obscured his face but she could see the gleam of triumph in his eyes. His body—molded by the sculpted black that accentuated his masculinity, his aura of danger, his seemingly reckless disregard—made the chair he sprawled in appear ridiculously fragile by comparison.

"How did you get in here?" she asked.

"The same way you did. Through the door."

"But the dogs—"

"You mean those playful pups?"

"You bastard. How long have you been here?"

"Long enough to find this."

He held something in his hand. Casually, he tossed it into the air, catching it neatly in his palm. She caught the flash of brilliant red before he closed his glove around it again.

The Blood of India!

"Sorry, kitten. The game is finished. You've lost. Let's see if you can accept defeat with as much grace as you waltz."

She stared at his closed fist, which concealed the gem she'd risked life and limb to find. So close, and yet as distant to her as it had ever been.

"Count Aveli, please. I need that ruby to save my father's life. He's been imprisoned and awaits execution. . . . There's a pirate in the Indian Ocean who . . ." She realized suddenly how pathetic she must sound and altered her tone. "Just believe me when I say I need this particular ruby. To you it's just another bauble. But to me it's everything."

If she'd thought to soften him, it hadn't worked. "You British," he scoffed. "So confident that you're at the center of the world. That your point of view is the only one that matters. It would never occur to you that I might have my own use for this specific gem."

"What could possibly be more important than saving an innocent man's life? Be honest, count. You want it to satisfy your personal vanity. You want it because of its size."

"You're breaking my heart, Mademoiselle Bernhardt. Such a pretty show of feminine supplication. Next thing I know, you'll be falling to your knees to beg the heartless landlord to extend the deadline for your rent. Not that I wouldn't love to see you on your knees before me. But you'd be wasting your breath."

She stood there, stunned by the mocking rejection of her plea. Rage surged through her, but she contained it with effort. She lowered her gaze submissively and said in a soft voice, "I *will* get on my knees if you like. Please, I implore you . . ."

She moved toward him and in a gesture of complete surrender, began to bend her knees. Halfway through the motion, however, she swung around and kicked his hand with the heel of her shoe, knocking the ruby high in the air. Still swinging, making a complete circle in the air, she snatched the ruby before he had time to react.

Reaching behind her, she withdrew from her waistband a long, thin Maltese dagger. Pointing it toward him, she said, gloating, "Now it's *your* turn to get on your knees."

Standing, he raised his hands briefly in a gesture of conciliation. "I never argue with a woman who has a knife at my throat. If you want the stone that badly, by all means, take it."

His tone was too smooth, too self-satisfied, for a defeated man. Suddenly suspicious, she raised her hand and took a close look at the stone in her palm. It was a brilliant faceted ruby about the size of a chestnut. Too small. Not the right shape. Not the Blood of India, after all.

"You contemptible scoundrel," she snarled, flush with fury. "You lied to me! If I hadn't taken this from you, you actually would have let me think you had the Blood of India. So I would give up and no longer be in your way. You don't have the slightest concern that it would kill my father."

"Your father is guilty. He deserves to die."

In a rage she lunged at him with the knife. But with one graceful movement, his hand shot to her shoulder and lightly pinched the tendon. The knife dropped to the floor. Kitty's arm was paralyzed. Waves of dizziness assaulted her. Gasping for breath, she dropped to her knees.

As the world swirled around her, flashes of memories skitted through her mind. She recalled, for the first time in years, Ngar teaching her a similar technique as a child—a temporary, nonviolent method of immobilizing an enemy.

Her heart was hammering wildly in her breast. She drew concentrated breaths until her head began to clear. How had he done that?

But when she looked up, he was gone. The chair was empty. The brandy snifter sat on the table beside the softly glowing lamp. The window was open. And she was alone in the room. Alone with the unasked question echoing in her mind.

5

The weather was perfect, cold and sunny, with just a hint of a breeze. Kitty glanced down at the crowd gathered at Hendon Field, their faces tipped toward the sky, riveted on her plane. She wore, as she always did for public exhibitions, a stunning costume all in white: silk aviator pants, open-collared silk shirt, tight jacket, knee-length boots, goggles, and a long white scarf that fluttered dramatically in the wind. She presented a striking picture in her white plane. Her auburn hair she allowed to fly free—to emphasize the fact that a woman was performing these aerial feats.

She'd climbed into the air, reaching her designated speed and height with ease, and was now approaching the first pylon—one and a half miles from her takeoff point. Another crowd had gathered here, where she would make a wide turn and then head back to land. A distance of three miles: breaking the record for English aviation she herself had set two months ago. It was time to begin the turn, but something held her back. She was consumed now by that rapturous sensation of absolute freedom in the open sky. She realized she didn't want it to end.

As the cold air lashed her cheeks into a rosy glow and her hair whipped about her face, the whispers that had haunted her the night before resurfaced. *Cameron.* But it was impossible. Cameron was dead. She'd seen him shot.

Still, the eerie sensation persisted. She thought again of her instant sense of familiarity with Aveli, the feeling that he was a mirror image of herself . . . of the effortlessness with which he'd bypassed the dogs . . . of the shoulder pinch that had sparked memories of her long-ago training with Ngar . . . the fact that Cameron had been so much in her thoughts lately . . .

It was nothing more than a flicker of intuition. She had no facts to back it up . . . indeed, the facts mocked her as a fool to believe Cameron could be alive. Yet there was something about Aveli that made her think of Cameron.

Below, over the steady drone of her engine, she heard a cry from the crowd, making her realize that she'd passed the first pylon and was heading for the second—another mile distant, farther than anyone had dared fly before. Once again, she'd allowed her mind to wander. If she didn't turn around quickly, she probably wouldn't have enough fuel to make it back. But still her thoughts nagged at her. *What could this connection between the two men be?* Was it possible, by some unthinkable quirk of fate, that Cameron was alive? That he'd assumed the identity of Aveli? But why? Even if he'd survived the shot that she'd assumed had killed him, why pretend to be someone else? Unless, having been left for dead, he'd remained a captive of the kidnappers. Unless they'd tortured him and played with his mind until . . .

Suddenly a thought jolted her. Perhaps he didn't remember! That would explain why he was so different. Dear God! Could it possibly be?

She was clinging to the merest glimmer of hope. But that hope was so seductive, so irresistible, so fulfilling, so . . . delicious that she couldn't resist it.

Suddenly, she couldn't wait to land, to get back to town and find him. To learn the truth. As she'd already gone beyond the second pylon, she maneuvered the biplane into a wide curve, heading back toward the airfield. Passing the first pylon again, she felt the Levavasseur engine begin to sputter. She pulled back on the throttle and tried to increase her height. Before her, she could see the crowd waiting for her return, wildly cheering and waving at her. The engine coughed and sputtered. She was out of fuel. Not designed as a glider, the Voisin fell toward the earth. But she pulled the aileron up and caught an air current.

The engine had completely stopped, but with a firm hand she guided the plane gracefully onto the field. As she stepped down, a crowd of spectators rushed her. She was instantly surrounded by well-wishers congratulating her, vying to shake her hand. Reporters surged to the front, pencils in hand.

"Do you realize you've just set a new world record of five miles?" one of them asked over the clamor.

"Could we have a picture, Miss Fontaine?" another called.

She felt impatient to be gone. She'd just made history, yet all she could think of was finding Count Aveli. But publicity was a necessary part of the game. So she struck a pose in front of her plane, standing so the words "The English Hope" were visible just above her head.

"Shake your hair, Miss Fontaine. And let's see if we can't get that scarf to fly in the breeze."

She shook the tangles from her hair obligingly then turned just a bit so the breeze caught her flowing white scarf. The photographers snapped their pictures as other newsmen called out questions.

"Do you now feel ready to fly the Channel?"

"Very nearly," she answered.

"Did you hear the latest comments of Professor Hoffman at Oxford University on that matter?"

"What has the esteemed professor said now?"

"He says it's one thing to fly above Sussex farmland, but quite another to fly over a body of water crisscrossed by some of the most treacherous winds in Europe. He says the Channel will likely never be conquered."

"Hoffman's a fool," she sniffed. "It's not a matter of 'if.' It's a matter of 'when.'"

"And a matter of 'who,'" someone added.

"Do you really think a woman has a chance?" another asked.

"Why not a woman?" she threw back.

"Doesn't the fact that our only serious contender is a

woman say something derogatory about English manhood?''

Kitty's patience was nearly at an end. "It says only that England's women are the equal of her men."

"But isn't it insanely dangerous for man *or* woman?"

Just then her gaze fell on a tall, dark figure at the back of the crowd. Max Aveli. The sight of him hit her like a blow. The handsome face with its strong jaw, dark eyes, and wickedly sensual mouth. His dark hair, tousling slightly in the breeze. That cat-burglar body, powerful, graceful, too ruggedly honed to be contained by the street clothes he wore. *Who is he?* She had to know.

She heard herself mouthing the phrase he'd said to her. "If it wasn't dangerous, it wouldn't be any fun."

Suddenly she realized what had made her freeze when she'd heard those words. Cameron, too, had found fun in danger.

One reporter crowed as he jotted down the quote. "I just love covering people who know how to turn a phrase. Makes my job all the easier."

Kitty couldn't tear her gaze from Aveli's face. Emboldened by the urgency of her need and the feat she'd just accomplished, she was determined to confront him. With a slight inclination of her head she indicated the hangars. He glanced toward them, then back at her. For a moment, he stared hard, as if wondering what she was up to. But he nodded and slipped away.

Lawrey had made his way through the crowd. "Congratulations," he told her, slapping her on the back with uncharacteristic cheer. "I don't mind telling you, my heart was in my throat when your engine died. But I thought I'd burst with pride when you caught that air current on the final approach. My hat's off to you, honey. It was a masterful bit of piloting."

"Thank you, Lawrey."

"I think it's time for me to install the big fuel tank. Suddenly that Channel doesn't look so daunting."

This was high praise, indeed. "Let's do it," she said.

Just then Charles Flemming elbowed his way through the crowd. He seemed much less pleased by her feat. "That will be all, gentlemen. Miss Fontaine has had enough excitement for one day."

"Tell us, Mr. Flemming," one reporter persevered. "How do you like being engaged to the Queen of the Skies?"

Gravely, Charles asked, "How would *you* like it?"

The young reporter laughed. "I don't think I'd mind a bit," he said, before saluting Kitty and moving on with the rest of the dispersing crowd.

She heard the announcer say, "Following Miss Fontaine is Captain Newton of Lincolnshire."

Captain Newton, dressed in a khaki aviator suit, walked toward her. "Congratulations on your daring achievement," he called. Then, with a fierce look, he added, "You can be sure I won't try to best it here today!"

Kitty turned to Charles. "Did you see me?" she asked.

"I saw."

"Everyone else here has congratulated me. Even my surly mechanic. Everyone except my husband-to-be."

Charles looked grim as he took her elbow and guided her out of earshot. "A fat lot of good you'll do your father if you're splattered all over Hendon Field to the delight of your bloodthirsty admirers."

"You're in a mood."

He turned on her. "It's dangerous and it's for nothing."

"Not for nothing. For England."

"England can do this without you. Let's go," he added. "I saw Aveli lurking in the crowd. I want you far away from him."

Her heart fluttered wildly. In a careful tone, she said, "Actually, it's because of Aveli that I must stay. I've a hunch I want to play out. I'm going to meet with him. You go on home. I'll take the train when I'm finished."

He stopped and looked earnestly into her face. "I don't like this, Kitty. The man is, after all, a criminal. A rogue. He could be a murderer for all we know."

Or he could be your brother, she thought "Well, he's not going to murder me before all these witnesses."

"I still don't like it."

"Charles, trust me. I shall be fine."

His face softened. "I can't help worrying about you. I love you, Kitty."

She cast a glance toward the hangars, eager to be off.

Charles continued. "And when you said you'd marry me . . . well, you'll never know how happy you made me."

"Charles, please . . . not now . . ."

"Is it so wrong for me to be concerned? I couldn't bear to lose you now."

A whisper of guilt fluttered through her. She owed him so much. But she had to discover the truth. What if Max was Cameron, only he didn't remember? What if she could help him? She touched Charles's arm. "You mustn't worry. Aveli won't harm me."

"How do you know?"

"I—I just . . . know. Go on. Tell your father I'll stop by when I return to town."

Reluctantly, he left. She watched him go, then made her way through the concession stands selling hot tea and chocolate and roasted chestnuts. The attention of the crowd was once again focused on the air as Captain Newton began his exhibition in a Demoiselle monoplane. She watched for a moment with a critical eye, then moved on.

It was dim and cold inside the hangar. A shaft of sunlight streamed in through the high windows, throwing the shadow of the parked Wright Flyer across the dirt floor. Kitty allowed her eyes to adjust to the absence of light, then scanned the room for Aveli. He wasn't there. Maybe he'd misunderstood her, after all. The stab of disappointment made her realize how desperately she'd wanted him to be here, waiting for her.

But then she heard his voice from behind her. "A private audience with the queen," he drawled. "A singular honor."

She turned and saw him standing in the doorway with the sun at his back. She couldn't see his face. Shivering, she pulled her jacket tighter about her. She was trembling with nervous excitement. The words she'd wanted to say seemed to catch in her throat.

Are you Cameron?

She was quivering with such excitement that she wanted to blurt it out. But she had to be careful. She must ease into it, despite her impatience.

He closed the door and stepped inside. His boots made no sound as he approached. She was suddenly aware of how alone she was with him, of how helpless she felt in his presence. She looked at him with new eyes, searching for clues. He looked older than she imagined Cameron would. And yet he *could* be Cameron's age. His skin was darker than most Englishmen's, as if he'd spent considerable time in the sun. He had faint sun lines around his eyes. Those eyes . . . so dark, so mysterious. Holding no key to who he really was. As if he assumed a mask of invisibility even when in plain view. Her senses bristled. Was it even remotely possible? That by some shattering miracle he'd returned to her?

"Why did you come today?" Her voice sounded hushed in the cavernous structure.

"Curiosity, perhaps. What is it like to fly through the air?"

Come, Baji. Come fly with me.

"It's like being a part of the sky."

If he remembered those words, he didn't show it. Instead he asked, "Why did you ask me here?"

"I wanted to know more about you."

He arched a brow. "Indeed? You don't strike me as a woman who's fond of social discourse. From what I know of you, you're more apt to come to the point."

"You've insinuated yourself into my life. It only seems fair that I know something about the man who's sworn to make a travesty of all my plans."

"It's enough, I should think, to know that I will."

"Call it curiosity, then. Where did you grow up?"

"In Italy, naturally."

"And yet you speak flawless English, without a hint of an Italian accent."

"A little trick I picked up. It comes in handy, you'll

agree, during midnight jaunts. Keeps the neglected English matrons from guessing who I really am."

"That's the question of the moment, it would seem. Who *are* you?"

"Ah, it's my life story you're after. Very well, if you insist. My father was Count Aveli. I was educated in Italy, but traveled extensively with my father until he died and I inherited his title."

"And your mother?"

"My mother and sisters were sadly killed in a train accident when I was quite young."

"Where?"

He hesitated, peering at her. "That's a topic I don't wish to discuss."

"Some exotic place, Lady Quimby said, although she couldn't recall just where. She knew your father, but oddly enough, never knew of the existence of a son."

"I can hardly be held responsible for the ignorance of silly Englishwomen."

"You don't seem to think much of the English."

"I loathe every one of you."

"And yet you came to England."

"You know why I'm here."

"I know why you *say* you're here. But is it possible you have an ulterior motive?"

"Such as?"

She shrugged airily. "Perhaps you came looking for something else. Something you'd lost and wanted to find. Something other than the ruby you profess to crave."

"As you once said to me, there's nothing else here worth taking."

"But that was a lifetime ago. Before last night. Do you remember your childhood?"

"Of course."

"Everything?"

"Vividly," he said with a touch of bitterness he couldn't disguise.

That answered the question of amnesia. Unless he couldn't really remember his childhood, and believed what he'd been told. "You're an Italian count, and yet you seem possessed of some extraordinary skills."

"You're not the first woman to tell me so," he said suggestively.

She blushed, remembering too well the effect of his trenchant sexuality. Even now, standing before him, she could feel his heat. He was like a magnet, calling her to him with a potent force that she could scarcely resist. Deliberately trying to distract her by seeming to misinterpret her words.

"Skills that are scarcely an Italian specialty."

"And how would you know?"

She sensed that she'd touched a nerve. Although his face didn't change, she felt a sudden wariness, as if he'd drawn around him a cloak of remote intrigue.

"That shoulder pinch, for example. Quite a handy trick. I suppose you're going to tell me some Italian master taught you that."

He was watching her closely. "You wouldn't expect me to divulge professional secrets."

"Secrets. That's at the heart of it all, isn't it? I know something about secrets. Secret skills that I learned as a child. Like how to slip past a pack of savage dogs without them detecting my presence. Or how to seemingly disappear into thin air. Come to think of it, I knew

someone else who could do those very things. Just as
you can."

"A magician, no doubt."

No hesitancy. No tremor of recognition.

"Or perhaps someone who was taught the same
things I was."

Silence. His eyes, cast in shadow, narrowed on her
face. "It must be true," he said at last.

Her heart skipped a beat. "What's true?" she asked,
holding her breath.

"That altitude plays tricks with the mind. I've heard
Professor Hoffman——"

"Don't play games with me," she snapped. "I have to
know. If it's true, you can tell me. I don't know why or
how. Right now I don't care. I only want the truth.
Because if it *is* true——"

He grabbed her arms and shook her. "Stop it," he
hissed. "Before you make a complete fool of yourself."

She stared at him, stunned. She stood before him,
vulnerable, small, feeling the tension of the room.

He wasn't going to make this easy. Either he didn't
remember, or he declined to admit it. But there was one
way she could find out. Cameron had been shot in the
chest. If what she suspected were true, this self-styled
Count Aveli would bear the telltale scar.

"I can't help making a fool of myself over you," she
said softly, moving closer. "You've done something to
me. You've made me . . . feel things I've never felt.
Made me want—what? What is it you make me need so
badly, Count Aveli? Why can't I forget you, even when
I try?"

She reached up with her hands and wove her fingers
through his crisp hair. Drawing his head down, she

kissed him. She could feel his resistance in his unresponsive lips, his refusal to play the game.

"Why did you call me dangerous?" she asked against his mouth.

"If you think you can toy with me—"

"But you must feel it, too," she purred, trailing a finger across the sculpted features of his face. The prominent cheekbones; the masculine jaw; the lush, full mouth that seemed to promise untold delights. "You called me sweet poison. You said I made you want me against your will." She felt his breath quicken beneath the touch of her hand.

"No man has ever said such words to me. You made me feel . . ."

"What?" he breathed.

"Truly wanted for the first time."

She sounded more vulnerable than she'd intended. Her eyes, fixed on his, showed too plainly the loneliness that had plagued her since the loss of Cameron so long ago. A painful longing gripped her, causing unexpected tears to swim in her eyes. She wanted nothing more than for this horrible yearning to cease.

"Kiss me," she pleaded. "Kiss me the way you did that first night."

Her mouth sought his. Again she felt him waver, holding himself back. But she wrapped her arms about his neck and kissed him hungrily until she felt him respond. Until his lips opened and his tongue darted in to taste the sweetness of her mouth.

"Don't you feel it?" she murmured. "This force that's drawing us together? Perhaps you don't remember. But surely you can feel its power. As if it's telling us this was meant to be."

She could feel him fight to hold himself aloof, even as his body responded to the touch of her mouth against his. He pushed her back, looking down into her face.

"You *are* dangerous," he growled.

"But if it wasn't dangerous," she whispered, "it wouldn't be any fun."

Her words seemed to crack through his resolve. As if he couldn't help himself, could no longer find the will to fight, he yanked her to him and captured her mouth in a scalding kiss. Waves of pleasure and longing swept her up, igniting her blood, causing her to moan her hunger low in her throat. He kissed her madly, as if driven by some demon he couldn't control, her lips, her cheek, bending to nibble frantically on the long column of her neck. His mouth found her ear, the play of his tongue and his hot breath electrifying her with shock waves of unbearable lust. His arms held her close, pinning her to him, even as his hands began an exploration of their own, slipping beneath her jacket.

He found her lips again as her fingers crept up to unbutton his shirt. Awash with desire, she couldn't wait for the unveiling. It was all she could do not to rip the buttons free. Her fingers trembled, faltering, because the lure of his mouth and his devastating kiss were rendering her insensible.

But finally the buttons slipped free. Her hands parted the shirt beneath his suit. She wrenched her mouth from his and brought it to his throat, trailing kisses downward as she heard his ragged gasp.

"Cameron," she murmured as her lips found their mark.

She felt him stiffen even as the incongruity registered. His chest was smooth beneath the tufts of hair.

Lifting her head, she opened her eyes and stared. The light was dim in the hangar, but there was enough to see. A virile chest, firmly muscled, covered with a smattering of dark hair.

But no scar.

6

She felt suddenly chilled to the bone. How could she have been so horribly wrong?

She looked up at him, her shock registering in her eyes. His handsome face was hard, cruel. "Your ardor seems to have cooled," he noted.

"I thought—" What had she thought? She felt so muddled, she couldn't seem to think straight at all.

"That I was someone else?"

"Yes," she all but whimpered.

"I'm still the same man I was a moment ago. The man who made you feel so wanted."

His words hit her like a slap in the face. She'd behaved shamefully. Had she lost her mind completely?

"You needn't rub it in. If you were any kind of gentleman, you'd allow me some dignity at least."

"Did I lead you to believe I was a gentleman? How remiss of me. I'll have to watch myself in the future."

She was too mortified to respond.

"So, you concocted a little fantasy, did you? Something to wrap all your jumbled feelings into a tidy package. Or did you perchance think to soften my black heart with this little charade? So I'll hand that ruby over when I find it? If so, you're wasting your time."

She felt close to tears. "I told you. I need that ruby to save my father's life."

He glared down at her unmercifully. "And I told you. Your father's guilty."

"How dare you!" she cried. "What do you know of it?"

"I know all about you, little girl."

"How could you possibly know anything about me?"

"I make it my business to know my enemies."

How could she have been such a fool? "Whatever you think you know, you're wrong."

"Am I? You've pried into my life. Now let's do a bit of prying into yours. I know, for instance, that you grew up in India. You were kidnapped as a child and your friend was killed. I might feel sorry for you, except that you've renounced everything you once knew."

"Renounced—"

"Your mother was half Indian. That could well be the most interesting thing about you. But you came to England and felt the sting of disapproval. So you began to believe the lie they live—the superiority of mighty Britain. You erased every trace of who you really are. You became more British than the British. You defy

death by day in an aeroplane and you defy the law by
night. To prove to the world what a brave little thing
you are. But you've built a fantasy world around you
where you'll be safe. You're nothing but a coward at
heart. Because you're running, little girl. Running from
who you really are."

She felt flayed by his accusations, as raw as if he'd
taken a whip and laid bare her skin. "Would a coward
risk everything to save her father?"

"A coward would *tell* herself she's risking everything
to save her father. When what she's really doing is
trying to save her own pride. If he's executed—if his
innocence is never established—what a legacy that will
be for you."

In a rage she flew at him, her hand poised to attack.
But he grabbed her wrist and held it in a biting hand of
steel. "You bloody bastard! You think I care—"

"That's right. I think you care so much what others
think that you're even willing to lie to yourself. Tell me
something, Miss Fontaine, and be honest if you can.
What bothers you more? The fact that your father stole
from people entrusted to his care? Or the fact that
people know he did?"

"My father," she ground out between her teeth, "is
innocent. He would never—"

"What do you really know of him? You haven't even
seen him for years. Like all the India British he packed
his pubescent daughter off to be taken care of back
home where she'd be safe from Indian influence. Have
you ever wondered why you're accepted here, despite
the fact that your father's been proved a thief? If he'd
stolen from proper Englishmen, as I do, you wouldn't
be able to hold your head up. But after all, he only stole

from a lot of poor 'wogs.' And where's the harm in that?"

She tried again to slap him, but he held her hand fast. She tossed back her head to shake the hair from her face. "To think I mistook you for Cameron. He would have understood. He was all that was brave and noble about the English. All I ever wanted was to live up to him. But I suppose that's a concept you don't understand. Don't they have a word for 'noble' in Italian? You, Machiavelli, aren't fit to utter Cameron's name. I'd rather he were *dead* than turn out to be you."

Her words reverberated through the silent enclosure. He stood, holding her wrist, staring at her through narrowed eyes.

"Then I do feel sorry for you," he said at last. "Because your Cameron doesn't exist. No, kitten, I'm not your sainted Cameron."

"You don't have to tell me that. Cameron wasn't cruel. He wasn't hard and bitter like you."

Again he studied her flushed face. An odd look crept into his eyes. "I wonder," he mused, "what your sainted Cameron would think of you now? If he could see how you'd . . . lived up to his ideals. But I'm not so picky," he said in a soft growl. "I'd take you right here, on the ground, without a second thought. I like you with your back up, little cat. I don't know about your friend Cameron, but I have no use for martyrs."

He pulled her slowly close. She could feel her breasts flatten against the hard surface of his chest. And then his mouth was on hers, firm, inviting, but not waiting for consent. Angrily, she jerked her head away. But his free hand twisted in her hair, bringing her face back to him. His mouth found hers again. She fought him, pushing at the chest she'd bared. She despised him. Not just for who he was, but for what he'd witnessed—her all too vulnerable need. She wanted nothing now but to be free of him.

"If your Cameron were alive would he kiss you like that?"

"Cameron would never—"

"Of course not. Not the revered boy of memory. He would, no doubt, be the perfect gentleman. And you hate it that I want to do things to you that your Cameron never would."

"Yes," she spat out.

"Is that why you kissed me the way you did? Or could it be that you're tired of worshiping a shrine? Maybe what you need is a real man for a change."

Without knowing how it happened, he was kissing her with furious force, crushing her lips, stealing her breath, causing her heart to pound like a frantic, primal drum. She pushed against him, desperate for release. But the anger and hatred she was struggling to preserve began to melt in the white heat of his devilish appeal. She felt mesmerized, lost in his kiss, as his arms crept about her back and held her close. Drowning in his domination. Completely lost in him. The fist she pushed into his chest softened, touching the taut skin. She heard herself moan repudiation, even as she kissed him hungrily now, meeting his tongue with her own, pressing herself into him until she lost all consciousness of self and became a part of him. Fury, humiliation, all the tangled emotions of her unveiled heart, flared into passion and her body surged to life. She experienced again the treacherous hunger, a longing so intense that it devastated all her aspirations to reject and humiliate him in turn. Heat and chill quivered alternately through her. Her head was spinning—dizzy now as she'd never been in the air or when scaling towering walls. Flying free.

But this wasn't Cameron. This was a complete stranger. A stranger she hadn't stopped thinking of from the moment she'd first met him. A stranger whom—God help her—she couldn't bring herself to resist.

He pushed her back against the plane. She felt the wood bite into her back as his erection branded her. He felt huge and lodestone hard. She threw back her head, gasping wildly, as his lips moved from her mouth to find naked flesh beneath her scarf. Lust stabbed her loins. She clutched his head and whimpered eager consent.

"Did your hallowed Cameron ever make you feel like this?" he asked as he worked at her clothes. "Did he ever make you pant with longing? Make you so hungry for a man that you'd give anything to relieve the lust raging through you?"

Somehow her jacket had fallen to the ground, and her blouse was open. His hand found her breasts, torturing her with sweet touches and gentle pinches that made her gasp aloud. "Because that's what I'm going to do to you. Right here, right now. I'm going to fuck you senseless."

She'd never heard that word before. It sounded raw, raunchy, wickedly arousing on his tongue. His voice, ever hypnotic, was like a whispered incantation, keeping her thoughts riveted on his words. His mouth found her nipple as his hands slipped her pants down her hips, a moist, warm, wonderful temptation. "I'm going to make you feel things you never have," he continued. "I'm going to make you scream and beg. I'm going to show you who you really are, beneath that cavalier façade."

Her breeches were at her ankles now. He kissed his way down her naked body to bend before her. His fingers found her between her thighs. She was wet, slick. She flinched at the initial contact, but he was relentless, exploring her so skillfully that she felt herself open to his touch. "You're wet," he told her. "That's what I love. A hungry, wet pussy, just for me. Does that feel good?"

Even as she trembled with desire, some part of her still wanted to deny him. She pressed her lips together, determined to remain silent. But he took his hand away, abruptly ceasing the marvelous mastery, leaving her feeling as if she were hanging from a precipice, waiting to fall.

"Tell me you like it," he demanded.

She tried to refuse. But he touched her once, just a brief flick of his finger, enough to make her shudder with need. When he withdrew his hand, she knew she couldn't stand another minute.

"Tell me."

"I do like it," she admitted.

"Would you like more?"

"Yes," she said on a sibilant sigh. "More . . . please . . ."

He obliged her. A single finger shot inside as his thumb found her tender bud and employed a bewitching rhythm. She felt startled and fulfilled all in the same breath.

"I'm going to give you pleasure like you've never

imagined," he told her. "But first, you're going to come for me."

She didn't even know what he meant. She only knew she'd never felt so wicked and free, so ravenous and sanguine all at the same time. Her hips were moving to the rhythm of his hand, like a snake caught in a charmer's spell. Liquid heat flooded her loins. She felt his hand on her, in her, as his other stroked her like a cat, her leg, her belly, her breast, caressing, teasing, driving her mad. She cried out loud.

"That's it," he cooed. "Give yourself to me completely. Feel my hand inside you. Christ, you're exquisite. There's nothing more beautiful than the sight of a woman coming for a man."

Suddenly she knew what he meant. She felt spirals of heat coil inside, felt herself burning with a combustion that exploded like a torrent, beginning in her core and shuddering through her like a blaze gone wild. Gripping the plane behind her, she trembled and gasped, her body seized by waves of pleasure that seemed too sweet, too torturous to bear. She shook helplessly against his hand, sobbing in delight.

And then she felt limp. So limp she couldn't stand on her own. She crumpled into his arms. She was faintly aware as he removed her boots, sliding her breeches down over her feet. Stripping her completely naked to his eyes. She felt herself lifted in his arms, swung easily as her head continued to spin, until she found herself resting on the ground. Then she felt him atop her, naked, leanly muscled, his body hard against her pliant flesh. He kissed her as his hands stroked her curves, igniting renewed passion and need. It wasn't enough.

She wanted more. More of this feral pleasure at his hands. All else was forgotten.

As he moved, tasting her, he rubbed his erection against her thigh. The feel of it, so rigid and insistent, thrilled her beyond measure. He took himself in hand and tested the aperture of her wet cove. Then, with a plunge, he shot inside.

Her scream ripped through the hangar.

Even when he froze, his body tense, immobile, the reverberation of her strangled cry seemed to echo through the eerily hushed hall.

"Sweet Christ," he swore. His hands gripping her hair, he commanded, "Look at me."

She opened her eyes. He was so perfect in his hard-bitten, masculine beauty.

She didn't want him to stop. The pain had eased, her body adjusting on its own to his assault. When he moved as if to pull away, she clutched his shoulders, holding him inside.

"Don't stop," she whispered. "Please."

He continued to peer at her, but she felt him burgeon inside. "If you'd told me—I wanted to punish you, but not like this."

"I don't want you to stop," she repeated.

He glanced back at the door. "I should leave you now."

"But you can't, can you?"

His eyes locked with hers. "No. Goddammit, no."

"Then give me what you promised. Take away the pain."

He could see, from the pleading look in her eyes, that she meant every word she said. Carefully, tenderly, he began to move inside her. He brought his hand between them and found her cleft, fingering it gently until he heard her moan. Slowly, gathering momentum, he fondled her breast, licking, sucking, teasing with his tongue and teeth, until she felt the surge of keen desire lift and carry her away. She felt so full, so complete, with him inside. As if the half of her that had been missing, unbeknownst, had finally found its rightful place. She wrapped her legs around him, lifting her hips in invitation. The pain had been transformed to startling pleasure. She wanted still more.

His hesitation crumbled at her unspoken request. His body began to move, confident now, finding its own rhythm. Even as he endeavored to hold himself back, the friction boiled in his blood.

"Better?" he asked.

"Sublime," she murmured dreamily. "It's like flying."

"Then fly with me."

The faint whisper of recognition shattered as he thrust into her hard, hurling her heart into her throat, causing her to gasp in joy. She met his thrusts eagerly now, shimmering in building heat and sparks of stark desire. And just as she felt herself soaring, gliding, she heard his growl and felt him spill his release.

They lay entwined for some time, breathing hard, clinging to one another, their bodies damp, their surroundings forgotten. Kitty felt so replete, so satisfied, that she felt herself floating still in some dreamy wonderland without substance or boundaries, a misty expanse of some higher consciousness than she'd ever felt before. As if she'd left her body and was nothing more than spirit. No worries, no cares. Everything forgotten but newly encountered bliss.

Then she felt him move and break the spell. "Jesus," he muttered. "What have I done?"

He thrust himself from her and stood to gather his clothes, covering his body bit by bit with swift, proficient moves. She saw the angry reproach in his face as if he was consumed by self-loathing, as if he'd defiled himself.

Then his earlier words came back to her—words she'd ignored in the ecstasy of feeling him inside her, fitting her so perfectly that she'd felt she'd been fashioned just for him. *I wanted to punish you* . . .

He didn't care for her. He hadn't made love to her, tenderly, sweetly, confessing with his body what he was loath to disclose. He'd done just what he'd said he would. He'd used her to satiate his lust, as a way of punishing her for the attraction he didn't want to feel.

Worse still, she realized too late, she'd allowed herself to think he could be Cameron because subconsciously she must have realized she might be falling in love with him. It was her mind's way of clutching at straws to justify feelings for a man she didn't want to care for. She'd abandoned her English practicality and had allowed her cursed intuition to play havoc with her mind.

Mortified, she reached for her scattered clothes. He was dressed now, eager to be gone. But he paused and tossed her a handkerchief. "Clean yourself up before you leave."

She glanced down to see the residue smeared along her thighs. She flushed with embarrassment and shame. And as he left, she heard the echo of his own recrimination.

What had she done?

7

No one was home when she arrived. Racing to the bathroom, she stripped off her clothes and scrubbed herself clean. She'd given herself to a man who thought no more of her than he would a whore. The worst of it was that even as she reviled herself, her body remembered the delicious provocation of his hands, his lips, his seductively murmured words that had driven her to such rash abandon. She cursed herself and scrubbed harder, until her skin felt raw.

Afterward, she went to Curzon Street to see Sir Harold. It took every ounce of courage she possessed. Her impulse was to hide herself away. She didn't know how she could face him. Or Charles! How could she ever look him in the eye again?

"Thank God you're all right," Charles greeted her. "I cursed myself all the way home, realizing I'd left you in the hands of that brute."

It was too soon, Kitty realized. She should have given herself more time. Tears of guilt and shame filled her eyes. And in that moment, she knew what she had to do.

As soon as he'd closed the door, she took his hands in hers and said, "Charles, you've been nothing but good to me. You've been patient and kind and understanding. That's why, for your sake . . . I can't marry you."

"What are you talking about?" he cried. "What's happened? What have I done? Is it because of my feelings about your flying? Kitty, you know I—"

"It isn't that," she assured him quickly. "It isn't you at all."

He frowned, suspicious now. "Has that brute done something to you? If he has, I swear I'll—"

"It isn't anyone. I can't explain. Please believe me, if there were any other way—but there isn't."

"Whatever it is, we can work it out. You must let me help you, Kitty. You're everything to me. I can't do without you."

"You don't understand," she insisted. "Something's happened to me. The events of the past months have unbalanced me somehow."

Sir Harold, having just entered the hall, asked, "Unbalanced you in what way, my dear?"

Before she could answer, Charles cried, "Father, she wants to call off the marriage. Talk to her—convince her—"

Kitty looked at Sir Harold, her tears threatening now to spill over.

"Charles," he said firmly, "let me speak with Kitty alone. Come into the study, dear."

Before she could follow, Charles turned to her with pleading eyes. "Please, Kitty, don't do anything rash. Think about it, won't you?"

By the time Sir Harold had closed the study door behind them, some of her tears had spilled down her cheeks. She swiped them away.

"Would you care to tell me what this is all about?" Sir Harold asked kindly.

"I don't know what's wrong with me," she sobbed. "Ever since Aveli has intruded into our lives, it seems that everything is falling apart. I can't concentrate. I think I must be losing my mind."

He watched her quietly for a moment, deep in thought. Finally he asked in a gentle tone, "Why do you say that?"

"I've made a complete fool of myself. I was seized by a delusion that . . . I don't even know how to tell you."

"I think you know by now that you can trust me."

"It isn't a matter of trust. I don't want to hurt you by opening old wounds. Perhaps it's best that I forget all about it."

"There's nothing you can't tell me. We're seeking the same thing, after all. Anything weighing on your mind could affect that goal." He softened his tone. "I can see the pain you're in. It may make you feel better to unburden yourself."

"You'll think me mad. I realize now how insane it all sounds. But there were all these clues. The dogs . . . certain skills he possessed . . ."

"Kitty, please, just tell me."

She looked at him for a long moment, gathering her courage. "For a time I actually convinced myself that Aveli was Cameron."

The color drained from Sir Harold's face. "Cameron's dead," he said in a dull voice.

"Of course he is. I don't know what I could possibly have been thinking. I feel like such a fool."

"Did you tell him of your suspicion?" he asked quietly.

"I did. I wish I hadn't, but I did."

"And how did he react?"

She flushed, remembering his awful words about herself, her father, England . . .

"He made it clear that I was out of my mind."

"I scarcely know what to say, child."

"The thing that hurts the most is, even though I knew Aveli to be a despicable man, I—" She stopped abruptly. She couldn't confess the most humiliating secret of all. That she was falling in love with a man she knew she should despise. And that she'd made a complete fool of herself in the process.

Sir Harold took her hands and said, "I think the strain of all this has been harder on you than any of us imagined. I want you to go home and rest. Don't think about any of this."

Kitty slept late the next day. She awoke feeling numb and overwhelmed. She'd tried to relax as Sir Harold had advised, but she'd found herself consumed with anxiety and regret. It was awful, having time to think. To relive her humiliation.

She'd actually wanted Aveli to do what he'd done. *She'd practically begged him.*

She quickly dressed and headed down the stairs. She longed for the sky. To clear her head. To seek some semblance of peace. But as she flung open the door, she found a messenger with his hand poised to ring the bell.

"Oh, you startled me, miss. Message for Miss Fontaine. Will you sign?"

Kitty signed and took the envelope back inside. Alone in the front parlor, she hastily read the contents. There were two pages. The first was a note, written in a bold hand:

As a matter of professional courtesy, I thought I'd pass this along to you. Not that it will do you any good, given the challenge it presents.

No signature. Nothing to indicate who it was from. She knew, of course, that Aveli had penned the note. But why?

She turned to the next piece of paper and discovered with a shock that it was a carbon of a memorandum sent from Chief Inspector Worthington of Scotland Yard to the head prosecutor at the Old Bailey. It read:

This office wishes to inform you that the accumulated stolen items recovered upon the arrest of the petty thief Robin Bascom contains an unusually large red stone, in all probability a ruby. As we have not yet ascertained the victim from whom the gem was stolen, said item should be analyzed and catalogued before the culprit is brought to the bar, as said item, were it found to be genuine, could be of sufficient value to elevate Mr. Bascom's charge to grand theft.

The Blood of India in the hands of Scotland Yard!

How had Aveli come across this? She read his curt note again, seething in anger. The nerve of the man! The unmitigated gall! She'd show him what good this news would do her.

But wait. How did she know this wasn't a dirty trick? It could be a clever ploy, working on her sense of competition, to have her arrested and out of his way. Leaving him free to seek out the ruby on his own. After yesterday, she'd put nothing past him.

Yet the memorandum bore all the signs of authenticity. It was typed on Scotland Yard stationery and stamped with the official seal of the chief inspector. Aveli could hardly have executed such a brilliant forgery in so little time.

She took it directly to Sir Harold.

"What if it's a hoax?" she asked. "What if Aveli's just trying to get me out of the way?"

Sir Harold looked at the document and shook his head. "It certainly looks authentic. And besides, what would he possibly gain by having you arrested? You know his identity. No, I think he'd deem such an action as being too risky to himself."

"So you actually think I should break into Scotland Yard!"

"The question is, what do *you* want to do?"

"I don't think I have a choice. Time is of the essence. Obviously, they don't know what they've got. Once they catalogue the ruby and send it to Old Bailey as evidence, the opportunity will be lost. Aveli will no doubt go tonight. I shall have to beat him there." She fell back into a nearby wing chair. "But good God! How does one do such a thing? There are sixteen *thousand* police going in and out every day. Since the last Irish troubles, it's been heavily guarded on all sides. How does one possibly sneak in?"

He sat in the chair across the reading table from her. "If you're determined to go through with this, I believe I know a way," he told her. "Years ago, when I was just a lad, the plot of land that Scotland Yard now stands upon was little more than a rectangular piece of swamp along the Victoria Embankment. Funds were raised to build an opera house on the site. I remember because my family put up a portion of the money. It proved a bad investment, as part of the building was constructed but never finished. Eventually it was torn down and, some years later, the new Scotland Yard built on the site. One of the arguments for the new location concerned a tunnel that had been built linking the platform of Westminster Bridge Station with the auditorium of the opera house, allowing patrons direct access from the station. It was later thought that this tunnel could, in an emergency, facilitate the arrival of secret police reinforcements from outlying areas. They could take the train to the station and proceed to Scotland Yard through the tunnel, unseen by the public."

As he'd spoken, Kitty had straightened in her chair. "The tunnel still exists?"

"It does. But it's boarded up now, as it hasn't been used for some time."

"Perfect," Kitty agreed, buoyed by the prospect of action. "With luck, I shall be inside while Aveli is trying to figure out a way to get past the outside guards." She took a breath, considering the enormity of it all. "Breaking into the very bastion of the Metropolitan police. It's rather cheeky, don't you think? Quite a feather in my cap, if I succeed."

And the perfect way to exonerate her humiliation at Aveli's hands.

From outside Westminster station, Kitty glanced across Bridge Street at her destination. New Scotland Yard, as it had been called since its inception in 1890, sat on the west bank of the Thames between Westminster Bridge and Blackfriar's, in the shadow of Big Ben. Hardly had the first spadeful of dirt been dug for the new structure than the dismembered body of a young girl had been found on the spot. The murder was never solved—some claimed it was a precursor to the Yard's subsequent inability to solve crimes—and the new headquarters rose on the site: a granite, turreted building with a tall mansard roof, part medieval fortress, part French château.

Lights were already coming on in the building. A stream of office workers and police officers were exiting through the south entrance, along the Thames. As she descended into the station—inconspicuous in a long, worn skirt, serviceable blouse, and old cloth coat borrowed from her chambermaid, her hair tucked beneath a dirty rag—a mass of commuters was rushing to and fro, most of them men.

She quickly found the opening to the abandoned tunnel and succeeded in prying loose the rotted boards that blocked it from the main platform. Then she waited for the next train to pull in. In the bustle of arriving and departing passengers, she was able to slip past the loosened boards and into the dark tunnel without being noticed. Now, lighting the lantern she'd stashed beneath rags in the bucket she carried, she began her journey. Rats scampered out of her path. The tunnel was damp and stale, with puddles of water here and there along the way. As her skirt dragged through them, she decided it would aid her disguise, giving her the look of someone who had, indeed, been scrubbing floors.

The door to the main building was locked, but that was easily taken care of. Opening it was another matter. She pressed her ear to the wood, trying to determine if any sounds were coming from the other side. It wouldn't do to have someone question why she was using a door that had been long locked and all but forgotten. Easing it open a crack, she peered inside. A group of policemen were passing, the sound of their boots thunderous. She narrowed the crack and waited. When they'd left, she took a quick look, to find the atrium empty. Carrying her bucket and broom, she slipped inside.

A brief survey showed her a flight of stairs across the atrium. This, she was well aware, was her greatest point of danger. For all she knew, she could run into the commissioner himself. Keeping her eyes down, assuming an air of humble anonymity, yet walking forward as if she'd done so a hundred times, she crossed the hall. The sounds of footsteps on the stairs above warned her and she quickly moved to the rail against the wall. With lashes lowered, she saw from the corner of her eye the passing of blue policemen's uniforms. They were deep in conversation, apparently discussing a case. They ignored her completely. It gave her a momentary thrill to know that she was moving, undetected, in their midst.

Halfway up the next flight, a lone office worker passed. But a few steps beyond her he paused and said, "Oh, you."

Kitty stopped. "Me, sir?" she asked, keeping her gaze on the floor.

"Of course you," he said with a tone of annoyance and self-importance. "There's a frightful mess in office 215. Attend to it, will you?"

"Yes, sir. At once, sir."

He stood looking at her. Kitty kept her eyes lowered, willing him to leave. He seemed to be studying her. She held her breath.

At last he snapped, "Well, get on with it, girl."

"Of course, sir." Ducking her head, she hurried on. When she heard his receding footsteps, she laughed inside. Perhaps one day he'd put it together, that the maid he'd chastised had boldly made off with a priceless ruby from beneath their very noses!

The upper floor was a jumble of narrow hallways and small flights of stairs, all thrown together with what seemed haphazard disregard for design. The hallways were dark, but she dared not light the lantern now, lest someone were to come up to the Registry Room, seeking records. In the meager light, she read the signs on the doors. Finally, at the far end of a winding hall, she found what she was looking for: the Property Room.

The door was open just a crack. This gave her pause. A lucky happenstance? Or had Aveli, impossibly, already made his entrance? She inched the door open with her foot. It was dark inside. No evidence of trouble.

Pushing the door open, she set her bucket and broom down just inside. She was reaching for her lantern, intending to cover it with a rag to dim the glow, when suddenly a light snapped on. She whirled to see Aveli standing across the room beside some old wooden cabinets. So he'd beaten her here after all. But as she looked at him, she realized, with a chill up her spine, the danger that awaited her. Aveli, standing there with a fierce scowl on his face, was handcuffed at the wrists.

She lunged for the door. But before she could reach it, a firm hand grasped her arm. She felt the bite of steel on her wrist. As she yanked it back, she realized with a sinking heart that it was a handcuff.

She looked up to find three gentlemen standing there with victorious grins on their faces. The man on the other end of the handcuffs was older, with deep bags beneath his eyes and reddish-gray hair and thinning mustache. She recognized him at once from pictures in the newspapers. Chief Inspector Worthington.

"Welcome, Miss Fontaine," he greeted her in a smug tone. "We've been expecting you."

8

"You *did* set me up," Kitty charged Aveli.

Holding up his cuffed hands, he growled, "Does it look like I had any part in this? We've both been had."

"True," admitted the inspector. "It was I who put together that irresistible memorandum and the notes that lured each of you here. Rather clever, don't you agree?"

Kitty had to fight to keep her panic from showing. If she were arrested and found guilty, her hopes of freeing her father would go up in smoke.

"We've known about you for some time," the inspector went on to explain. "We even took the trouble to collect samples of your handwriting and, in the event that you knew each others' script, commissioned a forgery by a notorious falsifier of documents we happen to be hosting at Wormwood Scrubs at the moment. In exchange for a lighter sentence."

"And how," asked Aveli smoothly, "might we avail ourselves of a similar . . . consideration?"

Kitty couldn't help noticing that Aveli had fallen back into his Italian accent.

"Funny you should ask," said the inspector. "First, let me introduce my esteemed colleagues. Lord Timsley from the Foreign Office—"

Aveli bowed, saying, "Lord Timsley, we meet at last." Kitty recalled that she'd first stumbled upon Aveli in the darkness of Lord Timsley's sitting room. An ironic reunion.

"You visited my house, I believe," Timsley was saying.

"You have proof of that, I suppose?" Aveli asked.

Worthington continued as if the interruption had never taken place. "—and Colonel Carrington from the Indian Secret Service."

"Distinguished company," Aveli muttered. "But tell me, even if we are what you assume, what would such illustrious representatives of the British Crown want with two such insignificant housebreakers?"

"Let's adjourn to my office," Inspector Worthington suggested. "We shall all be more comfortable, I daresay."

Kitty yanked her wrist so the metal cuff jangled. "Surely there's no need for this, Inspector. I can hardly overpower the three of you. And if I did, I should certainly never make it out of here."

"Not if you're thinking of escaping through the tunnel," he gloated. "Even now, we have men guarding the entrance."

How did he know? Had she been watched the entire time? Assuming nonchalance, she shrugged. "You make my point, Inspector."

Worthington glanced toward Colonel Carrington. He was a strapping man in his forties with a pencil mustache, deeply tanned, smartly dressed in his army uniform. "I see no harm," he admitted.

Reluctantly, Worthington unlocked her bracelet.

"And mine?" Aveli asked.

Colonel Carrington replied, "I shouldn't press my luck, were I you."

Kitty rubbed her chafed wrist as they made their way through the maze of dark hallways and down the flights of stairs. On the first floor, where the more important offices were housed, Worthington opened a door. As she passed, Kitty saw that there were indeed policemen stationed at the door from which she'd entered.

Inside, they found a stark office which, for all its expansive view of the Thames, offered little in warmth or luxury. A tidy desk, some heavy wooden chairs, and file cabinets were the only pieces of furniture.

The gentlemen took the proffered chairs. Aveli declined, going instead to stand by the windows overlooking the river.

"If you're thinking of making your escape out those windows, I wouldn't," Worthington warned. "I have men posted everywhere about the grounds."

"I wouldn't dream of it, *ispettore*," Aveli stated with a mock smile. "I confess you've intrigued me. You obviously have more on your mind than just throwing us in jail."

Worthington shot to his feet, his face flushed beneath
Aveli's insolence. "You think you're so clever," he
hissed. "That we're just fools. But tell me this. If we're
so foolish, how is it we know all about this ruby you're
after? This so-called Blood of India. How do we even
know that you, Miss Fontaine, are hoping to use it to
fund an illegal rescue of your father?"

"How could you possibly—"

"My dear girl, we *are* Scotland Yard, after all," he
huffed. "And you, Aveli. You want it for the same reason all thieves crave priceless gems—for vanity and
greed."

"Spoken like a man with a certain knowledge of
human nature," Aveli drawled in the same smooth tone.
"But tell me, *ispectore*. Your memorandum mentioned
that you had the ruby in your possession. Is that true or,
like our forged handscript—"

"We haven't got the ruby," Worthington snapped.
"We only pretended we did to lure you both here. Colonel Carrington, would you care to tell them where it
is?"

Carrington crossed one glistening boot over his other
knee. "After its theft from the Lahore Museum, the
Blood of India was passed about a few times—just
where is a bit vague. However, we've recently received
convincing evidence that it is now in the hands of the
Maharana of Udaipur. In Rajasthan, Miss Fontaine.
Your old stomping grounds."

Kitty suddenly felt weak. Slowly, she sank down in
her chair.

"Maharana?" asked the inspector, whose knowledge
of India was sparse. "Don't you mean maharaja?"

"Actually, no," Carrington explained. "A maharana,

strictly speaking, ranks above a maharaja. Centuries ago, the monarch of Udaipur was accorded the honor of the title because his state was one of the few that never surrendered to, or was governed by, the Mughals. Out of five hundred and sixty princely states in India, only Udaipur has a maharana."

"How do you know he has the ruby?" Aveli asked.

Carrington assumed a self-satisfied air. "Count Aveli, I assure you the Indian Secret Service is a competent organization. We have agents in every corner of India. If something is transpiring on the subcontinent, we are certain to know about it."

"Yes, yes, Colonel," Aveli said, sounding bored. "Like most schoolboys, I've read your Signore Kipling. *Kim,* wasn't it? Though how they call that a boy's book, I'll never—"

Carrington interrupted angrily. "The point is, we have discovered the whereabouts of the ruby you two seek."

The ruby. The Blood of India. Said to have once belonged to the Emperor Ashoka, the most revered leader in Indian history. The infamous stone that led to Ashoka's unification of India around 260 B.C., and was said to have determined the greatness of his reign.

"Indians are a superstitious lot, and they believe the gem holds magical powers," Carrington continued. "Thus, the underground Indian Nationalist Movement have been seeking the stone for some time. We're determined to deny it to them. The maharana is our ally, but a loose one. We can't be certain he won't eventually hand it over to those seeking independence from Britain, so they can use it as a rallying symbol."

Kitty turned to stare at Aveli. Here was a motive for

wanting the ruby that she hadn't considered before. Was it possible that Aveli, with his anti-British sentiments, his Rajput-like skills, and his knowledge of her background in India, might be connected to this movement? But it made no sense. What would a disreputable Italian count possibly have to do with Indian nationalists?

"If, as you say," Aveli asked, ignoring her suspicious glare, "the ruby is so important to England, why don't you simply purchase it? Or pressure the man into handing it over?"

"The maharana refuses to acknowledge his ownership of the stone, and we can't very well call him on it. We have an alliance and a political agent is in residence there, but the maharana is an independent monarch. One who, we suspect, considers the ruby a special source of power—a sword that, if necessary, he could put to our throats."

"And what has all this to do with us?"

"We thought you might jump at the chance to avoid some, shall we say, ugly consequences of your past actions. So we're offering you a bargain. The two of you will go to India and use your . . . talents to steal the ruby from the maharana, and turn it over to us."

In the silence that followed, Kitty turned pale.

"Why both of us?" Aveli finally asked.

"Because you both seem to be uniquely qualified for this sort of work—we assume you would be twice as effective working together. As a couple, you would appear less suspicious. And we happen to know that Miss Fontaine is the childhood friend of the wife of the resident in Udaipur."

"Victoria?" she asked. "What does she have to do with this?"

"She is one of the most important ingredients in our plan. Rajasthan is more closed off than other parts of India. Very few tourists and a relatively small British presence. A reunion with a childhood friend will provide the perfect cover for a visit. Otherwise you would most certainly be suspect.

"Understand," Carrington continued, "that we can't warn her or her husband of your true intentions. The maharana has spies everywhere. We don't even want you cabling her until you arrive in India. The less notice given, the better. We don't want to give the maharana time for background checks."

Max asked impatiently, "What do *we* get out of this?"

"You will avoid prison and a family scandal. The minute you turn the ruby over to us, your slate will be clean. You will be exempt from prosecution of all your crimes as the notorious Tiger."

"As for Miss Fontaine," Timsley added, "we will see to it that your father's conviction is overturned. The moment you hand us the ruby, he will be set free. Also with a clean slate. Of course this will postpone your plans for a Channel flight, but right now, this is more important to England."

Kitty had been churning inside as she'd listened. Now she rose abruptly to her feet. "I'll have to think about it," she said, her voice shaking.

This came as a surprise to the three gentlemen, who looked to one another for support. Timsley said, "Should you refuse, your father will be executed as planned, on the twelfth of May."

"I need time," she insisted.

"Very well," Carrington agreed. "Take an hour or so to think it over. We'll wait for your return."

In turmoil, she turned and fled.

A wind off the Thames cooled her face as she paced the Victoria Embankment. India! The source of all her nightmares, past and present. How could she ever face it?

Of course she had to go. It represented an extraordinary opportunity, infinitely preferable to paying blood money to a pirate and turning her father into a fugitive. If she succeeded, her father would legally be a free man. But a panic raged in her. She'd vowed never to set foot in India again. To do so would force her to confront her past, and all she'd rejected since coming to England. Where was she to find the courage? To seize control of herself and take the plunge?

Minutes later, she was standing in Sir Harold's parlor, telling him all that had occurred, confessing all her fears. "I'm not a coward," she told him. "I fly aeroplanes. I slip past armed guards to break into impossible vaults in the dead of night. And yet India terrifies me. The thought of returning . . ."

"My dear child, how may I help you?" he asked.

"I know I have to go. I have no choice. But how?"

"You're more courageous than you know," he told her tenderly. "Perhaps if you think of this as a blessing in disguise. You've been offered an opportunity to serve England and free your father in one stroke. Take courage from that thought."

Charles had been listening from the hall. He rushed

forward now. "Kitty, I'll go with you. I'll see you through this."

"No, Charles, they won't allow it."

"We can be married in India. Or even before we leave. They wouldn't dare deny your husband—"

"I've told you, Charles. I can't marry you."

"But I assumed—"

Putting a hand on his son's arm, Sir Harold cautioned, "Kitty needs time to sort out her feelings. You must give her that time. For now, she has enough to worry about." He turned to Kitty. "Do what you must, my dear. When you come back, we'll be waiting for you."

Half an hour later, Kitty walked into New Scotland Yard. She moved slowly through the guards, feeling drained. When she reached the door of Inspector Worthington's office, she opened it without bothering to knock.

She looked at them wearily. Inspector Worthington, officious and rather bored. Carrington, fit, tan, champing at the bit to return to India, back to the Great Game. Timsley, deputy foreign minister, holding her father's fate in his hands. And Max Aveli, thief, rogue . . . and what else? He watched her with a keen, questioning frown.

"Very well," she told them. "I'll go."

9

Bombay, India

*K*itty was in the recreation lounge on A Deck of the P & O steamer, *S. S. Southampton,* playing canasta with Carrington and Mrs. Ambrose, when the steward poked his head in and said, "We're nearly there. You can see it already."

At once, everyone in the room abandoned their cards, their embroidery, their week-old Suez newspapers, and went out to the port bow for a look. But Kitty remained, sitting like a statue in the now empty room. It had been a miserable two-week journey through Gibraltar, the Suez and Aden. She'd tried to keep her distance from Aveli, but couldn't avoid him completely. There were meals and inevitable encounters while strolling about the deck. His presence was for her like salt in an open wound, forcing to the surface a mélange of conflicting emotions. Under ordinary circumstances, such a journey would afford her an opportunity to get to know him better. But she didn't want to know him. She didn't want to face the fact that she so desired a man who, in some ways, seemed a mirror image of herself, yet who despised her—who wasn't above using her to sate his physical desire. That desire was palpable every time she so much as passed him in a passageway. He wanted no more to do with her than she did with him, yet the flash of his eyes told her that he too remembered their passion every bit as clearly as she did. Her body leapt to life every time she was near him, wanting him despite his rude rejection of her. So every meeting brought with it a fresh flush of embarrassment and humiliation.

Compounding this was her dread of finally reaching their destination. Her attempts at sleep were ravaged by the return of the old nightmares. Every morning, close to dawn, she awoke in a sweat, newly frustrated.

By now, she was weary of the emotional turmoil. Her desire to be done with this ordeal and return to England was so great that it began to overshadow her fears. Every throbbing nerve cried out to get the job done and be gone. From India. From Aveli.

Drawing a deep breath, she left the lounge and went to join the others on deck.

In the distance the coastline of India was slowly coming into view. Before long, they could see the curving harbor, the European buildings along the bund, the gentle rise of green hills in the background, reminiscent of the Bay of Naples. A number of cargo ships were anchored amidst a profusion of dhows—

small single-masted skiffs that carried the cargo into Bombay Harbor.

Bombay. The first city of India and the pride of the British Raj. Three hundred years ago, it was nothing more than seven islands inhabited by a few fisher folk known as Kolis. In 1534, the ruling sultan ceded them to the Portuguese, who in turn handed them over to Britain as part of the wedding dowry when Catherine of Braganza married England's Charles II in 1661. The British joined the seven islands into a single land mass and steadily built it into their major port in western India. The city's textile industries flourished during the American Civil War when blockades cut off the export of American cotton, and the world began to look to India to fill the shortage. It was during this time that Bombay was transformed into a progressive showcase of British colonialism: a city of grand Victorian buildings that rivaled anything in London. As they drew closer some of these buildings came into view.

Directly in front of the P & O dock was the city's most striking edifice: the Taj Mahal Hotel. The epitome of Raj ostentation, it combined late Victorian graciousness with a hint of Mughal exoticism to rise to a crown of arabesque domes built to resemble Agra's Taj Mahal. The central roof dome towered above the rest, looming over the harbor and the city like a sentinel—guarding, yet welcoming at the same time. One of the wonders of Asia. A timeless symbol, the gateway to India.

As they docked before the grand hotel, Kitty was hit by a sense of déjà vu, caused by the cacophony of sights and sounds and colors she'd so thoroughly repressed over the past fourteen years. The odor of curries aromatic with garlic, turmeric, chilies, ginger, and cloves.

Piquant oriental tobaccos, jasmine and sandalwood. The biting smoke of distant funeral pyres.

Even from the dock, the brilliance of the colors was staggering, the bright reds, greens, pinks, yellows, and blues of the women's saris all clashing together in a discordant rainbow. Birds were everywhere: emerald-green parrots nesting like clustered jewels in the trees, eagles and hawks circling the harbor, black squawking crows diving into the crowd for bits of refuse. After the silence of the sea, the noise of the city was a shock: the creak of bullock carts, the jangle of passing victorias and carriages, the thunder of horses' hooves, snippets of music combining the long-forgotten cadence of sitar and drums. The voices of so many people, speaking so many different dialects, all conducting business or gossiping in the open air. Overwhelming. Suffocating.

"Dear Lord," cried Mrs. Ambrose in an awestruck voice. "I've never seen so many people in all my life! I thought London was an enormous city, but there must be three times the number of people here."

As they disembarked, people surged about them in a confusing mass: Parsi businessmen, Bengali clerks, Pathan horse traders from the northwest frontier, half-castes from Goa speaking Portuguese, Mongol-featured peoples from Nepal and the Northeast. No two people looked alike. Those from northern India were pale skinned with light eyes; those from the south were short and dark. There were men in flowing robes of white muslin, men wearing dhotis, men with vividly colored turbans or skullcaps upon their heads, men in impeccably pressed uniforms. Hindu women wore saris woven with gold or silver threads and gold bangles, or pajama pants with knee-length tunics, while Muslim women were covered from head to foot in long black robes and veils. Many wore marks on their foreheads to designate their castes. A holy man roamed the crowds, dressed in ochre rags, his skeletal body visible beneath, his long, matted hair hanging about his shoulders, singing as he held forth a pail for donations. A boy sat atop a painted elephant, waving at the passengers with both hands. As soon as they stepped from the ship, they were assaulted by beggars, some young children with large, soulful brown eyes, some elderly men with deformed limbs, some mothers carrying crying babies and holding out a palm for alms.

One of the Englishwomen, a pretty young blonde, was so unnerved by the noise and confusion that she began to cry. "There's such a lot of everything," she sobbed into the chest of her husband, a new civil servant of the Raj.

"Yes," said Carrington, who was at home in such surroundings. "You'll get used to it in time."

The husband, as overwhelmed as his wife, asked, "How is it possible that so few of us are able to rule so many of them?"

"It does seem overwhelming at first," Carrington agreed. "Unlike England, India is not one thing. It's a million different things. Do you realize that they speak two thousand different dialects on the subcontinent? A dozen major religions compete: on some streets, I've seen Hindu, Jain, Buddhist, Zoroastrian, and Islamic temples all nestled side by side, each loathing and distrusting the other. In the northwest frontier, rival tribes have been butchering each other for centuries. We are the force that creates order out of this chaos. We set the example. Keep that in mind and it will always see you through."

As he spoke, Aveli had been watching him with a cynical sneer. To the couple, he said, "You must also remember the importance of taxing its people to poverty. Of conspiring with its maharajas to keep them destitute and hungry by suppressing any native industries that might compete with England's and offer them a living wage. Not to mention your sacred obligation to hunt its tigers to near extinction. Quite a chore, this white man's burden of yours."

He stalked off, leaving an astonished silence in his wake.

"Bloody cheek," the husband said, tightening his arm protectively about his wife's shoulders. "Who *is* that man?"

Carrington shrugged as if to dismiss him. "Just an Italian," he replied, as if that explained it all.

"Oh, quite," the husband concurred.

Aveli's outburst nagged at Kitty's suspicions. Unlike all other Europeans on seeing India for the first time, he didn't seem at all distressed by the immensity of it all.

She stepped to Carrington's side. In the course of the voyage, her resentment of his presence had transformed itself into a certain trust. They shared, after all, the same goal: that of attaining the ruby and freeing her father. A true English gentleman, he'd come to understand her anxiety during the trip and had put himself out to be charming. He'd taught her to play canasta and had bragged about her aeronautical daring before the other passengers at the captain's table. On a personal level, he didn't seem to hold her in low esteem for her burglaries. As a member of the Secret Service, he was

accustomed to dealing with all manner of people and
withheld moral judgments. His presence on board had
proved her single solace.

"I know why you can trust me," she told him now.
"I'll do anything to see my father safe. But what makes
you think you can trust Aveli? What's to keep him
from playing along with us and then grabbing the ruby
and taking off with it?"

Carrington seemed unperturbed. "The Aveli name is
an old and proud one. The senior Aveli had an impeccable reputation. Now that he's caught, he'll do anything
to avoid blackening the family honor."

"I hope you're right." But she had her doubts.

They checked into the Taj Mahal Hotel, intending to
stay for two nights in order to recover from the voyage
and plan their assault on Udaipur. It was one of the
great hotels of the world, no less luxurious than its
namesake: the eternal symbol of romance, the Taj
Mahal. Walking through its arched doorway, Kitty was
enveloped by an oasis of marble floors, lavish furnish-
ings, and service fit for a king. Its high-ceilinged interior offered a cool respite from the punishing heat. In
the center of the lobby, a flight of stairs leading to the
five upper floors was bordered by an exquisite wrought-
iron rail. From the atrium below, the railing created the
impression of a maze, a series of dizzying concentric
squares leading straight to the hotel's magnificent
domed roof, as if one were gazing up from within a
tiered wedding cake. The hotel's decorative motif both
inside and out was an inspired blend of Victorian state-
liness and Oriental whimsy.

Her room on the third floor was spacious, with a large bed and ceiling fan that gently stirred the air. Looking out from her window, she could see below a walled-off green lawn stretching to a swimming pool, a particularly modern luxury. Some of the guests lounged in chaises in the sun, the women holding parasols to shield their delicate skin.

She washed and changed clothes. Feeling better, she left the room again, pausing at the railing at the head of the hall to look down the deep stairwell, where she experienced a thrilling sensation of precarious height. She descended to the lobby, intent on taking care of her first order of business: wiring her friend Victoria in Udaipur and telling her they'd be visiting her in two days' time.

But as she approached the reception desk, she spotted Aveli across the lobby, heading out the front door. Alone. She crossed the floor and looked out the front window. As she watched, he waved off the doorman's attempt to summon transportation and began to walk south along the waterfront. There wasn't the slightest trace of hesitation in his stride. As if he knew exactly where he was going. As if he'd been here before.

Impulsively, she decided to follow.

She stayed well behind him as he trailed the waterfront for another three blocks. As she moved farther away from the bastion of the Taj Mahal Hotel, she felt herself increasingly swallowed up by the real India. Beggars, snake charmers, sword swallowers, postcard vendors, hawkers selling beaded necklaces, flowered garlands, peacock fans, any number of cheap trinkets, called to her, shoving their wares in her face. But as she left the Colaba tourist district, these gave way to the curious stares of the city's inhabitants, to narrow, crowded streets, to families clustered around cooking fires. Cows of all colors crammed the roads, some lounging in groups in the afternoon sun, some wandering leisurely through the traffic that slowed and swayed around them, even stopping to allow them to pass with their lumbering gait. The heat was oppressive. Already her clothes were sticking to her skin.

He suddenly turned right, glancing behind him as he did. Instantly, she crouched down behind a vegetable cart, watching from beneath until he moved on. She resumed her surveillance, keeping well behind as he meandered his way into a seedier district of bars and brothels that catered to foreign sailors. In front of the shabby cribs, the prostitutes stood vigil. Some were no more than children. They watched her pass with guarded stares, covering their faces with multicolored veils when she glanced their way.

She stopped short when Aveli abruptly halted his stride. Thinking he'd sensed her presence, she flattened back against a corner wall. But peering around it, she saw that a man had waylaid him. A pockmarked Gujarati wearing ragged black pajamas. Creeping closer, she heard the miscreant asking for money in broken English, obviously mistaking the well-dressed Aveli for an easy mark. Aveli brushed him off, intending to move on, but at a signal from the supplicant, two other men appeared from the shadows, blocking his path. In a rising voice, the first man now demanded money.

From where she was, she couldn't quite make out Max's response. But whatever he said, it didn't satisfy the brigands. They drew knives and charged. Aveli easily avoided their lunges, his speed and agility surprising the men even further. A taunting grin split Aveli's face, as if this were a welcome diversion after the stifling inactivity at sea.

Furious at the intended victim's attitude and his men's inability to touch him, their leader put fingers to lips and let out a high-pitched whistle. A dozen more men appeared, spilling from out of the surrounding doorways, each carrying a knife or curved sword. They were swarthy men, with glints of murder in their eyes. Forming a malevolent circle, they surrounded Aveli on all sides, readying their weapons for the slaughter.

Kitty watched with her heart in her throat. She should do something to help him, but what? Run for a constable? There was no time. Try to offer up a distraction? But that would likely bring the bandits down on her.

Remarkably, Aveli seemed unfazed. "So you want to play?" he jeered.

Kitty froze. He'd said this in perfect Hindi—Hindi that was so flawless, he could only have learned it as a child!

He widened his grin, flashing wolfish white teeth. "Well, play with this."

Reaching into his pocket, he pulled out a closed fist. As the group lurched toward him, he opened his palm with an upward sweep, spreading a cloud of dust into the air. The dust transmuted itself, forming a smoke screen all about him as the attacking men froze with superstitious gasps. When the smoke had cleared, Aveli was gone.

•   •   •

Max ducked into a side street, leaving his bewildered attackers in his magician's dust. From there his path followed a series of increasingly narrow alleys and warrens deeper into the black heart of gangland Bombay. He'd enjoyed the altercation immensely. The superstitious thugs he'd left behind were no doubt offering prayers to Lord Shiva even now. Likely they'd think twice before attacking someone like him again.

He felt alive for the first time in weeks. His blood was pumping, his skin flushed with triumph and devilment. It was all he could do to keep from laughing aloud.

Never realizing that Kitty had sidestepped his attackers and had once again picked up his trail. That she was watching him from the shadows.

She saw him stop before a small clapboard house at the end of Sikar Lane with the number 13 painted above the door. He stopped, took a cleansing breath, and rapped three times—one long, two short—upon the door. Momentarily, it was opened by a middle-aged Rajput man wearing a long blue cotton robe. His soupstrainer mustache showed flecks of grey, but his eyes were clear and commanding.

Eyes Kitty remembered from her long-ago childhood. Eyes that shocked her to the core of her soul. Eyes that belonged to her old tutor . . . Ngar!

"Namaste, Babu," Max said warmly, bringing his palms together. Greetings, Father.

His eyes lighting with pleasure, Ngar took Max's face between his callused hands. "My boy! I am so happy to see you. How long has it been?"

"Too long," Max replied, smiling into the older man's face.

Ngar had found the boy Cameron the night of the attack, lying abandoned in the Rajasthan moonlight. Most of the men had been killed in the attack, including Haghan, their leader. At first, kneeling beside the boy in the dust, Ngar had thought he was dead. But as he'd studied the body, he'd found a faint heartbeat. He and what was left of the band had taken the boy to safety and nursed him back to health, digging the bullet out of his chest and using special herbs to restore his skin to nearly its former state. There had followed torturous months for the boy, who'd healed slowly, unconscious and delirious most of the time. After his recovery, Ngar had wanted Cameron to stay with him. But the boy had wanted only to put distance between himself and what had happened. So he'd run away to Bombay. It was years before he would again seek out the man who'd saved his life and renew their old acquaintance.

They stood facing one another now, remembering, before Ngar pulled Max to him in a fierce embrace.

"You look well, my son," Ngar told him, leading him to a worn table and pouring a glass of tea. "How was your journey?"

Max took the tea and sipped the hot brew. "Uneventful," he said evasively. Actually, it had been a most uncomfortable trip. As much as he'd willed himself to ignore her, he'd found Kitty's presence on board a constant distraction and temptation.

When he'd first realized there was another cat burglar on his tail, he hadn't known it was Kitty, the grown-up incarnation of the child he'd once known.

He'd learned that she was in London, but he'd gone out of his way to avoid her, going so far as to leave social gatherings if she happened to be present. When he'd lifted her mask that first night at Timsley's and had seen who it was, he'd been shocked. But of course it made sense. She'd had the benefit of Ngar's training just as he had, even if it was only a fraction of what he'd learned in the subsequent years. It was a strange twist of fate that had placed them both on the trail of the same ruby. But also a stroke of luck for him. He'd been feigning resentment at being dragged along on this excursion, when in reality it couldn't suit his purposes any better. Carrington was right. The two of them, working together, would have twice the chance at success. Once he had the ruby in hand, he would ditch Kitty and give it to its rightful owners: Ngar and his freedom fighters.

What he hadn't counted on was his surprising and unwanted attraction to Kitty. He fully realized it could jeopardize his mission. He willed himself to be vigilant every moment that he was in her presence. Yet, despite his contempt for the world she'd embraced, despite the fact that he couldn't trust her, something happened to him every time she drew near. That day in the hangar, when she'd guessed the truth, he hadn't meant to carry it so far. He'd only meant to scare her, to behave in such a way that she'd convince herself that her suspicions were wrong. But once he'd taken her in his arms, something had seemed to snap inside his brain. It was as if he forgot everything—who he was and what he was after—and was possessed by someone else.

He knew the danger of this attraction. Being with her brought back to him a painful past he'd tried to shut from his mind, distracting him by opening old wounds. It was becoming increasingly difficult to keep his true identity from her. Kitty was no fool. He'd played with fire by turning the quest for the ruby into a game she could share, when he should have turned tail and run at first sight of her. He'd all but laid the truth in her hands. He couldn't afford to underestimate her again.

"Is she beautiful?" Ngar asked, breaking into his thoughts.

"Who?"

"Kitty, of course."

Max shrugged, turning away. "I suppose so." *Did you have to be this beautiful?* he'd asked.

"She was a beautiful child. I am not surprised. Also clever. You'll have to be on your guard. Whatever she was then, she is now English to the core. And very much her father's daughter. You must never let her know who you really are. Everyone has a point of vulnerability. This could well be yours." When Max didn't answer, he added, more forcibly, "Do I make myself clear?"

"You don't have to tell me what I already know."

Ngar studied him for a moment, noting the closed features, the blank and shuttered eyes. More gently, he said, "You would not be human if you were not drawn to the girl. The two of you felt a deep connection once. You share things others have no way of comprehending. The temptation to reestablish that connection may well prove difficult to resist. Do you find it so?"

Mentor, master. Ngar was so in tune with him that he could feel the conflict of his heart. "You needn't concern yourself on my account, Babu. I've dedicated my life to this cause. Should the temptation prove daunting, I'll remember who I am. I know what I must do."

"I have faith in you, my son. You have never let me down before. Remember all I have taught you. To control your emotions as you control your body, the way the ancient Rajput masters teach. This will hold you in good stead."

"I'll remember."

"To business then. This Carrington. What sort of man is he?"

"Clever. He knows his business."

"How clever?"

"Don't worry. He doesn't suspect who I really am."

"See that he doesn't. His spies are most thorough. We have ascertained that the Blood of India is, indeed, in the hands of the Maharana of Udaipur."

Max asked, "What sort of help can I expect from you?"

"We're attempting to make arrangements even now. But I don't know how much or in what form. When you arrive, there will be someone there to let you know. It is most fortunate that Kitty is friends with the wife of the political agent in Udaipur. It provides a perfect cover. Otherwise two European visitors would be most conspicuous in such a remote principality so far off the tourist path. Is it true the child flies in the air in a machine?"

"Yes. Quite good at it, too."

"That could suit our plans, as well. Our spies report the maharana is interested in flying machines."

Max saw the advantage this presented at once. "Tell me everything."

They discussed their plans at some length.

Finally Max glanced at his pocket watch. "I'd better get back to the hotel before I'm missed. Kitty is suspicious as it is."

As they stood up, Ngar took both hands in his and squeezed tightly. "I don't have to tell you how important this is to our cause. It is everything."

"I know, Babu."

"It is what all your training has been for. *Nothing* must interfere. Do you understand? Nothing—and no one."

Max looked into the eyes of the man who'd meant so much to him. His spiritual father. "I won't let you down."

In a daze, Kitty walked numbly back to the hotel. He *was* Cameron.

There was no longer any doubt. There was only one reason why Max Aveli would be secretly meeting with Ngar. It explained so many things. Their attraction for one another. How he'd known so much about her past. The Rajput-like skills. Despite the evidence to the contrary—the fact that she'd seen him shot, his denial that he was Cameron, the lack of a scar on his chest—her intuition had been right all along.

Cameron was alive! Impossibly, against all odds. She couldn't even imagine the events that had led to this moment. How was it possible that he'd survived—unscarred—the bullet that had ripped him apart? How, in God's name, had he ended up an Italian count? And why was he disguising himself from those who loved him? His father? His brother?

She remembered now the night she'd first met him in his guise as Count Aveli. She'd been dancing with him when Charles had come to interrupt. There'd been something—a look of profound sadness—when he'd seen Charles. But he'd masked it quickly and walked away. What madness had prevented him from speaking? From telling Charles who he really was?

Why did he refuse to acknowledge the obvious? Why hadn't he come to her, to let her know he was alive? Why didn't he want her to know?

There was only one possible explanation. He'd been left for dead, had remained with their captors, and had become one of them. He and Ngar must be working with the Indian nationalists who wanted the Blood of India for their own purposes.

This complicated things immensely. Not only did she have to worry about stealing the ruby and giving it to the British authorities in time to save her farther's life, but she was faced with the added pressure of having an enemy spy in her camp. A man who happened to be the grown-up boy she'd loved.

What was she going to do? She should tell Carrington at once. But it wasn't as easy as all that. She owed it to Cameron to at least try to get to the bottom of what was going on here before turning him over to the authorities. If he was involved with the nationalists, it was high treason. Could she possibly take her father's neck out of the hangman's noose only to put Cameron's in?

By the time she arrived back at the hotel, she felt completely drained by the shock. Despite her earlier suspicions, this proof was too much to take in all at once. Wearily, she climbed the stairs to the first floor, where the doorman had told her she'd find the Palm Court. There she could refresh herself with a cup of tea and decide what to do. The Palm Court was off the main hallway, a long, narrow, open room that spanned the front of the hotel, affording breathtaking views of the harbor. As she approached, she caught a glimpse of small tables before large wicker chairs, most turned to accommodate the view outside the long row of windows. At the entry she paused and looked about. The court was empty except for an attendant in a crisp white uniform and a lone woman, looking out the windows.

Kitty was about to take a seat when something about the woman caught her attention. She was visible only in profile, yet seemed strangely familiar. The fresh-faced beauty, the fragile elegance. She stood scanning the street below leading to the docks as if watching for someone in particular. There was something haunting in the way she stood so still, so intent on her purpose. Then all at once her face lit up as if she'd spotted what she'd been searching for. With a small cry of joy, she turned and ran from the room. As she passed, Kitty knew why she'd seemed so familiar. Victoria.

Startled, she turned and followed her. Victoria had rushed down the flight of stairs to the lobby. As she did, a young lieutenant came through the front door. He was tall, blond, strikingly handsome, virile in his khaki uniform. He walked with the brisk confidence of a man comfortable in his own skin. When he glanced up and saw Victoria he grinned, doffed his cap with one hand, and held his arms out to her. She rushed into them and he whirled her about before lowering his head

and giving her a passionate kiss that was so intimate,
Kitty squirmed watching them. Looking up into his
face, Victoria was glowing with happiness, lovelier and
more joyful than Kitty thought any woman had ever
appeared. The man, in turn, looked at her as if she were
something he treasured beyond measure—as if all the
crawling minutes of the day had culminated at last in
the pleasure of finding her here, waiting for him. Arm
in arm, they ascended the stairs together, passing Kitty
without noticing her.

What was Victoria doing here, of all places? And
who was this man upon whom she was bestowing such
wanton affection?

But more importantly, what would her unexpected
presence here do to their carefully laid plan?

The world seemed suddenly to be spinning around
her, out of control. Somehow, she had to grab on to
something solid, to anchor herself, to take some action
that would put things to right. But what?

10

She went to Carrington's room.

"Something's happened," she told him.

He ushered her in and closed the door behind her, the whisky and soda he'd been sipping still in hand.

For a moment, she considered telling him about Max. But she couldn't bring herself to do it. Not yet.

"What is it?" he prompted.

She informed him of Victoria's presence in Bombay. When he heard the news, he let out an exasperated sigh. "Damn it all. Why is it that in every operation, there's always the unexpected monkey wrench? Miss Fontaine, you must go to your friend and convince her to return to Udaipur with us. Her presence there as your hostess is essential to our success."

"It may be necessary for me to tell her what we're doing."

"Can you trust her?"

"Implicitly."

"Then tell her if you must," he agreed grudgingly. "But swear her to secrecy. Under no circumstances is her husband to know. As I told you before, the British residency in Udaipur is sure to be riddled with the maharana's spies."

He wanted her to speak to Victoria at once, but she decided to wait until morning. Victoria was, after all, having an illicit meeting with a man who wasn't her husband. She tossed and turned all night, the image of the boy Cameron and the man Max haunting her sleep. The knowledge that he was just down the hall thrilled her . . . and terrified her. He was Cameron, and yet he was her enemy. How had it come to this?

The next morning she dressed before dawn and went to wait in the lobby. Just after seven, she saw the handsome lieutenant come bounding down the grand staircase, whistling jauntily to himself. Kitty watched him climb into a tonga, then took the stairs once again to the third floor. Victoria's room was just down the hall from her own.

She knocked softly on the door. In a moment, it burst open. Victoria stood on the threshold, a long robe hastily knotted at her waist, her sun-kissed brown hair tumbling seductively about her shoulders, beaming her expectation that her lover had returned for one last kiss. But when she saw Kitty, the smile froze and a look of astonishment took its place.

"Kitty . . . my God!" she cried, her hand flying to the lapels of her robe and closing it tighter about her neck in an unconscious gesture. "What are you doing here?"

"May I come in?"

Victoria cast a flustered look back into the room. "Of course, dear. But how on earth—"

Kitty stepped inside. The room was much like her own, with a large bed and whirling ceiling fan. But Victoria's bed was rumpled in a way that sleep alone could not have caused. Her clothes from the day before were draped upon a chair, but some items—her stockings, a pretty lace corset—were strewn about the floor. Blushing, Victoria hurried to retrieve them and toss them on the chair. She flung the bedcover over the tangled sheets and said, "Please sit down."

It was an awkward reunion, certainly not what Kitty had envisioned. She sat perched on the edge of the bed, and told Victoria the whole story of why she was here. Everything except her suspicions about Aveli.

"You mean," Victoria breathed in wonder, "you were actually sneaking into peoples' houses? A thief in the night? I knew you were adventurous, but I confess this far surpasses anything I might have imagined. It's like something out of one of those penny novels we used to read under the covers."

"As I've said, I had no choice."

"I can tell you one thing, darling. You shan't have any trouble whatsoever when it comes to ingratiating yourself with the Maharana of Udaipur. He keeps a distance from the British as a rule, but he's an absolute fiend when it comes to aviation. He even owns his own aeroplane. Once he hears about you, I'm sure he'll be more than eager to meet you."

"But we must have a reason for being there. So you can see why it's essential that you return with us to Udaipur."

Victoria lowered her lashes, avoiding Kitty's gaze. "I've only just arrived. Mortimer won't expect me back for a week." With a sudden nervous quiver, she reached for her bag on the bedside table and withdrew a cigarette. "Would you like one?"

Kitty shook her head.

Victoria smiled sheepishly. "Mortimer hates it when I smoke, so I only do it here. My form of rebellion, I suppose."

"But not your only rebellion," Kitty observed.

"What do you mean?" came the cautious query.

"I know your secret."

Victoria paled. Lighting the cigarette, she exhaled a stream of smoke. "My . . . secret?"

"I saw you with your lieutenant."

Victoria leaned back against the headboard and brought her legs up, bending them at the knees. The smoke from her cigarette made little spirals in the air before disappearing in the stir of the ceiling fan.

"How can I make you understand?" Victoria asked at length, watching the blades turn. "I suppose you'll think it all rather sordid, although it's far from that."

"When you wrote me about finding your soul mate," Kitty told her, trying to ease her into the subject, "I had no idea. I assumed you and your husband had attained some new level of married bliss."

"With Mortimer?" Victoria gave a short, bitter

laugh. "I see now that I only married him to get away from Mother. Never realizing what it would mean."

"You weren't happy."

"Happy?" She took a puff on her cigarette and exhaled sharply. "No. I had my two children and settled in, serving as hostess to Mortimer's ambitions. I tried to be a good wife, but nothing pleased him. He grew increasingly critical of me. At the worst, he beat me so that I had to hide in my bedroom from my children. I felt so ashamed." She crushed her cigarette in the ashtray by the bed. "I wouldn't have put up with it except that he threatened to pack me off to England and keep the children. I couldn't bear that, Kitty. They're everything to me, all that kept me sane, living as I was."

"I could kill him," Kitty swore.

Victoria gave a small, sad smile. "That's what Ramsey says, although he knows I'd never stand for it."

"Ramsey?"

"He's the lieutenant you saw me with." Her face, so full of pain a moment before, softened, transforming itself into a gentle, radiant glow. "He's stationed here in Bombay, but he came to Udaipur on leave. The moment we saw each other we recognized something— I'm not sure what. We looked into each other's eyes and, for what seemed ages, couldn't look away. There was almost something mystical about it. As if we'd known and lost each other in another life, and had been searching for one another. It absolutely terrified me. I forced myself not to look at him. I tried, Kitty, I really tried to stay away. But I couldn't. Every time I looked into his eyes, my heart would whisper 'I know you.'"

Kitty felt her own heart constrict.

"I fell in love. Hopelessly, helplessly in love for the first and only time in my life. Suddenly my drab world seemed bathed in golden light. And when he kissed me for the first time . . . I finally knew who I really was. I knew I was meant to belong to him for all time."

"What happened then?"

"We began to meet in Bombay, here at our hotel. No one knows us here and we can be open and loving, pretending we have the right. Kitty, you can't imagine what it means to me to be able to come here, to be with him. He's taught me about love and joy, kindness and generosity. What it is to be celebrated just as I am. About gentleness and—passion. He's made my life worth living." She hugged her knees. "It's such joy to be with him, after my husband's constant criticism. I make him laugh. Do you know, I can't ever remember Mortimer laughing at anything I've ever said?"

"Do you ever feel guilty? About Mortimer?"

"I did at first. But not anymore. Had I met Ramsey first, I would have married him. Mortimer gave me my children, but to whom do I owe my allegiance, Kit? To my husband, who has treated me with nothing but cruelty and criticism? Or to the man who loves me unconditionally? The man who has given me the first true happiness I've ever had? The man I know to be my soul mate?"

Soul mate. Once again the words chilled Kitty. "You make it sound so simple."

Victoria sighed. "If I do, I'm a fraud. Nothing is simple for me, I'm afraid."

"But you're so happy."

"Yes, I'm happy much of the time. When I'm here,

with Ramsey. But there's sadness, too, and anger and frustration. Sometimes I feel I could spend hours just looking at his face—the face I love. I want to memorize it for the times when I'll never be able to see it again." Victoria sat silently for a time, her eyes lowered. When she spoke, her voice quivered slightly. "Kitty, sometimes I'm so frightened."

"Of what?"

"Of losing Ramsey. Mortimer has been making noises about putting a halt to my shopping trips. Kitty, I live for these secret trysts. The thought of giving them up is torture. I could go on meeting Ramsey this way forever. As much as I'd love to feel that I belong to him completely, I know that I have no right to expect more. But Ramsey needs more. He wants me to leave Mortimer and run away with him. He only wants to make me happy, to make up for all the pain I've suffered with Mortimer. But, as much as I believe we belong together, I can't help but care what people will say. They will look at my children and say their mother was a whore. That she cared so little for them that she could leave them without a thought. How can I do that to them?"

"Couldn't you take them with you?"

"Mortimer would never allow that. And I can't leave them. Knowing that because their mother preferred another man, Mortimer would take it out on them. They're my babies, Kitty. How can I leave them?"

Her eyes showed so much pain that Kitty reached to put her arm around her and comfort her.

"Ramsey and I have terrible rows. Both of us have tempers, I'm afraid, and at times it seems we bring out the worst in each other. The fights are awful. The fights break my heart. When we're not blissfully happy, we're quarreling about this. Kitty, I know I'm going to lose Ramsey. I feel it." She hesitated, then added softly, "He won't be happy when I tell him I have to return to Udaipur. He hinted this morning that he's made some special plans. It's been so long, you see, since we last met."

An awkward pause passed between them. Finally Kitty said, "I hate to have to ask it of you, Victoria. But I must."

Victoria reached over and put her hand on Kitty's. "Of course you must. Nothing is more important now than saving your father's life. Ramsey will understand. I shall speak with him tonight."

Kitty sat quietly for a moment, thinking.

"You mustn't worry, dear. It will be all right."

"I was thinking of something else," Kitty admitted.

"I can see you're troubled. Perhaps I can help."

Kitty told the story of her meeting with Max Aveli. And of her suspicions. How the absence of a scar had convinced her he wasn't Cameron. Of what she'd learned when she'd followed him.

"My God!" Victoria gasped. "But Kitty, this is a miracle! Your Cameron has come back!"

"But don't you see? He isn't my Cameron. I'm not sure I really know *who* he is."

"Do you love him?" Victoria asked.

"I think so. Unfortunately. And I was sure Cameron loved me. But I was just a child, and now I'm not sure what to think. I loved him as Cameron, but he's so different from what I remember Cameron to be. How could he be so changed?"

"You didn't know him very long. Sometimes when we lose someone we love, after a time we confuse the real memories with what we want to believe. It was a long time ago, after all."

"It's all so confused in my mind."

"Kitty, if you love him, you're going to have to love him for the man he is now. Not your memory of the past."

"How can I? When he hates me so? When he's such a threat to everything I want? I keep trying to sort it out in my mind. But there are so many contradictions that I can't seem to think what to do."

"You're trying to approach this in a logical, practical way. But the heart doesn't follow logic or practicality. In India, you learn to think differently. She's such a mass of contradictions. Her affluence and poverty, beauty and squalor, spiritualism and cruelty. You learn here that contradictions do coexist within one whole. You learn that your old way of thinking in absolutes has no bearing on the truth."

"I don't think he even wants to love me. It's as if he's fighting it all the time. Pushing me away when I get too close. Victoria, what should I do?"

"Find a way to make him realize that he loves you, I suppose."

"But how?"

"I don't know," Victoria said thoughtfully. "All I do know is that underneath any changes a person might go through, the soul remains the same. And the greatest longing of the soul is to be reunited with its mate. According to mystics, soul mates seek and find each other through countless lifetimes. Even after death, the soul mate's spirit guides its beloved, so we're never really alone."

"Which means . . . ?"

"It means if Max Aveli *is* your soul mate, he loves you, whether he knows it or not."

11

*K*itty lay on her bed that evening after dinner, feeling restless and edgy. She'd already packed in preparation for leaving in the morning, and there was nothing left to do.

Was it possible that all Victoria had said was true? That underneath it all Max really did love her? Once again her English and Indian halves were at war. It would be so simple to believe Max was her soul mate, that deep down he wanted her as much as she did him. But her long practice of shutting down her feelings and relying on logic left her wracked with doubts.

The first step was to make him admit he was Cameron. But what was the best way to approach him? If she stormed into his room and confronted him, he would no doubt try to deny it as he had before. What were the right words, the proper mood, that would break down his resistance? She didn't feel the time was right, yet it would have to come before Udaipur brought everything to a head. She would have to try and reach him before Max got his hands on the ruby.

A knock on the door startled her. Running a hand across her damp forehead, she opened the door.

Max stood in the hall in a white suit, looking tanned and windblown and deliciously rugged. She wasn't prepared for this. She needed more time to think.

He peered at her strangely. "You look a little flushed," he commented.

She turned from him abruptly. "Do I? It's the heat, I suppose. I'm not accustomed to it."

The words echoed hauntingly in her mind: *I know you're Cameron!*

After a pause, he came in and closed the door. Even with her back turned, Kitty could feel his presence. He seemed to fill the room and suck the air from it. "What do you want?" she asked.

"I looked for you earlier. Where were you?"

"I've been around the hotel." After a moment, she added, "And you?"

Without the slightest hesitation, he said, "I've been out reconnoitering. I make a habit of thoroughly researching every job before I begin."

"Where?" she persisted.

"Out there. The city, of course."

"But you don't speak the language." She was watching him closely.

"I pick up languages quickly. It's a gift."

What a liar he was. Why was it so important to him that she not know? "Who did you talk to?"

"People. Here and there."

"Very well. Be evasive. You *can,* I assume, tell me what you learned?"

"It seems our mark, the Maharana of Udaipur, has a passion for toys. The bigger, the more modern, the more costly, the better. He's just purchased a new gewgaw that has put the other princes with their fancy motorcars to shame. And what do you think his latest plaything is?"

"You tell me."

"A flying machine."

"Well," she said, barely concealing her sarcasm. "It seems you *do* do your homework."

He ignored her tone. "Carrington told me about your friend being here. She won't be a problem, will she?"

"No. She's agreed to return to Udaipur with us tomorrow."

"Good. Then all we need do is go there and let your friend spread the word that a renowned English pilot is stopping over in his state. If I don't miss my guess, he'll come to us."

"Are you always so thorough when you want something?"

Even to her own ears, it sounded like a sexual taunt. He swept her with a scalding look before abruptly averting his head. "It helps to know your enemy's weakness. Don't you agree?"

An odd stillness permeated the room. She suddenly felt the impulse to go for broke. Throw his lies in his face. But the moment was interrupted by the sounds of a commotion in the hall outside. Raised voices, a man's and a woman's. With a frown, Aveli cracked the door and glanced outside.

"Just a lover's quarrel," he told her dismissively.

He was about to close the door again when Kitty recognized one of the voices. "It's Victoria." She moved to the door and looked out.

She saw Ramsey, resplendent in his uniform, his face raw with rage. He'd obviously been in the process of storming out, but Victoria had taken hold of his sleeve.

"How can you possibly expect it of me?" Kitty heard Victoria cry. "To leave tonight—turning my back on my children?"

With an impatient gesture, the lieutenant ripped his arm from her grasp and turned, striding angrily down the hall.

The fights are awful. The fights break my heart.

Victoria ran after him, pleading with him to see reason. When he shrugged her off, she grabbed him and yanked him around. Kitty caught the word "unreasonable" but nothing more. Victoria began to struggle with her lover physically, trying to force him to stay and listen. But he was too angry. He fought her, flinging up his arm to push her away. As he did, as Victoria lunged at him, a horrifying thing happened. Somehow the lieutenant was hurled back against the waist-high rail so violently that he lost his balance and toppled over the side. One moment he was there, the next he was gone, falling down four flights.

Kitty's hand flew to her mouth. She heard Victoria's scream, saw her standing like a ghost, her white fingers gripping the rail, looking down, frozen in place. Kitty ran toward her, but Victoria was running down the hall toward the stairs, flying down them, and along the corridor to the next flight. Kitty was aware of others coming out of their rooms to see what the disturbance was about. At the rail she glanced down. There, far below, on the hard marble floor, lay the body of that beautiful young man, broken and bleeding on the white tiles.

Kitty raced toward the stairs, wanting desperately to console her friend. No one could have survived such a fall. Her breath was coming fast as she ran down the stairs, around the corridor, and down again, around and around until she came at last to the lobby. There, Victoria was on her knees, cradling the body of her beloved, his blood staining her clothes. As Kitty moved closer, she heard Victoria whispering. "Please God, don't let it be. You have to live, Dearest. For me. Please, Ramsey. I can't live without you."

Tears streamed down her face as she knelt there, rocking his body. The hotel night manager, rushing over from the reception desk, tried to pull Victoria away, but she shrugged him off and held her lover closer to her. People were coming downstairs, staring in horror, whispering, aghast. But Victoria seemed not to notice. She was pouring all her energy into the lifeless body in her arms, willing him to live for her sake.

Gently, Kitty touched her friend's shoulder. But she shrugged her off. Her own face wet, Kitty leaned over to try again, but she felt a firm hand take hold of her arm. When she looked around, she saw Max. He began to pull her away.

"Don't," he told her softly.

"I have to," she insisted. "She's my friend."

"She wouldn't want you to see her like this."

Despite her struggles, he drew her off, down a long hall, through large glass doors, out into the night. Kitty caught a glimpse of tables and wicker chairs, of plush chaises, of a large swing hanging to the side on gigantic gilded chains. The pool shimmered beyond in the lights along the path. A lovely, gracious world. But her eyes were swimming with tears, and her surroundings appeared indistinct, as if they were part of some horrible nightmare vision. A romantic setting soured by guilt and grief.

She began to sob. Racking sobs that sprang from her deepest reservoir of pain. She felt strong arms gather her and pull her into a solid chest, where she cried into his shirt. "It's my fault. If she hadn't agreed to come with us, maybe—"

"Stop it," he said. "It's not your fault. That young man wanted more from her than another few nights in Bombay."

"She said she was afraid of losing him," she gasped in a throbbing voice. "But dear God, not like this."

Max held her, saying nothing. She clung to him, wanting nothing more than to absorb his strength, to forget the scene she'd just witnessed, and the memories it unleashed. A young boy, standing in the moonlight. The roar of gunfire. Rushing to him, just as Victoria had rushed to Ramsey. Holding him, knowing he was dead. Wanting to die, if only her death would help him live.

"She's so young. How will she live the rest of her life without him? Too young . . . just as I was too young."

She cried into his chest, feeling his arms tighten about her back.

Max held her close, stricken with grief at her words. It all rushed back to him—the painful memories of his lost past, the life he'd been forced to give up and all that he'd renounced. It flooded him until he felt at one with her suffering. The reserves he'd honed melted in the flow of her tears. Tenderly, he kissed her hair.

"Too young to lose you," she added.

Everything stilled. His arms, holding her close, went limp and fell from her. Her crying ceased. She could hear the calls of night birds in the distance, hear the clip-clop of horses' hooves in the street beyond the outside wall. Slowly, her face wet, she looked up at him. "I know who you are," she told him, forgetting her earlier resolve. "I saw you with Ngar."

In the moonlight, his face seemed to have lost its color.

"I followed you," she told him. "I saw you with him."

In a strained voice, he said, "You saw what you wanted to see." But he knew it was a futile effort. It would have been only a matter of time, he realized, before she discovered the truth.

"Why are you holding back from me? Can't you see how much I need you? You loved me once. . . ."

The words seemed to hang in the still air. He raked a hand through his hair and looked away.

"Please," she whispered. "Just tell me the truth."

"Don't ask me to do this," he said through gritted teeth.

"Do what?"

"I don't want to hurt you."

She felt crushingly vulnerable. But she had to hear it. "How can the truth hurt me?"

Impulsively, she put her hand on his chest. It thundered with the beat of his heart. But he stood calmly, looking down at her hand outlined against the stark white of his shirt, doing nothing to betray his inner emotion. Then, slowly drawing a breath, he deliberately removed her hand and let it drop to her side. With forced patience, he began to speak.

"I told you before, the Cameron you knew died. But if he were alive . . . think about it rationally for a moment. How old was he when you knew him?"

"Thirteen, as you well know."

"And you?"

"Eleven," she whispered, wondering how he could possibly go on playing this game of denial.

"All right, then. Do you honestly think a thirteen-year-old boy is capable of loving an eleven-year-old girl with the intensity you've built up in your mind?"

She stilled. "What are you saying?"

"He might need her. He might even like her. But *love*?"

She felt a knife stab her heart.

In the same reasonable tone, he continued. "Say he did survive. Say he did go through a thousand life-changing experiences of which you have no knowledge. What makes you think he would even remember you, except as a child tagging at his heels? *Thirteen-year-old boys don't fall in love with eleven-year-old girls.* So you can see that you've invented the whole thing. It's nothing more than a demented fantasy."

She stood staring at him, stunned. Nothing he could say could have more forcibly yanked the rug from beneath her feet. It was as if Cameron had just died a second time.

"How can you say this to me?" she cried as tears once again stung her eyes.

He *didn't* want to hurt her. It was tearing him up inside. But he felt dangerously close to crumbling before the vulnerability in her eyes. He had to persist. He had to heed Ngar's warning that she could be his weak link. He had to convince her that he had no feelings for her. It would be kinder in the end. Wearily, he said, "The last I heard, you asked for the truth."

She stood before him, paralyzed, unable to think what to do or say.

Max stared at her, hating himself. Suddenly, he had to get away. Away from the awful look in her eyes. Away from the sight of her lovely mouth trembling at his betrayal. Cursing himself, he turned on his heel and stormed off. Leaving her alone in the moonlight.

12

She sat for a time, gazing about her—at the moon, the stars, the reflection of the hotel dome in the undulating ripples of the pool—with unseeing eyes. She was so battered by his words that she felt barren, numb to her surroundings, utterly drained of all emotion. Cameron hadn't loved her. She'd never really known him at all. A silly, inexperienced girl, she'd seen only what she'd wanted to see. She'd built her memories on pure fabrication.

And if she'd been so wrong about that . . . what else was she wrong about? Had all her perceptions been nothing more than illusions? She'd built those perceptions around the Cameron she remembered . . . building him up in her mind as the English prototype whom she could emulate in her quest for a definitive identity. But she'd never had the least idea of who he really was. She didn't know now. She only knew that she'd been a fool, deluding herself because, after her childhood tragedy, she'd needed to hang on to something that made sense. But it had all been a lie. How, she wondered now, could she ever trust herself again?

Eventually, she began to realize where she was and to remember the other events of the night. Victoria would need her now. She would have to shake herself from these immobilizing thoughts and go to her.

She went back inside to find that the front atrium had been cleaned up with remarkable efficiency. The body had been removed, the blood cleaned from the tiles. Only a few curious guests remained, still discussing the tragic accident in awed, hushed tones. Victoria was nowhere to be found.

Kitty went to her room and knocked. When there was no answer, she called softly through the door, "Victoria, it's Kitty. Please let me in." There was no response.

She tried again an hour later, and an hour after that. Finally, exhausted, she fell asleep in her clothes. When she awoke close to dawn, feeling worn out and bleary, she roused herself and knocked again. When there was still no response, she headed for the stairs. She couldn't help but shiver as she passed the rail where Ramsey had fallen. Just the day before, she'd stood there looking down, glorying in the sensation of height. Passing it now was like passing by a tomb.

At the front desk, she expressed her concern about her friend. She was shown to the night manager's office, where he was just preparing to go off duty.

"Your friend left last night," he told her. "I put her on the last train to Rajasthan. Horrible business. The authorities were most happy to write the mishap off as an unfortunate accident. But I didn't want the newspapers to get wind of the, shall we say, questionable circumstances of the lieutenant's stay here."

"Was she all right?"

"She seemed to be in shock, for the most part. Wanted to stay to see the chap buried, but obviously we couldn't have that."

"Did she leave me a note?"

"I'm afraid not."

Kitty left the office, deeply disturbed. She'd hoped to help Victoria through this. But her sudden disappearance created yet another problem. Would she be in any shape to help them in Udaipur?

She had to tell Carrington. She should also, she realized, tell him about Cameron. But what could she say that would make any sense? She glanced at the clock. They were supposed to leave for the train station within half an hour. She went upstairs and finished throwing her toiletries into her valise.

When she'd finished, she went down to meet the others. Aveli eyed her cautiously as she approached, keeping his distance. Their discomfort seemed to charge between them like a current. As the hansom cab that would take them to Victoria Station swung up before the door, Carrington rushed out of the hotel, looking officious and carrying a telegram in his hand.

"Bad luck," he told them. "I've been called south. Terrible trouble in Madras, I'm afraid. Unavoidable, but I should be able to join you within a week or so in Udaipur. I suspect it will take you at least that long to ingratiate yourselves with the maharana. I heard what happened with your friend. Damned inconvenient, but if it turns out she can't be of use, you shall just have to do it yourselves. We *have* had a bit of news that might help you, however. We now believe the maharana keeps the ruby in his bedroom. That should narrow the field for you a bit."

Kitty felt a momentary panic. "Can't someone else attend to Madras?" she asked.

"Afraid not. It's my old district. No one knows it better than I."

Kitty thought about it on the ride to Victoria Station. Should she tell Carrington right now what she knew to be true about Aveli? On the one hand, Carrington's presence protected her interests in the mission. But he was in a hurry, and Kitty realized even now how fanciful the tale would sound. There were still too many unanswered questions to present a convincing case.

Before she had time to make up her mind, they had arrived. Carrington hopped out first, saying, "Well, then, I'm off. I'll see you as soon as I can."

It was only after she and Aveli had boarded the Rajputana Express and it was pulling out of the station that the thought struck her. Aveli had shown absolutely no surprise at Carrington's change in plan.

"You arranged it, didn't you?" she accused.

He glanced at her with a guarded expression. "What?"

"Carrington's departure."

In an annoyed tone, he asked, "Is there no end to your suspicions?" With that he walked up the aisle to their compartment, leaving her behind once again.

She couldn't bear the thought of sitting with him, cramped and silent in their discomfort for untold hours, so she found an empty compartment and settled herself into a seat by the window. Leaving the station, the train chugged its way north, hugging the coast with the great expanse of the Arabian Sea below. After a while it turned inland. Beyond her window, the timeless landscape of India slid by: plump water buffaloes neck-deep in paddy fields; dry riverbeds awaiting the precious relief of the monsoon; groves of mango trees arranged in neat rows; hundreds of Hindu and Jain temples; even the occasional lion peering regally from the bush, here in the last habitat of the dwindling Indian lion.

Hours passed. Kitty sat without moving, feeling devastatingly alone. Outside, the breadth of northern India passed unnoticed. Before she knew it, the plains gave way to the rolling Aravalli mountains. Rajasthan! Wild, enticing, forbidding. Land of blood and sword, legends and kings. Home of the Rajput warriors, India's answer to Arthurian knights. And the land where, as a child, she was held captive for three months—months that would change her life forever.

Her aching heart began to mimic the rhythm of the wheels as they came closer to the very site where the kidnapped children had been held. Mount Abu. Only twenty miles to the east. The remote, mountainous hideout where fourteen years before Cameron had died—or so she'd thought. How ironic that she was being taken back on this very day, just after she'd finally learned the awful truth. What tortuous fate had brought her back, so close to this very spot, with this very man?

How many times had she wished Cameron were

alive? But not like this. As the thought struck her, a memory from the past floated to the surface of her mind. She'd had an Indian governess who'd cared for her in Jaipur. Once, the woman had said to her, "Be careful what you wish for, because if you wish hard enough, your wish will most probably come true. But not in the way you expect."

She shook herself, returning with an effort to the present. She couldn't afford to think about that now. She had to concentrate on her single imperative: freeing her father. And she had to be careful. This Aveli—this Cameron she'd never really known—was an impediment to that cause. He would stop at nothing to attain his goal. He would even break her heart.

But how could she concentrate? Her heart hurt so much that she wanted to rip it out. Her chest burned with unshed tears. Giving in to her despair, she put her face in her hands and cried until she felt hollowed out inside.

Just as the sun was setting, the Rajputana Express curved around a steep hillside and presented her with her first view of Udaipur. Clustered at the eastern end of beautiful Lake Pichola, it was a magical city. Its whitewashed arabesque buildings topped by graceful domes and elaborate cupolas, distinctive in their Rajput blend of the whimsical and the elegant, gave the impression of a charming community sprung from *The Thousand and One Nights*. Cradled by densely forested hills, the picturesque setting would in itself be remarkable, but here it served as merely the backdrop to three magnificent palaces: the fortresslike Monsoon Palace topping a hill four miles distant; the City Palace, a complex of buildings fronting the lake; and the much smaller, dollhouselike Lake Palace built on an outcropping in the middle of the lake, facing the City Palace. The last of the sun's rays cast a rosy glow over the buildings while the mist rising off the water gave an impression of mystical tranquillity.

Kitty had never been to Udaipur, but her governess had told her about its legend when she was a child. The Venice of the east, the Versailles of the desert. The most enchanted and dreamlike city in India.

As they disembarked at the train station outside of town, Kitty felt Aveli studying her. She averted her face so he wouldn't see her tear-reddened eyes, determined to present a cool façade that would hide the hurt and humiliation she felt.

The porters, all wearing white *kurta* shirts and colorful, elaborately coiled turbans, bore the distinctive Rajput trademarks: tall, light-complected, erect and proud, with various forms of the bushy mustaches that marked the men of Rajasthan. As they were looking about for a tonga, they were approached by an attendant who peered at them with a haughty demeanor.

"Memsahib Fontaine?"

Surprised, Kitty acknowledged the greeting.

"I was sent by the political agent, Mr. Hingham. His wife informed him of your impending arrival, and His Excellency requested that I meet each incoming train from Bombay until you arrived, so that I could welcome you."

"That was kind of him," she said.

"Mrs. Hingham is ill, so His Excellency regrets he cannot offer you the hospitality of his home. He suggested that I might show you to a nearby hotel. If you'll follow me."

He led them to a motorcar, arranged their luggage, and soon they were winding through narrow alleys, veering out of the way when a group of goats or a wild cow crossed their path. The high whitewashed houses that clung to the hillside and the cramped streets gave the setting a feel of medieval splendor.

"Mrs. Hingham has requested that you join the family for a reception to be given in your honor," the attendant explained. "Would tomorrow night suit?"

"If Victoria is ill . . ." Kitty began, not wishing to tax her friend so soon, but the attendant waved a hand, summarily dismissing her concerns.

"His Excellency will attend to the details, and feels certain his wife will be well enough to act as hostess. You have only to provide your consent."

Still, Kitty hesitated. But Aveli said, in his Italian accent, "Please inform the signore that we would be honored to accept his kind invitation. Tomorrow evening will be quite suitable."

The attendant checked them into the Royal Mewar Hotel and left them with the promise of sending a confirmation the following day.

Feeling awkward, Kitty turned to Aveli. "What do we do until tomorrow night?" she asked before they parted for their separate rooms.

"I don't know about you," he told her brusquely, "but I'm going to get the lay of the land."

Invitations had been sent out to the city's small British colony, inviting them to meet Kitty Fontaine, England's famed aviatrix. But Kitty knew they would come as much out of curiosity to gawk at the daughter of the notorious Colonel Fontaine—a man they professed to support out of loyalty to their own kind but had quickly abandoned once the guilty verdict was in. A connection with a condemned man could, after all, destroy one's career.

The British Residency was a solidly built redbrick building that looked out of place in the desert fantasy of Udaipur. Inside, the rooms were as coldly English as any manor house in Surrey. The only concession to India was a pair of ceiling fans that circulated the hot air about the rooms. The surroundings were formal, stuffy, clean to the point of sterility. Glancing about, Kitty could see nothing of the gracious, loving personality of Victoria.

Her husband, Mortimer Hingham, came forward to greet them, bowing stiffly to each in turn. Just a few years older than Victoria, he was young for his position, yet he wore it as ceremoniously as he donned his evening attire. Every word he uttered seemed calculated to further his ambitions.

"Miss Fontaine, it is indeed a pleasure to receive such a distinguished old acquaintance from home," he greeted her, sounding, beneath the formal courtesy, neither particularly pleased nor as if he remembered her at all, though she'd served as maid of honor at his wedding. He gave her the impression that, were it not for the coup of offering such a curiosity for the amusement of his guests, he'd prefer to have avoided the trouble of hosting this reception altogether. But she knew, from her childhood, that the British found the sameness of society in India to be dull and stifling. Any newcomer was an occasion, and she was something of a spectacle.

"And this is?" He turned to Aveli, who stood a head taller than he, dashingly handsome in evening dress.

Before Kitty could introduce him, Aveli gave a formal bow and said in his Italian accent, "Her husband, Count Aveli. At your service, signore."

"Indeed?" asked Mortimer, his brows rising in surprise. "We hadn't realized you were married."

"It came as rather a surprise to me, as well."

"But that would make you a countess," Mortimer concluded. "Splendid. We shall toast your success. Ladies and gentlemen, I present to you Count and Countess Aveli. Do greet them while I uncover the whereabouts of my wife."

Kitty cringed at his censorious tone. They were instantly surrounded by a circle of cheery British faces. Their compatriots muttered admiration for her feats in the air with one breath and condolences for her father with the other.

"This Hingham fellow is rather a cold fish, as you British are fond of saying," Max whispered.

"*We* British?" she challenged.

He ignored the taunt. "Did you notice he offered to toast not your happiness but your success?"

"No doubt a countess ranks higher on his list of acceptable guests than the daughter of a felon."

Kitty found that she was nervous about seeing Victoria again. Under the circumstances, this reception had to be a strain. She hadn't really expected Victoria to appear at all, rather to plead illness and remain in her room. But presently the assembled guests parted and Kitty saw her friend approach.

She appeared pale and drawn, in sharp contrast to the radiant woman Kitty had encountered in Bombay. She wore a simple black gown, impeccably cut but devoid of jewelry save the wedding ring on her left hand. Behind her, two small children, a two-year-old girl and a boy of three, hid behind her skirts.

She made her way through the guests and embraced her friend. Kitty held her close, feeling the trembling of Victoria's limbs, the frailty of her form. She wanted to tell her, "It's all right. I'm here. I'll help you." But with Mortimer standing off to the side, staring imperiously, all she could do was hold Victoria and offer wordless comfort.

When Victoria broke the embrace, the faintest trace of unshed tears were visible in her eyes. She masked them with effort and said in a soft voice, "I'm glad you've come." She included Max in her sad smile. He stepped forward and took Victoria's hand in his, bowing and gently kissing the back of her hand. Kitty heard him say, too quietly for the others to hear, "I'm deeply sorry for your loss." Victoria met his gaze for a moment, and Kitty feared that, in the face of Max's sincere condolence, Victoria might crumble. She was touched that he would go out of his way to offer comfort to her friend.

Suddenly she remembered what he'd said to her the night before. *I don't want to hurt you.* Perhaps, underneath his façade of ruthlessness, there was a core of kindness in Max, after all.

The little girl yanked at her mother's skirt, breaking the tension. Remembering her duties, Victoria added, "These are my children. Peter and Natasha."

Two freshly scrubbed faces peered out from their

mother's skirt, smiling shyly. They were adorable children with huge eyes and delicate faces, like Victoria. When Kitty smiled at them they giggled and ducked behind their mother's skirt to hide once again.

Kitty was charmed. But she heard Mortimer's stern voice admonish them. "Children, is that the proper way to greet your guests?"

Instantly, as if afraid of retribution, they snapped to attention. Coming out from behind their covering, Peter bowed while little Natasha dipped low in a wobbly curtsy. "Pleased to meet you," they murmured as one.

Casting a glance at her husband, Victoria dropped down so that she was level with her children's faces and took them into her arms, giving each a kiss on the cheek. "Run off to bed now, dears. I shall be up in a bit to tuck you in." Her voice was tender and full of love. When they moved to obey, she held them back for just a moment, clutching them to her until she sensed Mortimer's frown and reluctantly let them go. They bowed quickly to the guests and were about to run off when, as one, they stopped and, turning back, bowed formally to their father. A moment later, they were gone.

With quiet fortitude, Victoria played her role as hostess, introducing them to each guest in turn, instructing the servants on the serving of drinks and hors d'oeuvres. But she seemed like a ghost of her former self, going through the motions with effortless grace without seeming to realize what she was doing or saying. Once, Kitty heard a woman ask Mortimer, "Is Victoria quite all right? She seems so odd."

"My wife has been indisposed," he answered through gritted teeth.

"Poor dear," the guest sympathized. "Perhaps we shouldn't tax her."

"I assure you, she is perfectly capable of handling her tasks."

"It wasn't her tasks I was concerned with," the woman chastised gently. "It was her health."

Kitty remembered the vibrant woman she'd spent time with in Bombay, and she grieved for her lost friend. Even in her fear of losing Ramsey there had been passion, life. It seemed to her that Ramsey's death had accomplished what none of her mother's or husband's constant criticisms had: it had broken her spirit at last.

Kitty, in turn, played her part as honored guest with half a mind, answering questions about what it was like to be a woman flyer, when all she really wanted was to be alone with Victoria. It must be horrible to have to go through this charade, pretending her heart wasn't broken, having no one in whom she could confide.

The small talk seemed endless. Mortimer announced importantly, "We've invited the maharana, naturally. We always do, yet he never comes. He is known to be fond of aviation, though, so perhaps he will honor us this evening."

"I've heard, my lady," said one of the guests, "that it is your intention to fly the English Channel one day. Yet Professor Hoffman of Oxford says it can't possibly be done."

Finally one of the younger ladies asked Aveli about the Italian court, sparking a shift in the conversation. As they seized on him, and he answered their questions with effortless charm, Kitty saw her opportunity and drew Victoria aside.

"Is there somewhere we can speak alone?"

After a brief hesitation, Victoria whispered, "Come up to my room."

They went upstairs and Victoria closed the door behind them. Kitty found herself in a lovely, casual yet tasteful room, decorated in soft pastels, understatedly elegant yet feminine and delicate just as Victoria was. So different from the stuffy, masculine heaviness of the rest of the house. Mortimer, no doubt, slept down the hall.

"I'm so sorry for what happened," Kitty told her. "I tried to see you afterward but you were already gone."

Victoria gave her friend a bleak look. Now that she no longer had to put up a brave front, she seemed ravaged and shell-shocked. "The manager didn't want the scandal that would have resulted if I had been discovered there. As if I cared anymore. Oh, Kitty, I didn't even see him buried. I never had the chance to say goodbye."

"What happened?" she asked, thinking it might help to talk about it.

Victoria sighed and her lip quivered. "You recall he said he had a surprise for me? I waited in our room for him, wondering what sort of foolishness he was up to, thinking—oh, I don't know what I thought. I never expected—"

"What?" Kitty prompted.

"He came back with two one-way tickets he'd purchased on a steamer leaving that night. He'd decided that he would save me the agony of making the decision. I was appalled. Did he expect me to sail that night and leave my children without so much as a good-bye? We fought. In a rage of frustration, he stormed from the room. Suddenly, alone in that sanctuary where we'd spent so many intense and happy times, I knew I was going to lose him. I ran after him, pleading with him not to leave. But he wouldn't listen. We struggled. And in that awful struggle, he . . . fell."

The silence that followed her words seemed to throb in Kitty's ears.

"Even now, I don't know how it could have happened. My world stopped when I watched his slow—strangely slow—fall. The next thing I knew, I was running down those endless flights of stairs, around and around, praying frantically. I killed him, Kitty."

Kitty turned to her. "No," she told her. "No, you didn't. I saw it. It was an accident."

A single tear slipped down Victoria's cheek. "I did, though. I caused him so much pain." Her voice broke and she took a breath. "He was willing to sacrifice everything for me. Yet what did I sacrifice for him? Snatches of borrowed time—and ultimately, him. I was such a fool! If I had it to do over again—"

"You can't punish yourself," Kitty insisted. "You have to live, for him. For your children."

"What sort of mother will they have now?" Victoria's eyes as she looked at Kitty were empty, haunted. "I feel as if a part of me—the part that was real, that was happy, that was hopeful—left my body that night. As if that part of me is there still, watching from out of the windows of the Palm Court, for just one more glimpse of my beloved's face. That's the part of me that lives, Kitty. The rest is dead."

"I feel so responsible," Kitty told her. "If I hadn't pushed you to come back here—"

"No, Kitty. You mustn't think that. I never had a

chance to tell him. No," she added more softly. "The fault is mine."

"Was it worth it?" Kitty asked. "There was so much pain. Your happiness was so brief. If you had it to do over again—"

Suddenly there was a knock on the door. As one, they whirled toward it, startled, like two children caught in mischief. The door opened and Mortimer stood on the threshold, glaring disapprovingly.

"Have you forgotten your guests, Victoria?"

She lowered her eyes. "No, Mortimer, I haven't forgotten."

"The maharana has just arrived. He is affording me a distinct honor. I expect you to greet him accordingly."

"Of course, Mortimer. We shall be down directly."

When he'd gone, with a last disapproving glare, Victoria suddenly turned to Kitty, grabbing both her hands passionately in her own. "Kitty, if you've found the man you love, hold on to him and never let him go. Whatever pain you might suffer, however brief your happiness, it's worth every moment not to have to live like this. I made the mistake of putting my pride and my fear of what others might think above my soul mate. I shall live with that mistake for the rest of my days. But you don't have to. No matter what happens, no matter the pain or uncertainty, *don't make the mistake I made.*"

13

Like a sentry, Mortimer waited in the hall. The Maharana of Udaipur stood at the bottom of the stairwell, surrounded by his entourage of five bodyguards, utterly oblivious to the English guests, obviously waiting for the one thing he'd come here tonight to see: England's famous aviatrix.

He was a tall man in his forties with a regal bearing, dressed in a red brocade suit and matching turban. His huge mustache jutted out at right angles to his handsome, imperious face. His dazzling dark brown eyes followed Kitty down the stairs. He acknowledged Victoria's gracious greeting, but his gaze immediately returned to Kitty.

As she waited to be presented, Kitty glanced at Max,

looking at him with new eyes. *No matter the pain or uncertainty* . . . Victoria's words had cracked through her confusion. She remembered what she'd said in Bombay: *If he's your soul mate, he loves you.* She didn't know if she believed it. She didn't know what had happened to Max, why he was being so cruel. And she didn't know what could be so important to him that he'd stand by and allow her father to be killed because of it. But there was one thing she did know—no matter how long it took, no matter what she had to do, she was going to uncover the truth. Whoever Max really was, despite everything that had happened, she cared for him. If there was a chance that he could love her, she was going to find out. She was going to forge a new beginning. And soon.

She snapped back to the present when Mortimer said, "Your Majesty, may I present our dear friend, Katherine Fontaine—Countess Aveli."

"Delighted, delighted," the maharana said as he took her hand and touched it lightly to his lips.

The time had come to put all else aside and play her role. Kitty could feel Max's gaze boring into her. Still holding the maharana's hand, she curtsied and said in rusty Hindi, "*Namaste*—I am honored."

"A terrible shame about your father," the maharana responded. "I knew him, you know—if only remotely."

"I assure you my father is entirely innocent of the crimes of which he has been convicted."

"Of course, of course." He switched back to English and turned to shake hands with Aveli, who'd moved to her side to introduce himself.

"Italian, eh? I know about Italy. Julius Caesar, Marco Polo, Garibaldi. I read the English newspapers. I subscribe to the *Times*." He turned back to Kitty. "I have read about your exploits in the sky."

"I'm flattered."

"It may surprise many men that a woman would excel in such a dangerous and adventurous field, but it does not surprise me."

"Why is that, Your Majesty?"

"Because I know of your Rajput blood. Rajputana women are strong and independent and lead us Rajput men around like donkeys." He put his hand to his ear and pulled, as if to demonstrate. "The Rajput man may be the strongest, fiercest warrior in all the world. But there is one thing stronger—a Rajputana woman." He laughed uproariously, delighted by his confession.

"I'm quite sure no woman leads you around like a donkey," Kitty said with a slightly flirtatious edge to her voice.

"And do you know that we have something *else* in common? I too am a man of the skies. Yes, I am the proud owner of an Antoinette IV flying machine built by the great Léon Levavasseur himself in Paris, France." He waited for her surprised reaction.

"That's a magnificent machine. I had no idea one even existed in Asia."

"I have all the modern conveniences. I own five Rolls-Royce automobiles. I have a phonograph. I have a Lumière machine that shows moving pictures on the wall. I am a most forward-looking man."

"I'm sure you must enjoy flying such a marvelous aeroplane."

He frowned. "Alas, I am no pilot. But perhaps you would oblige me by taking me up in the air."

"I'm afraid that won't be possible," Max stated in his best husband tone, learned, no doubt, from Mortimer.

The maharana ignored him and addressed Kitty as before. "You can fly the machine, yes?"

Kitty glanced at Max, realizing that he was denying the maharana's wish to make the chase more inviting. "I suppose, but—"

"Then you must be my guest. You must teach me how to fly like the birds in the sky."

"I'm afraid, Your Majesty that would be—"

"Out of the question," Aveli finished. "We have a schedule to keep. We have firm reservations for a private tour of the Taj Mahal in Agra at the end of next week. Our visit has been timed to coincide with the full moon."

The maharana dismissed this with a wave of his hand. "What is the Taj Mahal? A gaudy tomb. Rajasthan is the real India—not the Taj Mahal! Moreover, it is your heritage! You must stay here at least a month. No, two months. I can show you the great desert cities of Jaisamer and Bikaner and Jodhpur. I shall . . . I shall show you. . . . Tiger hunting! You English love to kill the tigers, yes?"

"Yes, the English do indeed love to kill tigers," Aveli muttered.

"Then we shall kill the tigers. As many as you like. There is no thrill like bringing down one of the great striped beasts just as it is about to pounce on your bearer!" The very thought of it seemed to excite him. "What a time we will have!"

The image repelled Kitty, but she tried not to show it. "I admit the prospect *is* enticing."

"And pig-sticking! That other great sport of our beloved Raj. Have you ever had the pleasure of lunging a lance into the side of a snarling wild boar? The sound of the animal's squealing is more stimulating than anything you can imagine."

"I'm sure it is, indeed"—she looked at him with a slightly seductive glint in her eye—"stimulating. And I do so wish we could take you up on your kind offer—"

"Where are you staying tonight?"

"We have rooms at the Royal Mewar."

"The Royal Mewar is a pigsty! I won't have England's greatest flying woman staying in such a hovel. You will be my guest at the Lake Palace." He snapped his fingers at his entourage and gave instructions for them to fetch the couple's belongings.

"We will have *such* fun. Think of it! We will picnic at the ruins of Chittogarh. We will ride elephants in the moonlight in Ajmer. And we will fly my machine through the beautiful skies of our beloved homeland."

"Your Majesty," Aveli said, rather more sharply. "You don't seem to be hearing us. I am telling you that we have other arrangements. Besides which, now that the countess is my wife, I'm not certain I approve of her flying anymore."

Kitty bristled beneath his autocratic tone, but she was beginning to formulate a plan of her own. Steering the maharana aside, she whispered, "You see my dilemma, Your Majesty. My husband disapproves of my avocation. Such a nuisance, really, but what's a woman to do?"

"Ah," said the maharana with a conspiratorial gleam in his eye, "but husbands can be taken care of, yes?"

"So you see—" Max continued, but the maharana—

erect, proud, every inch the king—looked down his nose and interrupted.

"Enough!" he ordered. "You will be my guests. I insist."

His tone was enough to alarm Mortimer, whose position depended on the goodwill of the sovereign. "Perhaps Count Aveli could adjust his plans," he suggested. "I should be happy to wire ahead and reschedule your itinerary."

"Then it's settled." With that, the maharana turned to his host. "Let us eat, then. It seems I have worked up quite an appetite." He couldn't resist casting a suggestive glance at Kitty as he spoke.

As they filed into the residency dining room, Kitty beamed at Max and said under her breath, "I'm beginning to think it might not be such a task to get into this man's bedroom, after all."

Max returned her smile with a glare of suspicion. "What are you up to?"

With an airy shrug, Kitty told him, "Just following your lead."

A frown of annoyance flicked across his face. She smiled inwardly. He'd so carefully built his house of cards, protecting it at all costs. He didn't know it yet, but she was about to knock it down.

She spoke to him now with a light, bantering air. "What a fearsome scowl you have. Is it my imagination? Because it appears to me, Machiavelli, that you've developed an instant, and most *unprofessional* dislike for His Excellency, the Maharana of Udaipur."

She sashayed into the dining room and accepted the seat of honor at the right of the maharana.

．　　　．　　　．

As they were leaving, Kitty drew Victoria aside. "Thank you for everything," she told her. "I know it wasn't easy for you to do this."

"I only hope it's sufficient. Do be careful, Kitty. Don't underestimate the maharana. He's clever, and he's proud. I shouldn't want you to come to any harm."

"It's like you to worry about me when you have so much on your mind. But you needn't be concerned. I have too much at stake to risk failure now. I'll come by and see you before we leave—"

But Victoria shook her head. "No, Kitty. You'll think me rude and selfish, but—"

"You'd prefer I didn't come back, is that it?"

Victoria averted her gaze. "I don't think I can bear it just now. Seeing you brings it all back to me. It's too fresh. You understand?"

Kitty did. She hugged her friend and wished her well, knowing there was no help she could offer. What Victoria needed now was time to try and heal a wound that, Kitty knew from experience, was unhealable. With a last kiss on the cheek, she turned to Max and the challenge ahead.

The maharana took them in his Rolls-Royce through the narrow streets toward the City Palace, where he and his wives were in residence. The façade facing the lake was lit up, casting its grand reflection on the water. Off to the side of the palace was a large archway leading to a dock where a majestic launch waited.

"My man will take you across the lake to the summer palace," the sovereign told them. "Tomorrow morning he will collect you and we shall go to see my beautiful

flying machine. I regret to say that it won't be possible
for me to join you for dinner tomorrow night. I have a
previous obligation—affairs of state and all that. We
will dine together on the following evening. Now, my
friends, enjoy the hospitality of my Lake Palace and we
shall meet in the morning."

The launch resembled a miniature version of a Carib-
bean pirate ship, furnished with plush cushioned seats
upholstered in red velvet. Resplendently uniformed
oarsmen rowed them on a meandering course, maneu-
vering around the myriad lotus flowers that covered the
surface of the water, scenting the night air with their
sweet perfume. At the stern a sitar-and-drum ensemble
serenaded them. The music drifted on the lake to min-
gle soothingly with the night mist.

Shimmering in the soft glow of night lights was the
fabled Lake Palace. Covering every inch of the island's
nearly four acres, it was a dreamlike confection of white
marble. Writers throughout the centuries had described
it as "one of the most romantic creations of man"—a
pleasing potpourri of elegant courtyards, cupolaed pa-
vilions, and fountained gardens designed to catch the
breezes that drifted in off the lake. It seemed to Kitty
that the moon and stars had been created as nothing
more than a backdrop for this jewel in the water.

Momentarily they came alongside the north wing of
the palace and docked before a short flight of marble
steps. Entering the inner courtyard was like stepping
through a looking glass into a world of imaginary
splendor. Arched doorways, fanciful murals, mirror
work embedded to form lovely frescoes on the walls,
stained glass, glimpses of fountains bubbling in the
gardens beyond, all contributed to the impression of

having been transported back in time to an era when kings were omnipotent and princesses lay about on luxurious chaises nibbling figs.

They were led around the inner, open courtyard where *kathakali* dancers were re-creating a scene from *The Ramayana* as a welcome. One woman balanced eight ceramic pots atop her head, each growing smaller until they towered four feet in the air. When the guests were spotted, a servant stepped upon a ladder and added three more pots, which the woman stabilized while swaying to the beat of the music.

They were shown to a room by a male attendant. A spacious chamber decorated in shades of white and gold, lushly exotic. The windows facing the lake were shuttered by latticed arabesque screens, and draped in a tangled profusion of gauzy white and gold veils. The bed was a large four-poster covered with a white cloth with tiny mirrors sewn into its surface. Across the top of the canopy, small gilt chains were slung, dangling in delicately cascading loops. The furniture was white, gilded with gold leaf. The only splash of color came from a large, plush wall hanging made from bright blue and green peacock feathers, spanned out to re-create the flamboyance of a peacock's tail. Tile floors were softened by a scattering of hand-woven silk carpets that appeared white and gold when viewed from one side yet changed to shades of pastel blues and greens when viewed from the other.

"Your things have been unpacked," the attendant told Kitty in Hindi. Obviously the maharana's underlings had passed along the word that she spoke the language. He was nothing if not thorough, she realized. "There is fruit and wine on the table." He opened a door to reveal a small enclosed octagonal balcony, shuttered with latticed screens, that jutted out over the lake from the front corner of the palace. An enchanting little outlook perched atop the water furnished with a diminutive table and two deeply cushioned chairs. The circumference was such that only two people could comfortably sit without feeling cramped. But the sense of privacy was sublime. A perfect place, Kitty realized, for a Rajputana princess to sip her tea and observe the forbidden outside world without fear of strangers seeing her face.

"You may breakfast here if you wish. It provides a lovely view of the lake and the City Palace at dawn."

As they returned to the room, he opened the windows overlooking the lake, lit several candles about the room, then switched off the light. The chamber was instantly transformed. Thousands of tiny mirrors imbedded in the ceiling took on the aspect of twinkling stars as the breeze from the lake made the candles dance. "It is a Rajasthani art," he explained when Kitty gasped in wonder. "Designed to form the impression of being surrounded by the night sky. If you need anything at all, you've only to pull the rope on the wall and it will be provided. Sir, if you'll follow me," he added in English, "I will show you to your room."

When they'd left, Kitty stood transfixed in the middle of the room, staring at the ceiling. The flickering candles shifted the light constantly so the mirrors twinkled and shimmered, reflecting the luminous glow. She did, indeed, feel as if she were surrounded by the night sky. It was breathtakingly beautiful, charmingly romantic.

She fingered the gilt chains that formed the canopy

for the four-poster, the diaphanous veils that served as drapings over the windows, the exquisite wall hanging made from peacock's feathers. On a small table she found a basin of warm water perfumed with jasmine. Stripping off her evening gown, she stood in her silk petticoat and bathed her hot skin with the sinfully soft cloth provided. The scent of jasmine filled her senses. She could feel the breeze from the water cooling her damp flesh. She could see the water of the lake lapping against the embankment and the lights of the City Palace, stretching along the banks like a fairy fortress. The moon cast its silvery glow on the water, dancing with the gently shifting current. With the mirrored ceiling shimmering above her, she felt truly one with the night.

She heard a sound and turned to find Max coming in the door. He'd removed his dinner jacket and untied his cravat so that it hung loose on either side of his open collar. A smattering of dark chest hair drew her gaze. He looked devilishly disheveled, as if he'd loosened the encumbrance of formal attire in haste. As he stood there he ran a hand through his neatly combed hair so that it fell over his forehead in rakish fashion. He was so handsome that her heart skipped a beat.

"Have you ever seen anything more beautiful in your life?" she asked. "It's like a fairyland."

"It's a prison," he announced curtly, sounding none too pleased. "While you were looking at the stars and the lights on the water, I was noticing that the lake is infested with crocodiles. I've never seen so many tails swishing in the water."

She shuddered at the thought. Crocodiles!

"There's only one way here and back," he continued,

"the maharana's launch, which they've sailed back to shore. Guards stand watching the docks on either side. Which means your friend the maharana has got his thumb firmly planted on our movements. Making it next to impossible to get to the palace and the ruby."

"I don't think we'll have to worry about the guards or the launch or the crocodiles," she told him confidently.

"You must know something I don't."

"In a manner of speaking."

"And what is that?"

She turned and looked at him. In the twinkling lights of the mirrors he looked like some romantic hero from a storybook. "Because I'm going to get into his bedroom without the impediment of crocodiles or guards . . . or you."

He frowned at her. "How do you expect to work that little miracle?"

"I'm going to seduce him."

14

tter silence followed her breezy statement. He stood glaring at her, his gaze sweeping down the length of her so she became aware that she stood before him in nothing but a thin silk petticoat. "The hell you will," he growled at last.

Her spirits soared. She'd planned to test him with her statement, to determine if he were capable of jealousy. She'd caught a whiff of that possibility at dinner, when he'd glared his annoyance at the maharana's obvious interest. But just how far could she push him? Enough to break through the layers of his resistance?

"The foundation has been laid," she told him in the same insouciant tone. "He's made it clear that he . . . desires me. He thinks I'm married, so he likely has no fear that I would have further designs on him. You've already laid the groundwork by playing the part of the disapproving husband—rather too well, I might add. One would think you'd had practice."

"I had a good example in your friend Mortimer," he said conversationally, trying to gauge her mood.

"And we know how well you can assume a role to conceal your true self," she said sweetly, as if complimenting him. "You played your role so brilliantly, in fact, that now all I have to do is appeal to his masculine instincts. I think he'd rather fancy having the wife of an Italian count seduce him behind her husband's back."

"That wasn't part of the bargain."

"What wasn't?" she asked, feigning ignorance.

"You don't have to bed a stranger to get the ruby. There are other ways."

"What ways? You've already told me how impossible the situation is. Besides, I bedded you, as you so elegantly put it. One more man hardly makes much of a difference."

"That was different. You thought I was—"

"Cameron? Well, that's neither here nor there, is it, since it seems I've never really known you—as Cameron *or* Max. Which makes you as much a stranger to me as the maharana. So I hardly see the distinction. In any case, what do you care? You've made it clear you have no feelings for me. I'm an independent woman. This is 1909. The sexual emancipation of women is at hand. I'm free to do whatever I choose. With *whomever* I choose."

He was gazing at her speculatively. It was clear he didn't believe a word she said. "As I recall, you haven't . . . seduced many men in your time."

"Oh, well," she said dismissively. "How difficult can it be?"

"You have a strategy for seduction, I suppose?"

She pondered the possibilities for a moment. She had no intention of following through with this plan. But if she was to force his hand, she had to convince Max otherwise. "Given that the maharana desires me, which we've already established—we *have* established that, I presume?"

"I think it was obvious to everyone there tonight," he conceded grudgingly.

He *was* jealous, after all! "Then given that, I suppose it's a matter of playing it by ear. Relying on my feminine instincts, as it were."

"Such as?"

She pretended to consider. "Well, you have more experience with seduction than I. What approach do you think best? Should I be coy? Pretend innocence? 'Your Majesty, don't look at me with those hot eyes. You make me blush.' Or perhaps play the tease? Brush up against him as if I didn't realize what I was doing?" She walked toward him slowly and brushed against him as she passed, lingering with her back to him. "Let him know—subtly, of course—that a stolen kiss wouldn't be amiss?" Turning, she stood on tiptoe and brought her mouth close to his. She saw his gaze drop to her parted lips and stare. She watched, mesmerized, as his mouth moved closer to her own as if drawn by some sorcery too potent to resist. She could feel his breath, tinged with brandy, mingling with her own. But before he could move closer, she lithely darted away.

"Perhaps I could drop something and bend over so he might catch a good glimpse of my . . . shape?" She turned again and bent, slowly, lingeringly, as if retrieving something from the floor, affording him an excellent view of her backside. Glancing over her shoulder, she saw his gaze glued to her. A hot, hungry gaze that suddenly made her feel ready for the chase.

"Or do you think a more direct approach is in order?" She stood and moved with a slow, grinding gait toward him until she was all but touching him. "I understand, Your Majesty," she purred, inching her lips closer to his, "that you have some remarkable gems tucked away. Perhaps you might show me?" As she said this, she reached forward and rubbed her palm against the bulge in his trousers, feeling him leap to attention beneath her touch. "Oh, my," she said innocently. "That seems to work nicely."

"And what," he asked in a strained voice, moving her hand aside, "if your little scheme should backfire?"

"Backfire? However do you mean?"

"What if the eminent maharana isn't the gentleman you suppose him to be? What if he takes matters into his own hands?"

"You'll have to explain yourself, I'm afraid. As I say, I'm not as well versed in the art of seduction as you seem to be."

"What if the sorely tested maharana should turn into one of the tigers he so likes to hunt? He's apparently fond of prisons. What if he were to confine you? What if he took your wrists in his hands"—he caught her wrists in a punishing grip—"and locked them together so?" With a slow, deliberate force, he moved her hands behind her back and held them tightly together. Thrust up against his chest, she felt her heart flutter wildly.

"But you forget, Tiger. I excel at escaping from impossible situations. Even from wild beasts." With a quick twist of her wrists, she broke his grasp and flitted away. "He won't get near me—unless, of course, I want him to." She tossed him a lascivious grin.

"He might pursue you."

He stalked toward her. The muscles in his thighs strained against his pants, drawing the material tight as he walked, outlining an erection that seemed more than eager to play the game of passion she'd concocted. She stepped away from him until her back came up against the nearest post of the bed. When he was in front of her, he rounded her with his arms, and clasped the post so that she was caged before him. He inched closer. She felt his erection, rampant now, at the juncture of her thighs. Slowly, with catlike grace and control, he ground into her, imprisoning her loins against the power center of his body, rubbing her relentlessly. Thrills shot through her as longing, raw and primitive, coiled within her. Her mouth dropped open and she gasped at the splendor of sensation.

But then she saw the flicker of triumph in his dark eyes. She ducked and twisted so that she escaped his hold. Leaping onto the bed, she skimmed the mirrored coverlet to grasp the bedpost opposite and swing to the floor on the other side of the bed.

She caught the glimmer of something unreadable in his eyes. But a moment later, he shrugged, conceding defeat. "Very well. You've proved you can elude him. What then?"

In the darkness, with nothing but the candles and the glinting mirrors to light his features, he seemed remote. Was he giving up so easily?

"Rajput rulers are fond of dancing girls, are they not?"

He shrugged again. "Who isn't?"

She couldn't determine if he was being serious or sardonic. "I could dance for him. Show him the goods, so to speak. Let him lick his lips and survey the feast he might consume if he's fortunate enough."

She'd seen him flinch at her allusion to showing the maharana the goods. But he only asked in a mild tone, "Can you dance?"

"I'm a cat. One thing I do know is how to move."

She went to him and put a hand to his chest, pushing him backward across the room until his progress was arrested by a chair. With a single shove, she sent him sprawling backward.

"Watch and learn," she said smugly.

She didn't really know how to dance. Not like this. She had vague memories of seeing a belly dancer at a party once when she was a child. She'd thought it silly then, all the grinding and wiggling of hips. She couldn't understand why the men had seemed so enraptured. But now, as Max lounged back in the chair, his eyes half-lidded and deceptively drowsy, she felt a simmering in her loins that caused her body to move of its own accord. As if he were an instrument, strumming a tune that commanded her limbs to dance for his pleasure, his arousal. As if she were responding to his silent song.

She moved before him. With leisurely, fulsome movements, stretching with feline grace, her eyes locked with his, undulating to his melody. And as she did she felt the stirrings of arousal, the sharp awareness of displaying her scantily clad body—so forbidden, so sublime—to his heated gaze. Scalding dark eyes biting into her, taking note as her nipples hardened, becoming tight little buds that thrust out against their thin covering, her breasts swelling, throbbing, swinging voluptuously as she dipped and swayed, bringing them close then pulling back, denying the ravenous hunger of his eyes. And as she played this heady game, she felt for the first time the hum and glow of the seductress, felt the power of her female flesh, displayed yet tantalizingly hidden, to arouse the beast of lust in a man.

Her hands grazed her hips, following a sleek line up her waist, caressing her breasts, lifting them to his gaze. She reached up and found the tortoiseshell pins in her hair. Taking one, she held it before him and let it drop to the floor. One by one, the rest of the pins followed until her heavy auburn curls tumbled in glorious disarray about her shoulders, naked but for the thin silk straps. He watched, transfixed, as she ran her fingers through the tresses, watched the contrast of deep flame slither over creamy white flesh.

As she danced before him, she used her hair as a shield, hiding her face, holding a thick strand across her eyes, her lips, before moving it aside to reveal the bounty underneath. She'd never thought too much about her looks. She hadn't longed for the attentions of handsome men the way most young women did. Even with Charles, she'd felt more like a sister than a siren. But as she caught the leap of appreciation that lit Max's eyes, she knew for the first time what it was to feel truly beautiful. Unconsciously, he licked his lips and told her it was so.

Some part of him knew what she was doing. His mind rebelled, determined to resist her goading charm.

She was such an innocent, really, playing at a game whose dangers she couldn't even fathom. His heart slammed shut like a cell door. But his body felt the pain of her enticement. His erection pulsed with an appetite all its own, heedless of his finely honed denial and control. He gripped the armrests with a hold that threatened to split the wood in two.

Emboldened by his grudging response, Kitty moved closer, teasing, to bend over him and drape her hair like a curtain about his shoulders and his face. As she did, he caught the sweet fragrance of jasmine. It filled his senses, warm, erotic, a distinctly womanly fragrance mingling with the faint yet infuriatingly arousing musk of her sex. He sat like a rock as she provoked him by moving her head and shoulders so her curls were drawn back and forth across him, slowly bringing trailing tendrils to brush across his cheek. Rounding him, she tracked her hair across his shoulders, from the side, from behind, so he couldn't see her, could only feel the slither of silky hair, and smell her scent. The cell door opened just a crack and he found his hand, of its own volition, jerking up to grasp the tendrils tantalizing his senses. But she smiled slyly and skipped away, maddeningly out of reach.

He'd never responded to a woman with such wanting, such intense and aching longing. But this wasn't just any woman. This was the girl he'd all but forgotten in his desire to shove the painful past from his mind. No more, no less than that. But the thought of her parading herself for any other man was suddenly intolerable. He'd never felt possessive about a woman in his life. He hated that he felt it now. She was simply trying to spur him into revealing secrets he could never divulge. He knew it. He had to remember it. Even as his body swelled with wanting for this bewitching creature—child of his past, coquette of his present—a woman he could never have.

She felt his withdrawal. He was strong. His will was sharpened by years of practice until it had become an indomitable force. But she was every bit as determined as he. She'd crack through his reserve, his rationale, all the defenses he'd built up to harden his heart to her.

She snatched a gauzy white and gold veil from atop the window, and used it to further incite him, covering her face then disclosing it a bit at a time. His mind fought the effect as she gave him fleeting glimpses of a smoky green eye, a tip of her pert nose, the lush folds of a mouth pursed and ripe for his kiss. He caught a fleeting movement of her hand beneath the veil, releasing the bows of her petticoat just enough so her breasts tumbled free. He saw just the heavy sway, sheathed, indistinct, but his body responded with a resounding jolt. She continued her dance, her breasts a sweet temptation beneath the veil, allowing him brief and futile glimpses of rosy nipples riding mounds of sumptuous swaying flesh.

He was on fire. Once again his body moved of its own accord, involuntarily lunging upward, his hands poised to grab. But she laughed—a low, wicked mewling in her throat, damningly seductive—and bringing up a bare foot, gave him a gentle shove. "Oh, no, sire," she purred, continuing the pretense as he tumbled back into the chair. "I'm not through with you yet."

She danced across the floor, using the veil to alternately shield and display. She looked in the glint of the candles like a white flame undulating in the breeze. Her movements mesmerized him as she reached up and delicately plucked a peacock feather from the wall. The veil fluttering as she moved, revealing as much as it concealed, she dropped the petticoat to the floor. Now her body shimmered beneath the sheer weave of the cloth, obscure in the faint and shifting light of candles, perceived in soft curves and fragrant flesh, yet frustratingly withheld from view. His erection nearly exploding, he watched with gritted teeth as she used the feather as an instrument of pleasure, trailing a delectable path across her cheeks, her mouth, her upthrust breasts, the gentle curve of her hips. Skimming the barely discernible dark triangle between her creamy thighs. Telling him with the smallest smile, *This is what you might have . . . and this . . .*

Moving toward him, close but out of reach. Bending and extending the feather a fraction at a time, making him wait and wonder, forcing him to track its progress, closer . . . closer . . . until at last it grazed ever so delicately against his cheek. She used it to tickle his eyelids, to kiss his mouth with its soft touch, to guide it slowly, suggestively, down the length of his tight chest, his flaming belly, to the pulsing erection jutting up from his lap. She saw his swelling organ jump at the contact as his hand snaked down and closed on the obtrusive feather, yanking it from her.

She laughed as if to say it didn't matter. What was one discarded toy when she had other weapons in her arsenal? Scampering away from his piercing glare, she stopped halfway across the room. There, she glanced at him from over her shoulder. The veil had shifted. A healthy portion of her backside was uncovered to his gaze. Long, pale flesh and a high, tasty curve. He was sitting uncomfortably erect, his languid pose ripped to shreds by her promise of delights just out of reach, her pleasure in displaying herself for his feasting eyes. The naivete of it only made her actions seem sexier by contrast. She was playing with explosives and she didn't know it. But he knew. His seething gaze told her so.

With a gesture that transmitted a gentle scolding—tut, tut, tut—she covered her flank once again. And then she lowered herself to her hands and knees and began to crawl across the luxuriant carpet toward him, her hair dangling, her eyes locked with his. Along the way, the veil caught beneath her knees and fell loose, displaying her breasts to his gaze. She came closer, the veil tangling under her so long, slim legs were revealed as she executed her steady crawl. As she approached, he leaned forward, his lust raging now in the sultry heat of the room, his senses full of her scent, the sound of her breath, the torment of her succulent flesh. She felt his hunger jolt through her with a shock.

"You play a dangerous game with your virtue," he warned.

She turned, crawling away from him now, her legs and backside swaying seductively, calling him to follow if he dared. He didn't move. Glancing back over her shoulder with a saucy smile that was half promise, half pout, she breathed contemptuously, "I face greater danger than this nearly every day of my life. Should His Majesty respond as tamely as this Tiger, I have nothing to fear. My virtue, it seems, would remain intact."

Inside she laughed at her challenge, knowing he couldn't resist, knowing that she held him captive now. So certain was she of her triumph that it came as a shock when she felt a grip like a vise around her naked ankle.

Something snapped in Max. A cold and frightful rage, railing at her willful provocation, gripped him like a fever. He'd leapt like the tiger she'd called him, twisting her leg, bringing it high, her ankle confined by the castigating grip of his fist, driven past the point of control. "I've got you now," he growled.

She whirled about to see him standing over her, eyes blazing. He looked like a madman, his eyes feverish, the lust pumping through his veins driving out all rational thought. This wasn't what she'd planned. The playful air of seduction shattered and in its place there was something dark and dangerous, something she'd never seen in his eyes before. A fierce and carnal determination to crush every ounce of control she thought she'd gained.

Fear fluttered through her, an awareness of having gone too far. "Let me go," she gasped. The leg he held began to tremble like a wire held taut and yanked with cruel force.

He laughed harshly. "I give the orders now."

Something in his voice frightened her even more. It's a game, she wanted to say. But it wasn't, and she knew it. In the struggle, she'd pushed him beyond the boiling point, beyond the boundary of restraint, baiting his vulnerability until she'd unleashed the true tiger he kept so tightly reined within.

She struggled wildly, trying to disengage her ankle, but it only pained her as he tightened his grip. With ankle in hand, he dragged her across the carpet toward the bed. Determined to be cruel, to punish her for forcing to the surface something he didn't want—couldn't afford—to face. Some demon drove him, crushing out the horrible longing to hold her gently in his arms, beating away at any tractable impulses, feeling nothing now save the need to overpower, to force her to his bidding as she'd sought to overpower him.

"What are you doing?" she cried in alarm.

"Showing you what can happen when you toy with a man like the maharana."

"He'd never come near me," she spat out, trying frantically to grip the edge of the carpet and slow his abduction.

"I did," he pointed out. "And now, my fine captive, I'm going to show you what tormented Rajput warriors do to little vixens like you who test their patience."

"This game is over," she said angrily, fighting for dignity with a scathing tone.

"This game," he breathed softly, "has only just begun. So you want to know what might happen if you set out to seduce the maharana, do you? A man with a thousand willing concubines in his harem. What would you do, clever cat, if he tied you to the foot of his bed like the plaything you'd no doubt be?"

Pinning her to the carpet at the foot of the bed, he snatched up the discarded veil, using it to secure her ankle to the bedpost with swift tugs.

All her struggles couldn't keep him from his task. She jerked around and lunged for the knots. "You think he'd keep me long?"

He seemed to tower over her like a god. As she worked at the knot, he studied the gilt chains hanging from the canopy of the bed. "He would," he said, "if he had his servants secure you with chains."

Reaching up, he yanked a chain loose. She heard its delicate rattle as it fell to the tiles outside the boundary of the carpet beneath her. As he bent to retrieve it, she halted her attempt at escape and stared at him with wide, horrified eyes. "You wouldn't!"

"But we're not talking about me. We're talking about a man who, in his palace, is surrounded by hundreds of guards, eager to do his bidding."

He was actually going to chain her to the foot of the bed! "You vile, despicable——"

Chain in hand, his mouth curved into a mocking grin. "You say that now," he said.

She saw him coming closer, a stubborn gleam in his eyes.

"Never!" she cried.

"Is this your idea of seduction?"

He caught her wrist and began to pull it toward the other footpost. She fought him with all her strength, turning onto her stomach, yanking at her wrist. But he was far stronger than she. Catching her other hand, he pinned both wrists to the post and secured them with the chain. She was now spread naked before him, her right ankle and both wrists imprisoned, a captive to his will.

She continued to struggle, breathing hard, tearing at her bonds. She was fleetingly aware of his jacket falling beside her, of the cravat that followed close behind. She could feel his eyes burn into her, so her backside sizzled beneath the awareness of his gaze. Then she felt his weight on her bottom as he straddled her, holding her down. "You see now," she heard him rasp out, "the real danger of your thoughtless game." His breath was hot against her cheek. "The maharana now has you in his power, to do with you what he will."

"I'll never submit," she swore.

"You'll have to learn better manners if you plan to please him enough to get that ruby."

She felt something at her back, soft, tantalizing, sending shivers up her spine. Belatedly, she realized it was the peacock feather he'd snatched from her earlier. Shifting slightly, he trailed it along the backs of her legs. Rebellious shivers racked her naked body.

"The maharana is a man of sophisticated tastes," he told her in an ominous tone. "He's used to making slaves of his women, rendering them helpless, driving them insane with pleasure until all they can think of, all they can hope for, is the chance to give their master pleasure."

"I don't believe it," she snapped.

"Believe it, darling. He'll make you believe it soon enough."

The feather tickled her bottom, insinuating itself up into the crease between the cheeks. She tried desperately to free her hands, to reach back and stop the torture that was sending helpless thrills of pleasure shooting through her. But her efforts only emphasized her defenselessness. She gave a strangled, frustrated cry.

A moment later, she felt fleeting relief when the feather was taken away. Then the palms of his hands, warm and strong, were pressing into the exposed flesh of her back. They glided upward, along her rib cage, to the sides, then underneath to lift her slightly and capture her breasts in containing palms. She gasped, feeling brazenly invaded even as she felt a primal lust shoot through her loins.

He kneaded them with infuriating skill, straddling her so his erection through the fabric of his pants seemed to brand her. She found, to her shame, that her breath was coming fast and hard. She tried to tame it, but his fingers played with her nipples, rotating with a mastery that portended the loss of her resolve.

Then one hand moved out from under her and a moment later she felt the tip of the feather on her thigh. The jolt of pleasure was unbearable. She grit her teeth together, moving away as best she could with his weight pinning her down. He nudged her free leg aside, capturing it with his knee, so she was spread open before him. She couldn't see what he was doing. She could only wait, suspended in anticipation of his next move. Then she felt it. The velvety tip of the feather teasing her inner thigh until ripples of longing caused her legs to tremble. It moved slowly, licking at her with merciless expertise, inching closer to the throbbing core between her legs.

And then he found her, brushing with agonizingly delicate strokes along the sensitive cleft, moist and dewy, traitorous in its response. All she could do was lie there beneath his unrelenting assault, feeling her resistance weaken in the luscious torture he inflicted. Her head began to reel. She wanted more than anything to deny the sweet sensation that was hurtling her higher, sending her soaring like a gliding plane, but she knew, as her body thrilled beneath his touch, that she was lost.

"Please," she whimpered. "It wasn't supposed to be like this."

"It wasn't supposed to be at all," he corrected. "But you asked for it. Now take what you wanted."

She couldn't help it. Her senses exploded. Between the agony of his hand at her breast and the torment of the feather, she felt her body surrender, felt the stars converge and become one with her consciousness. She shook and cried her abdication as coil after coil of unbearable pleasure turned her pliant and breathless beneath his unmerciful hands.

Then the feather was gone and she felt his hand tugging at the fastenings of his trousers. An instant later she felt his unsheathed erection, soft yet pulsingly rigid, against the flesh of her ass. She lifted her hips to receive him, beyond caring now, so hungry for him that pride and plans were shattered in the wake of his domination. Gasping aloud as he plunged inside, filling her to the brim, sending shock waves through her so she could almost feel him in her throat.

His gasp blended with her own. The clash of pleasure as he burgeoned inside her was so startling that it caught him off guard. He drove into her, immersing himself in liquid heat, bucking and lunging in a fevered effort to purge the demons assailing his soul. Bent on driving her physically, forcefully, from his mind. Her cries of pleasure and pain lashed at him, propelling him on.

But then he heard her gasp in wonder, "My God, it's so sweet!"

The word "sweet" penetrated the fog in his brain. Shame purged his lust. Suddenly, he became aware of the softness of the body beneath him, of the delicate fragrance of jasmine on her skin. He leaned forward, inhaling her scent, hearing the melody of her enforced delight in his ears. And then, because he couldn't help himself, he was kissing her back, trailing her shoulders with his lips, burying his face in the luxurious texture of her hair. The madness evaporated like mist in the sun, and he knew her in a way he never had before. He felt her in every pore, in every fiber, every muscle. He tasted her, smelled her. Felt himself merge and become one with her.

Slowly, in a trance, he withdrew from her and reached over to yank loose the ties. Gently, as if picking up the remnants of a crushed flower, he turned her over onto her back. As he did, in the shimmer of mirrored lights, she caught the look of abject apology in his eyes. And she knew in that moment that she'd won this round at least.

She reached up and took his head in her hands. He was looking at her as if he'd never really looked before. As if something had opened his eyes to who she truly was. Tenderly, wondrously. She pulled his head toward her and he dipped it low, taking her mouth with his, kissing her now as if she were something fragile that might break beneath his brutish touch. She lifted beneath him, deepening the kiss, and he groaned low in his throat. Her sweet surrender, her willing opening of herself to him, cast off his reticence, and he kissed her now like something cherished and forgotten.

And then he felt her hand on him, on the painful erection that had been denied too long. Denied for years the gratification of finding a true home. She guided him as she clung to his mouth, tasting all he had to give, steering him into her warm cove. The fit of their bodies was so perfect they seemed fashioned for one another.

As if only she could envelop him in such a way as to bring this shuddering joy.

He began to move inside her. But he was a different man. Gone was the need of the abductor to torment and punish. In its place was a lover bent on ravishing this gift with love and gratitude for the fulfillment of such a moment as this.

He couldn't get enough. His hands were on her, touching, caressing, exploring the body for which he'd hungered so long. His mouth kissed her, blazing fervent trails along her flesh, nuzzling her breasts, her shoulders, every inch of the silky skin of her neck, her face. Feeling her pull him close, her breath becoming one with his as if they'd been making love like this for eternity. Instinctively, her tongue found the spots that could drive him wild. The lobe of his ear, the flesh behind, the lower lip that she sucked into her mouth before pulling him in for a kiss that seared all consciousness and left nothing in his senses but her.

They came together with such a fusion of beauty that afterward he lay atop her, damp and shuddering, weak beyond measure, and, for the first time in years, at peace. He kissed her in the dreamy aftermath, tasting faintly of her sweat, feeling her soft arms wrapped around him as if she would never let him go.

And then he knew the awful truth. He loved her. His little Baji. Had he loved her all along, and never known it? At once, the peace was gone, the serenity of drifting shattered. Damn her soul for forcing him to this. This sweetness he could never own. The pain of longing he could never ease.

He pushed himself from her. It was the hardest thing he'd ever had to do. Her arms held him back, reluctant to let go of the magic of the moment. But he had to. He knew if he stayed, he might never leave.

He disengaged himself from her loving arms and rose to retrieve his coat and cravat. He hadn't even un-clothed himself in his haste. It took everything he had to look at her now, lying naked and rumpled and dreamily sated on the carpet at his feet. But he dove inside himself and retrieved a harsh, unrevealing tone.

"You'll seduce the maharana over my dead body," he said before stalking from the room.

"Whatever you say," she whispered after him. She felt, in the wake of his parting, a strange mixture of loneliness and longing. And something she hadn't felt in some time. Hope . . .

15

The next morning, Kitty couldn't wait to see Max. How would he behave? Would he acknowledge the miracle that had taken place the night before? Would their shared experience open him up, make him more willing to share his secrets and his heart? She felt light-headed and breathless as she waited for him in the courtyard, almost giddy with anticipation.

But the moment she saw him, she knew her hopes had been in vain. He appeared tired, as if he hadn't slept. He didn't meet her eyes. Instead of giving her the tender greeting she hoped for, he immediately got down to business.

"I need to get into the City Palace," he told her. "To get the lay of the place."

She swallowed her disappointment. "How do you intend to do that?" she asked, keeping her tone light. If he wanted to pretend last night had never happened, let him. She could wait.

"I have a plan," he told her.

They were taken across the lake, where the maharana met them at the city launch with his Rolls-Royce waiting nearby. His cheeks were glowing in the early morning sun, and he appeared as excited as a young boy at the prospect of their outing. He wore a long duster and cap with goggles pushed high, as one might expect of a man about to take a flight in an aeroplane. Except that his duster was made of embroidered yellow brocade, adorned with semiprecious stones.

"Good morning," he greeted with robust cheer. "A marvelous morning for sport, don't you agree?"

Following Max's plan, Kitty allowed him a moment to look sullen, then asked the maharana in a low tone, "Your Majesty, may I speak with you a moment?"

They stepped off to the side. The maharana was all but licking his lips in anticipation. "I'm in a bit of a spot," she told him confidentially. "The count is none too happy about our proposed flight this morning. Naturally, you could order him along and he'd be obliged to obey, given your most generous hospitality. But he'd spoil the fun. With him waiting impatiently on the ground, I fear we should feel compelled to shorten our flight. I should hate for anything to mar this experience for you."

The gleam in his eyes told her he thought she was trying to finagle some time alone with him. "What do you suggest, countess? I am at your disposal."

"The count has a particular weakness, Your Majesty.

He's peculiarly fond of palaces and castles. I can't tell you how many dreary tours I've been forced to endure for his sake."

"Then I have the perfect solution," he cried, snatching the bait. "I shall have my man give him a tour of my City Palace. That should keep him occupied while we attend to . . . more pleasant business."

"An excellent idea, Your Majesty! You are, indeed, as clever as your reputation."

When she turned back to Max with a wink, she caught the faint glint of warning in his eyes. It encouraged her. She left with the maharana for his makeshift airfield with a light heart.

It took her a while to familiarize herself with the controls of the aircraft. But once she did, she took him up into the vast blue Rajasthan skies, showing him a bird's-eye view of his kingdom. He was delighted, laughing in boisterous tones, forgoing the dignity of his position in his immense enjoyment of his latest toy.

Once in the air, there was little for Kitty to do except keep the craft aloft. It was too noisy for conversation, although the maharana was shouting above the roar of the engine. It left her free to think about Max. She'd felt so bonded with him the night before. For those brief moments, she'd felt that she had touched the real man. But he wasn't ready to surrender yet. He was like a gem covered and hidden by mantles of hard rock and the ravages of time. But little by little, she would chip away at his exterior until at last she exposed the jewel underneath. Max was a formidable foe. But she had time on her side.

By now Carrington should have realized Max had tricked him, and he'd no doubt be on his way to

Udaipur. Once here, he would ensure that the ruby reached Port Blair and freed her father. In the meantime, she would work on Max again tonight. Nothing as brazen as her exploits of the night before. Just enough to remind him of the bliss they'd found. Just enough to make him long for more.

It was nearly dinnertime before Kitty returned to the Lake Palace, since the maharana had insisted on driving her up to the Monsoon Palace. Max had been back for some time, having seen all he needed to see of the City Palace. They dined beneath the stars in the garden courtyard on course after course of rich food—legume soup seasoned with red chili peppers, okra, eggplant, jackfruit, wild boar spare ribs marinated in yogurt, onions, garlic, ginger, and coriander, tandoori mutton, with sweetmeats and juicy mangos for dessert. Dancers were brought for their entertainment. They were never out of earshot of the servants. But Max was in an uncommunicative mood anyway. He avoided her gaze, instead watching the dancers intently throughout the meal. She tried to make small talk, but he answered her in monosyllables.

Strangely, the fact that he held himself aloof from her made him seem all the more appealing. In the soft and gracious surroundings of the pleasure palace, he appeared as rugged and inscrutable as the Rajasthani hills. Achingly handsome. The sight of his mouth flared memories of hot kisses and helpless sighs. His clothes cloaked the cat-burglar body that had shown her so much pleasure the night before. His hand, resting on the table, long-fingered yet utterly masculine, caused her to tingle at the recollection of his fingers playing with her and making her gasp. She felt herself simmering. It was all she could do not to shove back his chair and drop into his lap and kiss him madly, showing him the fallacy of his apathy.

But his withdrawal also made her realize how lonely and one-sided his life must be. "What do you do with the rest of your life? Do you ever forget about your mission and just live?"

He looked startled, as if he'd never thought about it before. But the fleeting expression was quickly masked by a shuttered look that told her it was none of her business. He pushed back his chair and said, "I'm tired. I'm going to bed."

Watching him leave, Kitty realized she'd struck a nerve. It was as if he were afraid that if he let his guard down, his defenses would crumble completely. If he was trying to give her the impression that their lovemaking the night before had left him unfazed, he was failing miserably. His enforced distance from her only served to prove that she'd touched him more deeply than he cared to admit.

She stewed about this alone in her room, pacing restlessly. He was vulnerable to her. If she gave him the time he was demanding, he might well succeed in convincing himself that the emotional bond they'd shared for so brief a time had been imagined. It would make it all the easier for him to turn away.

She went down the hall to his room. There were no locks on any of the doors so she softly turned the curved brass handle. Expecting to find him lying in a fever on his bed, she found him instead standing by the open window wearing the tight black body-fitting suit that he wore for burglaries.

"What are you doing?" she cried.

He froze and turned to her, his body stiff, his demeanor wary and alert. About his waist he wore a belt with a small watertight pouch affixed to the front in which he kept the tools of his trade.

"You're going to get the ruby, aren't you?"

He studied her a moment, his eyes narrowing. Finally, reluctantly, he said, "I discovered today that it has to be tonight or never. The reason the maharana can't dine with us tonight is that he's entertaining an envoy from the Russian czar. With the intention of discussing the purchase of a certain ruby. If the maharana accepts the envoy's price, the Blood of India may well be gone by morning."

"You were going without me!"

His face hardened. "That's right. It's too dangerous to take you along."

"Dangerous or not, I'm going. If you try to go without me, I'll scream bloody murder. I'll bring the house down. I'll follow you and alert them to what you're up to. Whatever I have to do."

He stood glaring at her. "All right," he said at last. "Get changed. But if you're not back in two minutes, I'm going without you."

When she returned, he was holding a walking stick he'd purchased at the market earlier that day. He broke it in half over his knee. Taking the smaller of the two fragments—a stick about two feet in length—he slapped it into the palm of his hand as if to test its strength. Satisfied, he slid it under his belt.

"What's that?" she asked.

"Insurance."

"Insurance against what?"

"Crocodiles."

She froze. "You can't possibly expect us to swim across the lake?"

"That's exactly what we're going to do."

"I can't."

"You *can* swim?"

"Yes, but . . ."

"But what?"

"I'm not going anywhere near those crocodiles." Her old dream filled her mind. She and Cameron fighting a crocodile for their lives. Watching helplessly as Cameron lost his battle and drowned. She'd always thought her dream was symbolic of the events that had transpired the night she'd thought he'd died. Now it seemed too frighteningly like a premonition.

"I'm terrified of crocodiles! Don't you remember— that day with Haghan . . . ?"

"There's no other way."

"Maybe we can steal the launch," she suggested desperately.

"You know as well as I that they keep the launch on the other side."

"Then maybe we could use something as a raft. Anything."

"Look," he said. "Crocodiles are like any other animal. If they sense your fear, they'll pounce on you. So we must display *no* hint of fear. The way to do that is to lose all thought of ourselves and become crocodiles. We *are* crocodiles. We don't fear them because we are one with them. If they bump into us—and they may—we don't panic. They're our brothers. Say it: 'I am a crocodile.' "

Slowly, she repeated, "I . . . am . . . a crocodile."

"Good. You can do this. Together we can do this. You understand?"

He'd said something similar to her when they were children. It was as if he were asking her if she understood the underlying meaning of his message. She nodded.

"All right, then, let's go for a swim."

Carefully opening the lattice screens that covered the window, he looked down to see that the water level was only about a foot below them. In the distance, lights had come on to illuminate the seemingly impregnable fortress across the lake: the City Palace. Half a mile of water separated them from the landing dock. And maybe a hundred hungry crocodiles.

"Let's go," he said.

As she climbed over the windowsill and dropped into the water beside him, she felt her body enveloped in a balmy warmth. It was like the water of a bathtub. Above them, the Rajasthani night sky was ablaze with stars, reminiscent of her room the night before. Moonlight beamed down on them.

With smooth strides, they glided through the calm lake in the direction of the shoreline. As she occasionally gulped a breath, Kitty couldn't help opening her eyes and noticing ahead of them what looked like a flotilla of logs but was actually the backs and tails of crocodiles: a gauntlet of jaws and teeth waiting for them. *Concentration and focus . . . no fear . . .*

Two hundred feet into their swim, the first of the monsters brushed against her. She felt the hard, scaly skin rub the length of her body, the force of its impact jarring her. Then it happened again. And yet again. The creatures appeared to be investigating them. *What are you?* they seemed to ask.

I am a crocodile, she forced herself to answer. *I am a crocodile.*

As they continued to swim, making solid progress now, an entourage seemed to be following them, escorting them, still testing them. Then, as Max paused a moment to get his bearings, she made the terrible mistake of looking straight at one of the reptiles. She couldn't help but feel it—a sharp stab of cold, primal fear.

The animals began to speed up their motions, their long, muscular tails whipping the water, swimming in ever-smaller concentric circles around the two intruders who were quite obviously now *not* their brethren.

"It's time to go under," he signaled. "Stay behind me, and feel the motion of my feet kicking in the water to lead you."

Kitty took a huge breath and went under, diving into the depths. Below the thermal layer, the water was icy. She opened her eyes and saw nothing but utter blackness. But she could feel the ripples of Max's kicking feet as he swam underwater ahead of her. She followed him as if he were a beacon leading the way to safety.

The beasts seemed to lose them. It was sweet relief to not feel their loathsome, leathery forms slithering against her. She wanted to be brave. Indeed, this fear felt foreign to her. But the dream haunted her. She'd awoken in terror too many times to ignore it now.

She swam and swam. A minute passed. Still she felt Max's presence ahead of her. Still she felt the relief.

Then she experienced the first ache of her lungs. It was soon excruciating, unbearable. She had to get to the surface at once. But ahead of her Max continued to swim on. She willed herself not to think about it. More agonizing time passed. What? Another minute? Her lungs were bursting.

Just as she thought she could stand it no longer, she felt Max's hand grab her arm and pull her toward the surface. They broke free with a gasp.

The air was delicious. Breathing hard, he said, "They're quite a distance behind us now. But it won't be long before they're back on our trail. Swim for all you're worth."

She did. But after progressing another fifty feet or so, with another two hundred to go, she felt that horrid sensation once again—a crocodile slithering against her. Only this time, the experience went on and on and on. This creature was twenty feet long at least. The grandfather of all crocodiles!

Before she had time to contain the onrush of panic, the monster made one more quick circle and, with a single lash of its mighty tail, made its attack. She saw the flash of moonlight in the monster's eyes. The wide-open jaws. The rows of razor-sharp, crooked teeth. She wasn't a crocodile now. She was pure terror.

She felt the teeth clamp down on her arm. Involuntarily, she screamed and began to struggle, trying to rip her arm from the demon's grasp. She felt her flesh tear.

But suddenly Max was at her side. He beat at the mammoth jaws until the creature loosened its hold and veered, charging Max now. Acting as a decoy, he lunged away from Kitty, drawing the crocodile in his wake. As the jaws were about to descend upon him, he disappeared in the water, followed closely by his attacker. For a few seconds that seemed an eternity to Kitty, the water all around was eerily calm. Then all at once a form exploded to the surface. Max and the giant reptile were locked together. They rolled as one before dropping below the surface once again. Once more the agonizing calm. One second passed . . . two seconds . . . three . . .

It was her nightmare all over again. But this wasn't a dream. This was real. Just as her dream had foretold, he was going to drown . . .

She couldn't let it happen. She wouldn't. In a panic, she dove beneath the surface, searching for them. She didn't know what she would do, she only knew she had to try. She couldn't lose him. Not again.

But it was impossible. The water was too black to see. Finally, weeping in frustration, she found the surface once again. All was calm. There was no sign of man or beast.

Just as she was losing hope, the crocodile burst to the surface again, slapping the water with its immense tail and making a roaring sound. Something was in its huge mouth.

In the moonlight, she could see a thick stalk wedged inside the creature's mouth behind its teeth, prying its jaws apart. A portion of the walking stick Max had brought as insurance. Frantic, helpless, shrieking its frustration, the animal flopped around in the water, then disappeared.

Max surged to the surface beside her. In a rush, she lunged at him, wrapping her arms about him, mindless of the pain that ripped through her left arm where the crocodile had taken hold. "You're all right!" she cried.

He saw her fear, and the subsequent relief. Gently, he pushed a strand of dripping hair from her face. "It pays to be prepared."

Relieved, exhausted, flush with genuine admiration for his ingenuity, she laughed and allowed the fear to drain from her body. "You're almost as clever as I," she teased.

"You see? Dreams don't always come true."

"Sometimes they do."

They stared at one another for a long moment. Her eyes were filled with love and gratitude. He saw it and turned away. "We'd better go. Can you swim?"

Ignoring the pain in her arm, she told him, "Just try and stop me."

Together they *could* do anything. Optimistic now, she swam by his side. The shoreline was only fifty more feet ahead of them. The water was shallow enough that she could feel the mud of the lake bottom touch her toes as she kicked. In another few moments they came out on dry land.

As they rose from the water, Kitty felt her limbs ache from the exertion of the swim. Her left arm was numb, the broken flesh showing through the ripped sleeve. Ahead of them, near the small ferry dock, a squad of the maharana's guards were posted. Crouching low, their bodysuits giving them camouflage, they crept around the dock to reach the base of the gigantic wall of the City Palace.

"This, at least, offers little challenge," Kitty said, studying the wall. It was fashioned from large stones, unequally piled atop one another, with plenty of nooks and crannies for someone with their skills to get a hand and foothold. "There are no guards anywhere along the base of the wall. Or, from what I can see, the top."

"I'll show you why." He took her hand and placed it lightly on the plaster wall. She felt something sharp, like the edge of a knife blade.

"The wall is covered with a layer of *suruchi*."

"With what?"

"Nails, broken glass, and pieces of razor-sharp metal mixed with plaster and cemented over the wall."

"But how do we climb—"

"No one can climb over *suruchi*!"

"Then it's over."

"Not by a long shot."

He stepped over to the wall where he retrieved a coil of thick rope that he'd obviously either put there himself or had arranged to be placed at his disposal. She glanced up to study the smooth summit of the wall. She could see nothing on which to anchor the rope.

"How are you going to secure it?" she asked.

"Watch this."

He quickly knotted the end of the rope to form a loop. Then, twirling it above his head a number of times to gather momentum, he hurled it toward the towering rampart. Watching, Kitty was amazed that anyone could fling a rope to such a height. In one try, one end fastened itself as if by magic to the side of the uppermost wall.

"How did you do that?" she gasped.

"I have a spy planted in the palace. He secured a metal hook over the top of the wall where no one would see it."

"And you learned to throw a rope like that in the wild west of Italy, I suppose?"

Ignoring her, he snapped, "Are you going to stand here gawking or are you going to climb?"

"Oh, by all means, you first."

"Remember. Keep your feet flat on the wall. Don't let any part of your body touch it, or you'll be cut to ribbons."

With that last warning, he hoisted himself up and began to shimmy up the rope. When he paused and glanced down at her, she followed.

Higher and higher they climbed. At a hundred feet, she looked behind and saw the lights of the Lake Palace: a twinkling gem in the water. She realized suddenly that she was enjoying the sensation of being here, alone with this man. The danger on all sides of them added to the irresistible sensation. *Come, Baji. Fly with me . . .* Higher, higher. Another fifty feet. And another. Climbing together as they had climbed the sheer rock cliff that night as children.

Finally, they reached the top of the rope and mounted the flat rampart overlooking a courtyard below. Musicians played softly, sending their melody into the night air. Looking back, Kitty saw Max give the rope a tug and release it so that it fell heavily to the ground below.

"How are we going to climb back down?" she whispered.

"We're not. Once we get the ruby, there'll be a horse saddled and waiting for us in the lower courtyard."

"Your spy again, I suppose?"

"He arranged for the horse and planted some changes of clothes in the saddlebags. I didn't know you'd be with me, but there should be enough for both of us. The guards never check people going out as closely as they do coming in. We're going to ride out of here right under their noses."

The center square of the rooftop courtyard was lined with neem trees. On either side, large graceful swings were suspended from marble overhangs. Along the opposite wall, brightly dressed women danced for the pleasure of the men who sat with their backs to the intruders, lounging on enormous cushions, smoking hookahs, and nibbling sweetmeats as they watched the entertainment. Servants stood unobtrusively about, awaiting their master's pleasure. The music would obscure any sounds they might make, but they could easily be spotted by anyone who happened to turn their way.

"Where's his bedroom?" she asked, her mouth to his ear.

"Carrington was wrong. It's not in his bedroom, it's in the treasury. Across the courtyard and up a flight of stairs."

"How do you know? Oh, don't tell me. Your spy again."

"He slipped me the information during my tour."

"My, you *are* thorough."

When he didn't answer she surveyed their surroundings. They'd have to pass the servants' line of vision. Steeling themselves, they descended to the base of the ramparts, hugging the wall, shielded by the darkness. They inched their way around the outside of the court- yard, pausing only when a servant turned their way.

Then she heard the maharana's voice. He was speak- ing to his guests through an interpreter. But no Russian was being spoken. The translation was from Hindi to Tamil—the language of South India. She looked at the guests. They weren't even European!

Once out of earshot, she whirled on him. "You son of a bitch! You lied to me!"

16

"There never was any Russian envoy trying to buy the ruby," she hissed. "So there was no reason why you had to get in tonight. You weren't sneaking off because you were afraid for my safety. You knew if you didn't get it before Carrington comes back, you'd never have another chance to grab the ruby and run. Leaving me holding the bag. Tell me something, Machiavelli. Just how ruthless can you be? How far *will* you go to get what you want?"

Anger darkened his eyes. He took her arms and pushed her back against the wall, pinning her body as his eyes captured her gaze. "You listen to me," he ground out low. "The games are over. I have work to do and I can't afford to be saddled with someone who can't keep her mind on the task at hand. If you get distracted, you could cost us both our lives. Do you hear me? Now either you get your mind focused, or get the hell out of here. I'll do this alone."

She jerked her chin, chafing under his autocratic tone. "I'm not the one playing games."

He peered at her for a moment, then sighed heavily and altered his tone. "All that matters now is getting that ruby."

"You excel at that, don't you? Ignoring everything and everyone to get what you're after."

"You're damned right I do. And it's that focus that's going to get us out of here in one piece. So you've got a choice to make. Either you're with me or against me. If you're with me, keep quiet and do as I say. If you're not, leave now."

"How can I trust you when you'll stoop to anything to manipulate me into doing your bidding?"

"Did it ever occur to you that I have my reasons?"

"I'm not a child, nor am I half-witted as you seem to suspect. It's your reasons—and your intentions—that are in question."

"Christ!" he swore, casting a glance at the hallway behind him. "What can I say to convince you to let this go and get to work?"

"There is something," she said softly.

"What?"

She put a hand to his arm. "When we do find the ruby . . . if we succeed in getting it out . . . you could just—" She felt uncharacteristically awkward, as clumsy as a toddler babbling her first words. Drawing a breath, she managed, "He's my father, Max. I can't let him die."

His eyes shuttered, he looked at her through half-lowered lids.

"You're the only one who can help me. I need you. I don't ask you to promise. Only think about it, will you?"

For a moment, it seemed that his gaze softened. "If I promise to think about it will you do everything I say without question?"

"Yes."

"Then I'll keep it in mind."

It wasn't much of a pledge. But she had no choice. She had to believe he would come through for her in the end.

She followed him up the narrow, winding passageway. No guard was posted at the entrance to the treasury. Max withdrew a file from his tool kit, and within a second had picked the lock. He lit the lamp by the door. It was a room about twenty feet square. In the far corner was another door: metal with a small window covered with iron bars. This door opened on stairs that led to another room—the inner treasury—which was a flight above them. This sanctuary also had a window covered with iron bars.

Max stepped to the second door and examined the lock. He shook his head and turned to Kitty. "I may need you after all."

Kitty watched him, uncertain of what he had in mind. It was unsettling not to know his plan ahead of time. She was accustomed to having at least a general idea of what might transpire when she pulled a job such as this. But now, it seemed that he was revealing his scheme in bits and pieces as a way of keeping her off balance.

"This lock was made two hundred years ago by Kankroli, the great Rajput locksmith," he said. "It's so intricate that no one can pick it. There are only two ways to get it open."

"What ways?"

"One is with the key. The other is a technique so advanced I haven't mastered it yet."

"Then what can we do?"

He considered, then pointed up to the window of the inner treasury. "You're going to squeeze through those bars."

No more than five inches separated one bar from the other. It was preposterous to think she could squeeze through.

"You should have warned me not to eat," she muttered.

He ignored her sarcasm. "With my bulk, I couldn't possibly make it. But you can, if you follow my instructions. Can I depend on you?"

"As much as I can depend on *you*."

A brief frown creased his brow. But he crouched low, helping her onto his shoulders, then stood so she was level with the bars. "This isn't possible," she told him. "It's much too narrow."

"Just concentrate on what I tell you. Completely. Focus. All that matters is this moment. Erase everything else from your mind."

Taking a deep breath, she sharpened her focus as he'd instructed.

"Now think of yourself as energy. Your body is only solid mass if you perceive it to be. Feel yourself capable of shifting like liquid. Hold that image. No thought, no emotion. Allow nothing to interfere and cause your body to expand."

Ngar had spoken of working with energy. How a true master, using the force of his will, could control energy and work feats that would seem miraculous to ordinary men. But he'd never taught her this. He had, however, taught her to become one with her surroundings. She took his teachings and incorporated them with Max's instructions. His voice was hypnotic, rendering her body limp and pliable.

"Perfect," he encouraged. "Now turn to the side and stick your hands through."

She did.

"Feel your body weight shift to your hands and lower arms."

Again she did as he'd said.

"Now your head and torso."

This was tougher.

"Relax completely. Call up your visual mantra. . . . Now breathe in deeply and, as you exhale, feel the energy of your body shift and slide through as I push your feet."

She allowed herself to follow his lead, feeling like liquid flowing through a sieve. Miraculously, within minutes, she'd squeezed her entire body through the narrow space.

"Quickly. Look around."

She found herself surrounded by a king's ransom in gems, spilling over from open chests. Emeralds, diamonds, and pearls, each worth a fortune in its own right. Boxes of gold. Priceless relics encrusted with precious stones. Amidst the clutter, haphazardly arranged, was a pedestal with a white velvet covering. And nestled in the folds was a ruby such as she'd never seen. Unmistakable. A deep, seductive red that seemed lighted from within by a flame. The Blood of India. *My God,* she thought, *it's the size of a man's fist!*

Suddenly, she heard the outer door open. Looking down, she saw that a guard had entered the treasury behind Max. Seeing him, the man shrieked and ran out again. "Thief! Thief!"

"Quickly," Max hissed. "Get out of there."

She snatched the ruby and raced for the bars. But surprise and panic had turned her body once again into a solid mass that wouldn't budge. "I . . . can't. What do I do?"

He glanced behind him. "Throw me the ruby!" he called.

The sound of running feet. What was she going to do?

The footsteps grew louder in the outer hall. "Throw it, dammit!"

She stood frozen, staring at the iron bars.

"Baji, throw it."

Her eyes met his. Baji! She thrust her hand through the bars and tossed the stone down to him.

He caught it easily. As the running feet approached, his words seemed to hang between them. He glanced up and met her gaze. What she saw in his eyes chilled her blood. A gleam of determination that would accept no bounds.

The room flooded with men carrying swords and pistols. Max charged them, breaking through and running past. Two of the guards raced after him, screaming in alarm. The others moved toward Kitty as one. Never in her life had she been so completely trapped.

They stood as if waiting, speaking in low tones. Within another few minutes, the voices lowered and the maharana entered the treasury with two bodyguards. When he saw Kitty behind the bars, his eyes blazed and his nostrils flared in fury.

The two guards who'd chased after Max returned, breathless. "We lost him, sire," one of them said, bowing low, his demeanor one of trepidation at having to disclose such news. "But we have sounded the alarm. He will not go far."

The maharana motioned to a guard behind him holding a large brass key. He used it to unlock the door, and the two bodyguards entered. As they grabbed for her, Kitty darted away and made a dash for the door. More guards rushed her. Two of them took hold of her, but she twisted her arms and once again wrenched herself free. At the furious maharana's order, all the guards charged at once. One grabbed Kitty by the hair and she bit him savagely on the wrist. As he swore, the others grabbed her by the arms and legs and carried her out. Her struggles were fierce, but they were brawny men and they soon succeeded in immobilizing her.

Another guard made a quick search of the inner treasury, and finding the empty pedestal, he held it up for his master to see.

As the guards held her, the maharana stepped over and slapped her hard across the face with the back of his hand. "So you thought to play me for a fool," he snarled.

Before Kitty could answer, another of the palace guards entered the room and announced in Rajasthani that the other thief had escaped the palace. He'd been seen galloping down the road to the city.

Max had deserted her after all.

The maharana screamed orders to his men—to fan out into the city to find him—then turned back to Kitty. "Where is he going with my ruby?"

"I wish I knew."

He raised his hand and slapped her again—even harder than before. "Vile thief," he sneered. "Do you think you are safe from my wrath simply because you are British? The British have no power in my state!" To his guards he said, "Bring her to my bedchamber."

Fear shuddered through Kitty. She recalled in a flash the things Max had said about toying with such a man. The implications of a woman's fate in the maharana's hands . . . sex slaves . . . chains . . .

She was dragged from the treasury, through the courtyard, and up two flights of narrow stairs to a sumptuous room that overlooked the lake. The maharana gave more orders and the guards continued to hold her by the arms. He unsheathed a long Sariya sword that was attached to the wall. Ivory handled, decorated in gold, a simple and elegant instrument of death. "You *are* going to tell me where he is."

Max's betrayal had left her feeling flayed and vulnerable. But pride pushed to the fore. She'd be damned if she let them see her fear. Raising her chin, she said in a steady voice, "I don't know where he is."

"I am going to ask you the question once again," her captor said calmly. "If I do not get an answer, I will deprive you of your right hand. You may not find it so easy to fly an aeroplane with your wrist. If you still refuse to cooperate, I will relieve you of your other hand. Then your feet, arms, legs, ears, eyes, and so forth. Sooner or later you *will* tell me. At what point you decide to cooperate is up to you."

Kitty felt a stab of blind terror. But she was telling him the truth. Had Max intended this all along? He'd lied about the Russians. He was now free and in possession of the ruby—and she couldn't give him away because she had no idea what he was up to.

"All right, then. Where is he?"

"I don't know."

The maharana motioned to his men and one of them grabbed her hair again while the other stretched out her arm in front of her.

"I'm telling you the truth," she gasped.

The men forced her arm onto the surface of a small serving table by the bed.

"This is your last chance, my little fiend of the skies. Where is he?"

He raised the sword in preparation. She stared at the blade. One swipe and her hand would be neatly severed. "Bombay!" she lied. "He's going back to Bombay. The Taj Mahal Hotel. We were to meet there if we got separated."

The sword swung down, crashing to the surface of the table.

It missed her hand by a mere fraction of an inch, making a deep slice in the sandalwood surface.

He smiled with cruel delight. "The next one will be right on target. Now, once again. Where is he?"

"I'm right behind you."

Max!

He'd come back for her!

The maharana swiveled around to face the intruder,

the sword still in his hand. "Where is my jewel?" he demanded.

Max removed it from his pocket, bounced it in his palm three times. "Shall we make a trade? The girl for the stone? And our free passage out of here, of course."

The maharana swiftly considered the proposition. "Very well—a bargain."

He took Kitty by the arm and stretched out his other palm to receive the ruby—as if to make the trade simultaneously. But as Max handed the stone to him, the maharana yanked Kitty back and barked orders to his men. "Seize him!"

Although he held Kitty, his attention was fixed on Max. Snatching the opportunity, Kitty swerved and kicked the maharana's hand, knocking the ruby from his palm. As if the maneuver had been prearranged, Max grabbed it in midair and swerved to his left, avoiding a sword blow from one of the men. Then he swerved to face the two guards who were now rushing him, and with a succession of savage kicks, sent them sprawling.

As the maharana screamed for more men, Max grabbed Kitty and flew from the chamber. They raced across the courtyard, where they were accosted by two more of the palace guards. Without hesitation, Max executed a perfect Rajput double elbow block. Pulling his fists together and extending his elbows to make a straight line, he leapt forward and hit each of his attackers in the face, knocking them out cold.

At the far end of the courtyard, they encountered two more men. One had a long Afghan rifle. As he raised it and took aim, Aveli pushed Kitty aside and faced the men. Between the time the trigger was pulled and the bullet would have hit its target, Aveli had disappeared.

By the time the bewildered man realized what had happened, Max was on him, knocking him and his colleague to the ground.

Once again grabbing Kitty's hand, he pulled her through the narrow passage leading to the lower courtyard. Here, two horses were saddled and waiting. He'd run off as a diversion, only to return and to find another horse for their escape. He helped Kitty onto one and mounted the other. But, by this time, word of the robbery had reached the heavily guarded front entrance. A whole platoon of the palace soldiers were in place to block the way.

Max said, "There's nothing to do but ride through them. Are you game?"

She kicked her heels into her horse and sped off toward the wall of armed men, startling the hundreds of crows perched in nearby trees so they squawked and scattered into the air in all directions, blocking out the lights of the palace like a shroud. Max quickly followed and together, side by side, they burst through the barricade.

They made it through, but the men, at first caught by surprise by such a bold tactic, quickly recovered in time to fire a volley at their backs.

Kitty had glanced behind so she didn't realize they were coming upon the section of the courtyard that served as elephant parking—huge indentations in the stone drive large enough to fit an elephant's prone body, where the animals lay down to sleep. She heard a loud blare and, turning to look ahead, saw that one of the elephants was lurching to its feet. Her horse reared and Max's followed suit. As he veered to avoid the obstruction, a bullet hit his horse in the flank and it dropped beneath him, sending him flying to the ground.

More elephants roused themselves as the men reloaded their old breech-loaded rifles, milling about the drive in a confused mass. Kitty doubled back and reached down to Max. He took her hand and leapt onto the back of the horse. Using the bewildered pachyderms to shield them from the second volley of bullets, they galloped off, their horse's hooves clattering on the ancient stones of the causeway, the sounds of shouting men and bellowing elephants left behind.

They rode up the narrow alleys and tore out of town, toward the forested hills that surrounded the king's enclave. When they'd outdistanced any signs of pursuit, Kitty reined in the horse and turned to Max, sitting behind her.

"You came back for me," she said wondrously.

"I couldn't very well leave you—"

"Why? If all you really wanted was the ruby? You could easily have run off with it, the way you'd intended. So why come back?"

He was staring at her, the words burning in his eyes. "Max, please. Tell me . . ."

"Tell you what?" he growled. "That I love you? That ever since I saw you that first night, you've been like a fever in my brain? That it hurts to think of you because I want you so badly? That I can't think straight because of this longing that eats at me and won't let me be?"

"Yes," she said. "All that."

"All right. I love you, dammit. Are you happy now?"

Happy? She smiled and touched his mouth with

trembling fingers. "I'm happy, dammit," she whispered. "So very happy."

He stared at her for a moment. Then his arm snaked out and clutched her to him, holding her head hard against his chest. She felt his lips in her hair. "God help me, Baji, I do love you. I think I loved you the first time I saw you in London. I just didn't know it. Not until last night."

She reached up and kissed him, the first truthful, openly loving kiss they'd ever shared.

17

"We have a problem," he said, still holding her.

"Such as getting out of here alive?"

"I'd planned to be on the Ujjain Express, but it left fifteen minutes ago. With only this one horse, there's no way we can intercept it now."

Kitty was struck by an idea. It was absurdly bold and dangerous. But it might just work. "We'll intercept it. Leave that to me."

"Are you going to make this horse fly?"

"Not him. Us."

"The aeroplane! Of course."

She gathered up the reins and said, "Hold on." Then she kicked their mount and sped off in the direction of the maharana's airfield east of town. Urging the horse on, they rode through the hills like phantoms in the night.

Finally Kitty saw the silhouette of the Antoinette IV monoplane sitting idle on a flat patch of field. No guard was posted since no one in India knew how to fly the machine and stealing from the maharana was unthinkable. She reined in horse beside the craft and slid off.

"Have you a match?"

Max reached into his tool kit and handed one over. Kitty lit it and checked the instrument panel. Luck was with them. It was fueled and ready to go.

While she'd been checking the fuel gauge, Max had rifled through the horse's saddlebag and had withdrawn the clothes that he'd had planted earlier. "Put these on," he told her, handing her a pair of *kurta* pajamas. She slipped into them, adjusting the folds to fit her smaller frame, then waited as Max wrapped a turban about her head. He did the same for himself, saying, "They won't be looking for Indian travelers."

As they slipped into their sandals, he glanced up at the night sky. "Can you fly in the dark?"

"I've never tried it. But the moon is fairly bright tonight. Once we spot the train, we can use its lights to guide us. It's a bit chancy. But then," she added, turning to him, "if it weren't dangerous—"

"It wouldn't be any fun." He grinned, his teeth shining in the moonlight.

A rush of tenderness caused Kitty's heart to swell. She went to him, taking his hand lightly in her fingers. "Come, Cameron," she said. "Fly with me."

She caught a brief flash of something unreadable in his eyes. But following her instructions now, he spun the propeller with a mighty thrust, then climbed into the rear seat. She started the engine and felt the familiar stirring of her senses, the anticipation one might feel in the moment before the lifting of a theater curtain, the expectancy that told her she was truly alive. "Are you ready?" she called over the noise of the engine. He nodded and she started down the field.

Kitty eased the throttle back and they rose swiftly into the air. When she reached her desired elevation— about two hundred feet—she leveled off. Below them, the moonlight bathed the Aravalli Hills in silvery splendor. Above them, the stars illuminated the cloudless sky, twinkling like brilliant diamonds just out of reach. She felt his arms reach from behind to encircle her as his lips grazed her flowing hair. In her ear he called rapturously, "I never dreamt anything could be so sublime!" A sense of peace and oneness flooded through Kitty, bringing with it a surge of exquisite bliss. She wanted the moment to last forever.

But after flying south for only a few minutes, they saw the light of the train as it snaked its way through the hills.

Max leaned over to scan the landscape. "Can you land down there, on that promontory?" he called.

It was a small plateau that ended on a sheer cliff overlooking the tracks. The train, rounding the curves of the hills, would reach this point within a few minutes. "It's a bit short for a landing," she admitted, "but I can try."

"Better make it quick," he said. "We have company."

As she began her descent, Kitty could see a detachment of horsemen charging down the road that paralleled the train tracks, about a mile behind the train.

"We must have been spotted taking off," he called. "The maharana obviously wired his southern garrison and told them to intercept us when we land."

Kitty curved west and dropped from the sky onto the plateau. The wheels touched the ground with a crashing thud. She could see at once that they were landing much too fast. There wasn't enough runway. She cut the engine, but the force of their momentum was sending them hurtling toward the cliff. "Hold on tight," she screamed. When she felt his arms grip her tightly, she yanked the controls to the right, sending the aircraft veering toward its starboard side, screeching piercingly as the three wheels, not built to withstand such pressure, one by one collapsed. Still the plane skidded toward the cliff, the engine spewing sparks into the night like a child's sparkler on Guy Fawkes Day.

As Kitty prepared herself for the plunge over the cliff and onto the train tracks, the plane suddenly, miraculously, stopped. But it was half on and half off the cliff, the front suspended in midair. One move, one minute shift in the precarious balance, and the plane would topple forward to crash to the ground below.

Behind them, they could now hear the galloping hoofbeats of the maharana's approaching cavalry. They'd obviously seen the plane land and were charging onto the plateau in frantic pursuit. Below them, from the other direction, they heard the chug-chug-chug of the train's steam engine. There was no way of determining which would arrive first: the train or the cavalry.

Within a moment, the band of riders galloped into view behind them. The train curved around a bend.

Suddenly the plane lurched forward. It was losing its hold on the precipice.

Max took Kitty's hand. "When I say jump . . ."

The maharana's men increased their speed. The train was getting closer . . . closer. Once again the plane jolted beneath them.

Max squeezed her hand. "Jump!"

Together, they leapt from the plane. As they did, they felt it give way, hurtling to the ground to crash in a fiery explosion beside the railroad tracks just as they landed atop the boxcar with a thud. The force of the impact together with the rickety momentum of the train as it approached the curve sent Kitty sliding across the top. Grasping for something to hold on to to break the slide, she felt her fingers come up empty. Her slide continued until she felt her legs touch the edge. Then her knees, her waist . . . she was falling off completely.

Suddenly she felt a hand grab her wrist. Max had latched onto a brakeman's handle with one hand and had narrowly caught her with the other. She fought the wind to anchor her feet against the side of the car. Then she cast a quick look behind her. The maharana's newest toy burned brightly in the black night. Their pursuers had now reached the promontory. They were dismounting and preparing to fire at them.

But just as the rifle shots exploded, the train rounded the curve and headed for the interior of India.

For hours, they clung to the top of the boxcar, choking on coal fumes, unable to communicate over the noise of the locomotive, but grateful to be alive. Kitty began to feel chilled in the rushing night air. Max pulled her to him and warmed her with his arms wrapped tight around her. She lost track of time. Silhouettes of trees flashed by. Open fields. A village here or there. Exhausted from the rigors of the night, she allowed herself to drift in Max's arms.

Finally, some hours later, the train began to slow. Sitting up, they saw before them the station at Ujjain. When the train had stopped, they waited for the few passengers to disembark, then climbed stiffly down. Adjusting their unraveling turbans, they entered the station.

"What next?" Kitty whispered.

"Next we catch another train. But we have to be careful. The maharana will have wired ahead. They'll be looking for us."

Before she could answer, a wandering *sadu* bumped into them. No one but Kitty would have noticed that the holy man inserted something into Max's pocket.

As the old man wandered off, Kitty asked, "What was that all about?"

Max withdrew a slip of paper and held it up. "My ticket to Chatarpur."

"Your ticket? What about mine?"

"I didn't know you'd be with me, remember? But don't worry. It's a first-class ticket. You'll go along as my servant."

"But where's Chatarpur? I've never heard of it."

"It's near the center of India—in a no-man's-land far removed from the British Authority or any of the princely states. There's a place there where we'll be safe until this all blows over. It's all been arranged."

"Why not just take the ruby directly to the British resident here? We've done our job."

"That's exactly what the maharana will expect us to

do. He'll have men watching the residency. No, we have to get as far away from his influence as we can, as fast as we can."

Reflexively, she balked. The intricacy of his secret plan was chilling. He'd had men in Bombay, in Udaipur, inside the City Palace, and several hundred miles away here in Ujjain. But then she remembered all that had changed in that one moment when he'd returned for her.

When they were on the train heading east, Kitty asked, "What's at Chatarpur? Why are we going there?"

"We'll just be passing through."

"Where are we going, then?"

He glanced at her with a strange spark in his eyes. "It's a surprise. But I think you'll like it."

They slept through much of the journey. When the train reached Chatarpur, they were the only two passengers to get off. It was a dusty village that served as little more than the marketplace for the two hundred farmers in the area. A tall man who eyed Kitty suspiciously was there to greet Max. Max gave him some instructions and the man left, returning shortly with two saddled horses. After a quick meal of rice and curry, they rode north.

The country here was completely deserted—a wilderness of brown eroded desert that gradually shifted to jungle as they headed farther north.

As the afternoon wore on and the shadows lengthened, the jungle became increasingly dense. As dusk began to settle, they came out into a broad clearing. Suddenly before them Kitty saw an extraordinary complex of ancient Hindu temples, their conical towers entwined with vines, giving them the effect of some storybook lost city.

"What is this?" she gasped.

"Khajuraho."

"My God! It's stunning. Why have I never heard of it?"

"A thousand years ago it was the spiritual capital of an ancient Hindu people called the Chandelas. When their civilization crumbled, it was completely forgotten. This area is so remote that the temples have been perfectly preserved. The Mughals didn't even know they existed, so they couldn't destroy them as they did so many others. Sixty years ago, a British expedition stumbled upon them. But the British and Indians alike have kept it a secret."

"But why?"

"Come. I'll show you."

He took her hand and led her to the closest of the structures. The light was beginning to dim now, but she could see that the outside of the temple was adorned with sculptures—carved likenesses of men and women making love in a bewildering variety of positions. Naked bodies. Stiff erections. Full-breasted women with ripe and shapely hips. Groups of people participating in carefree orgies. Plump lips on rigid male staffs. Couples kissing. Couples engaged in every conceivable form of pleasure. Unashamedly erotic. Graphic. A celebration of the joy of love.

All around the compound, some distance from one another, were over a dozen other temples, all similar.

She couldn't believe what she was seeing. "How did this happen? Who made these?"

"No one knows for sure. But the theory is that the Chandelas belonged to a Hindu cult that believed sexual fulfillment in all its forms was holy, the purest way to blot out the evils of the world and achieve nirvana. You can imagine how shocking this was to the British who stumbled upon these tantric sculptures in the 1840s, and even to the modern Hindus, who tend to be as puritanical as the British."

They gathered wood and made a fire in the center of the clearing. Then, by the light of makeshift torches, they explored some of the other temples. There were thousands of what he'd called tantric sculptures, expressing a staggering panoply of sexual possibilities. As darkness covered the still earth and crickets chirped and night birds sang, Kitty felt the spirit of the place steal over her, at once spiritual and stirringly erotic. As if the souls of all who'd come to worship at these joyous shrines lingered still, paving a rose-strewn path for her to follow.

At the temple dedicated to Surya, the sun god, Max came up behind her and put his arms about her. "It's from these temples that the engravings of the *Kama Sutra* were taken."

"*Kama Sutra?*" she asked, a little breathless now.

"Sacred texts that outline the path to spiritual union through sexual bliss. You're a part of this, Baji. The blood of the people who created this flows through your veins. It's the part of you I love best."

Ordinarily, his words would have unsettled her. He was asking her to accept the portion of herself that she'd longest denied. But standing there, in the serenely hushed darkness, in the golden glow of the torches, she felt the spirit of this magical place take hold. A beautiful, benevolent spirit. As if the goddess of love these forgotten people had come to worship had become one with her, infusing her with a warm inner light of openness and love.

"Is it possible?" she asked.

"What?" he whispered.

"All that this place promises?"

Tenderly, he turned her around to face him. "Let's find out."

He kissed her softly, his lips like velvet, as he gently enfolded her in his arms. Cameron's arms. Holding her for the first time devoid of the tangled emotions that had kept them from coming together in harmony and truth. All defenses down.

She felt something stir in her that was fresh and new, yet faintly remembered from some distant time. Love so overwhelming, so tender, that it washed through her, bathing her in its pure, unvarnished radiance.

As they shed their clothes in the sultry Khajuraho night, she felt the stripping away of their outer selves, of all the pain and suffering and uncertainty. They touched and kissed and explored in silence, swallowed by the night. And yet their silence spoke as no words ever could. Each sigh became a covenant, each moan an exhalation of joy in this enchanted place. She heard, like the sweetest melody, everything his soul had waited so long to express. She felt—in his breath, his kiss, his caress—that they'd been summoned to this place to discover who they really were.

Time was meaningless. The hours drifted by without impact, as if all the world stood still. With their mouths, their hands, their bodies, they laid claim to one another as no one else ever could, knowing in their suspended state they'd been created for this. That they belonged each to the other.

It was so much more than a union of humming bodies. They breathed as one, moved as one, loved as one. Together they experienced a breathtaking intensity that few lovers ever gleam. Weeping their joy, washing away the grief, the loneliness, the despair.

It took them some time to come back to their surroundings. When they did, they gave a last kiss, then stood to dress since the night was growing chill. Still, they didn't speak. The companionable silence seemed a part of the magic night.

Spotting a bush of wild flowers close by, Kitty plucked one and ascended the steep stone steps to the Temple of Surya. Inside the small enclosure, she laid the flower on the altar, giving thanks for all that had passed this night. For the first time, she felt that she was a part of all this, of mystical India and her varied splendors.

When she'd descended, they walked arm in arm to the center of the clearing and stoked the fire before settling back into the soft meadow grasses. Lying in each other's arms, feeling the heat of the fire warm them, they gazed at the night sky, so vast above, with its canopy of brilliant stars. Immersed in the contented afterglow of lovemaking.

Snuggling against him, Kitty felt the need at last to voice her satisfaction. Kissing his strong jaw, she murmured, "When I think of all the years I lived without you, missing you, longing for you. All the time we've wasted. You've made me so happy. Cameron, darling, I love you so."

She felt his muscles tense. "Will you do something for me?" he asked, his voice sounding hoarse.

"Anything."

"Don't call me Cameron."

She pushed herself up to look down on him. The firelight played with his stark features. "Why?"

He was silent for a moment, as if gathering his thoughts. "I didn't lie to you when I told you Cameron was dead. He died that night. Cameron is a product of a past I can't embrace. Can you understand?"

She touched his lips tenderly with her fingertips. "Help me to understand."

He sat up and ran a hand through his hair, as if the tale required too much effort to reveal while lying vulnerably prone. As she sat up beside him, watching his face, he allowed his mind to go back to the past, peeling away the years in his memory, to put himself once again on that moonlit shelter beneath the towering pinnacle of Mount Abu, fourteen years before. He began to speak slowly, telling her how Ngar had found him and nursed him back to life. How he'd wanted him to stay. But how, wanting to put the past behind him, he'd run away.

"Over the months I begged my way to Bombay. There I lived on the streets, using my wits to beg or steal enough to scratch out a meager existence. By then my skin was so brown that I easily passed for an Indian."

"But I don't understand. Why didn't you turn yourself in to the British authorities at once? Why didn't you go to your father?"

"I'll have to ask you to be patient. I have to tell the story in my own way."

"Very well." She willed herself to restrain the burning questions.

"I don't know how long I was there in Bombay. Months. Dressed in rags. Eating when I could. I became a master pickpocket, preying on foreign visitors, using what Ngar had taught us to blend in with my surroundings and disappear when there was trouble. One day I saw a well-dressed Italian who was just coming out of the Taj Mahal Hotel. I picked his pocket. To my delight, the billfold was bulging with rupees. I could live like a king for months, maybe even a year. But as I was gloating over my good fortune, a newspaper clipping in the billfold caught my eye. It told of a fatal train crash in Darjeeling just the month before. There was a picture of the man whose pocket I'd picked, and under it the story of how his wife and three daughters had been killed in the crash on their way to join him in the mountains."

"That was Count Aveli."

"Yes. He lost everything he cared about that day. I knew what that was like. Some spark of decency made me go to the hotel. They tried to oust me, but I refused to leave until I'd spoken with the count. They summoned the police, but by the time they arrived, Count Aveli had come down. I confessed what I'd done and returned his billfold. He was so touched, he took me up to his room, gave me a bath, and sent for new clothes for me to wear. As I was eating the dinner he'd ordered for me—a feast by my standards—we began to talk. We recognized in each other the same sort of loss and loneliness. Anyway, to make a long story short, he adopted me. To take the place of the family he'd lost."

Once again, Kitty restrained herself from asking, *Why didn't you go to your father?*

"We traveled around India for months, then on to other countries. He was a wanderer. He'd been adrift since the loss of his family, and wanted to see the world. He treated me from the first as if I really were his son. Eventually, he decided that if I were to inherit his title, I'd need an education. So we went to Italy. I spent the next few years there, going to school. But a month after I graduated from the university, Count Aveli died. Leaving me as his sole heir."

"But that didn't satisfy you."

"No. I was at loose ends. It seemed that I was . . . searching for something. I spent a few years drinking and whoring my life away, evading the matchmaking attentions of wealthy Italian mothers. But India continued to call out to me. Finally, after a week-long binge that ended when I woke up in a Milan gutter, I'd had enough."

As he spoke, Kitty felt an overwhelming sadness for those lost years. She reached over and took his hand.

"I returned to India. It took me months to find Ngar, but I finally did. I wasn't sure what to expect, but he welcomed me like a long-lost son."

Long-lost son! Kitty wanted to scream out: *But you have a wonderful father!* Uncomfortable, she took her hand away.

"I spent the next five years at his side, training once again in the Rajput arts, as we traveled around India and he worked for the cause of freedom from Britain. I saw Mother India through his eyes, and what I saw shamed me. When I told him that I too wanted to work for his cause, he was overjoyed. I learned so much, Baji.

More than I'd ever learned in the stuffy halls of the university. More than we ever dreamed of when we were children. I learned to do things I never would have thought possible."

The steadiness and intensity with which he told the story planted a small seed of dread in Kitty. What was he leading up to?

"Gradually I began to understand that all my training was leading toward one supremely important quest. To find the long-lost Ashoka ruby—the ancient symbol and talisman of the unity of India. Ngar believed that if we could acquire this treasure, it would give us the credibility and spiritual power to unite all the warring factions and tribes and religions of India into one force that could drive the British from our shores."

She couldn't contain herself any longer. "But Max, *you're* British! The people he wants to drive out of India are *your* people. *Your* father . . . Why didn't you have Count Aveli contact him? Or why, when you came to London, didn't you let us know who you really were?"

"I didn't want you to know. I even left parties if I saw you were there."

"Your father's heart was broken the day he thought you died. When I think of all the years he suffered— how we suffered together! How could you do that? How could you let him go on missing you, grieving for you, when all the time you were alive!"

He turned on her, and she saw a flash of anger in his eyes.

18

Once again she felt his withdrawal. He clasped his hands together and dangled them over his bent knees. The anger vanished as he stared out into the night. "I can't talk about that now. Not yet." His voice throbbed with some deep emotion, and he dropped his head wearily.

"It's all right," she told him, sensing his fatigue. "You can tell me when you're ready."

"The important thing now is that I've promised the ruby to Ngar. Tomorrow night he'll meet us here and we'll turn it over to him. I've given my word."

When she didn't say anything, he prompted, "You *do* understand?"

"What about my father?" she asked quietly.

His eyes were sad. "Baji . . ."

"He's not guilty."

"I know you don't want to hear this. But he is."

"How do you know that?"

"Ngar—"

Impulsively, she put her fingers to his lips, halting the words. "Hush," she said, pulling him close. "Don't talk anymore. Just hold me for a while."

Lying beside him, Kitty watched as Max slept. He looked almost childlike, his hair ruffled, his strong features relaxed. She'd never seen him so at peace. As if the burden of keeping his secrets so close for so long was finally gone, affording him his first tranquil slumber in years.

All around her, everything appeared unchanged. The stars were every bit as bright in the velvet Khajuraho sky. The temples and the jungle beyond enclosed her like a protective barrier against the world outside. Yet for Kitty, everything had changed.

At any other time, under any other circumstances, she might have taken comfort from the sight of her lover sleeping so tranquilly by her side. From knowing that he'd found the solace of sharing his torment at last. The knowledge that he wasn't alone. Except that this repose was a horror to her. Because she knew now what she'd never comprehended before.

Max had never been the enemy. It was Ngar. A zealot who'd kidnapped children for his own selfish gain. Who'd taken a wounded, nearly dead, boy under his wing with the sole and pernicious objective of molding him into a mindless soldier for his cause. Winding

him up like a machine. Convincing him that her father
had stolen from Ngar's people as a way of using him for
his cause. She churned with anger at his callousness.

It was Ngar she would have to fight. For her father's
life. And for Max.

She knew what she had to do. She knew too that Max
would see her actions as betrayal. But she wasn't be-
traying him. She was doing the only thing she could to
wrest him from Ngar's corrupt web.

It was only a few hours before dawn. She rose quietly,
careful not to rouse him, and reached for the tool bag
that lay by his head. Holding her breath, she opened it
and removed the Blood of India. And with it, half of his
rupees.

Putting them in the pocket of her pajamas, she crept
to the temple where the two horses were tied. She saddled one of them, climbed on its back, and took the
reins of the other horse in her free hand. With a gentle
kick to its flanks, she rode off with both horses. She
hadn't made it fifty yards from their encampment when
she heard Max's incredulous voice calling after her. A
voice that heralded his betrayal at her hands. Reso-
lutely, she closed her ears to it. He would thank her in
time.

She broke into a gallop. Kicking her mount and
holding the reins of the other horse, she raced through
the tangled jungle and over the dark countryside beyond. Willing herself not to think about the enormity
of what she was doing, or the man she'd left behind who
was now, no doubt, frantically pursuing her on foot.
Concentrating all her energy on reaching her only hope
of escape: the railroad spur line that connected
Chatarpur to Allahabad.

Finally she spotted the tracks. She followed them until she came to a place where they made a steady incline up a steep grade—where the engine would lose speed. Here, she shooed the second horse away, and remained mounted on the other.

The wait seemed endless. She could almost hear Max's footsteps as he pounded after her. She could feel the panicked rhythm of his heart. Hurry, she willed the train. *Hurry!*

At last she heard the train to Allahabad chugging onto the horizon. As it slowed down to maneuver this steeper grade, she gave her horse a kick and began to race alongside the line of cars. Several passengers watched inquisitively from their windows as Kitty leapt from the animal, grabbing onto the handle of one of the compartment doors. A startled attendant opened the door and helped her in.

She purchased her ticket and settled in. Outside her window, the sun rose over India, bringing with it a sharp new pain. India, in the guise of Ngar, had destroyed Max's life. Just as it had nearly destroyed her father's and her own. The temporary concession she'd found with her native land was smashed anew, and in its place was the old, familiar threat. Suddenly she couldn't wait to reach her destination. The prison she'd cursed for keeping her father captive seemed now the ultimate British sanctuary. The place where she would realize her dream at last. The place where she would find help for Max.

She knew he'd follow her. He'd find a way to stop her if he could. He knew India and had resources at his disposal the magnitude of which she couldn't even fathom. But if she could beat him to Port Blair, she knew she could save him. They would take him into custody, in the one place where Ngar and his cronies couldn't get their hands on him. Then she and her father would take him back to England, to his real family. To those who loved him.

The train reached Allahabad four hours later. It was a lively town and a major railhead, situated on India's famed Grand Trunk Road: the four-thousand-year-old route that crossed the width of the subcontinent from Peshawar to Calcutta. From Allahabad, the main rail line ran parallel to the Trunk Road directly to Benares and then on to Calcutta.

Allahabad was a surprisingly beautiful city with a large British cantonment. She remembered that Mr. Kipling, the author of *Kim,* had lived here for many years, writing his stories and working as a reporter. Tokens of comfort, symbolizing her connection to England. For a moment, she considered taking the ruby directly to the British commander here. But that could prove foolish. The forces manipulating Max obviously had spies everywhere. Even if she reached the cantonment safely, how would she know whom to trust? Which of its sepoys—the Indians who made up most of the British Army in India—were loyal and which were traitors? No, not even Calcutta would be safe. She had to get to Port Blair.

At the ticket office, she discovered that another train from Chatarpur was scheduled to arrive within the hour. If Max had run all the way to the tracks, or had intercepted one of the horses, he could be on that train! With great haste she bought her ticket for Calcutta and climbed aboard. After an excruciating forty-minute delay for no apparent reason, the train finally pulled out of the station, just as the Chatarpur train—and, no doubt, Max—pulled in.

Since the next Calcutta train wasn't scheduled to leave for another two hours, she once again felt reasonably safe. She settled into her seat, watching the passing scenery along the Grand Trunk Road. Every motion of the wheels seemed to bring her one step closer to safety. Soon the churning wheels began to lull her. Exhausted, she fell fast asleep.

She awoke with a start in Benares. As the train chugged to a halt at the station, it occurred to her that Max would likely have compatriots in this city on the Ganges: the holiest in all of India to Hindus. He could have wired ahead from Allahabad. If so, they might intercept her here!

But when the train pulled out five minutes later, she saw no sign of anyone looking for her. Had he not wired ahead because he feared it would compromise her safety? After all, he must know that these men wouldn't hesitate to kill her to get the ruby.

She slept with that thought for the remainder of the trip to Calcutta. It was early the next morning when they pulled into the vast central Calcutta train station. From the large wall clock, she noted that they were an hour behind schedule. When she asked, a porter told her that they'd stopped in the night to clear the tracks after a minor earth slide. The next Calcutta train would be only minutes behind them.

She hired a tonga and had the driver race the pony across town to the Kiddapore Docks. Once again her luck held. The Andaman Islands ship was just about to leave. As she boarded, a final call was given and the ship left the dock. From the railing, her eyes scanned the city skyline, taking in the sight of the gigantic Victoria Memorial, the Calcutta Maiden, and Fort William. But then, glancing down at the dock, she saw Max running up to the landing.

For a moment, their eyes met. The emotion she read in his wasn't anger, or even pain. It was sadness. Sadness and fear. But fear of what?

He broke eye contact to scan the pier that ran the length of the harbor. Spotting a schooner, he dashed toward it, jumped aboard, and with agitated gestures, negotiated with the owner to follow the ferry. As her ship curved to the south and headed down the Hooghly River, Kitty saw him arguing and pointing her way. Finally, he took out a roll of bills and shoved them into the man's palm. The deal was made just as Kitty's ship surged toward the open sea.

She paced the deck nervously. While the schooner was sail powered and would ordinarily offer no competition to a steamer, there was a strong wind today that would keep him close on her heels. Her plan hinged on her arriving well before him, so she would have time to reach the prison and make arrangements to have him safely taken into custody. He would hate her at first. But once he understood, he would see that it was all for the best.

When the ship finally tied up at Port Blair, Kitty could see the famous Cellular Jail at once. It was the main structure of this sleepy capital of the Andaman Islands, dominating it from every angle: a complex of six wings radiating from a central tower, completed just last year after a full decade of construction. Looking at it, Kitty almost wept in relief.

At the entrance, she identified herself to a young Welsh corporal. He eyed her native garb curiously before snapping to attention. "Yes, ma'am! We've been expecting you, sure enough."

He opened a huge, heavy metal door that closed behind them like a tomb slamming shut. They entered a passageway that led to another heavy, locked door and yet another hallway, then out into the prison yard. The closing of each door brought added comfort to her troubled mind. All around her, Kitty could see impenetrable fences topped with vicious coils of barbed wire. Armed sentries watched from four guard towers, one in each corner of the yard. Ngar and his legions would never be able to penetrate this fortress.

The Welshman left her with a sergeant major sporting bushy muttonchops. He looked her over and said, "Wasn't there to be a young man with you?"

"He may be on the next ship that docks—a schooner. When he arrives, please take him into custody until I have a chance to speak with him. Be careful. He may resist, but he isn't to be harmed. Just detained."

"I understand, ma'am. Now if you'll follow me, I'll take you to the warden."

They climbed a steep flight of stairs to a large office in the central tower that held a commanding overview of the prison courtyard and the Port Blair harbor. The warden was a thin, almost cadaverous, colonel named Holcomb. He came around from his desk to greet Kitty effusively.

"Miss Fontaine, you made it after all. We were worried on that score. You've had a difficult journey, no doubt. May I offer you tea?"

"Thank you, Warden. But I'd prefer to see my father first."

"Do you have the ruby?"

She patted the pocket of her pajamas.

"Wait just one minute, then. Please have a seat."

He left the office. She waited, allowing herself to sink into the cushioned folds of the chair. Portraits of King Edward and the Houses of Parliament offered safety and assurance. The next time that door opened, her father would step through it—a free man. He would know how to save Max. He would protect them both.

While she waited, she could see another ship from the direction of Calcutta come into view. Was this the boat Max had hired? If so, it wouldn't be long before he arrived.

Within another moment, she heard the sound of boots coming up the stairs to the warden's office. She turned toward the door. *Father!*

The door opened, but . . .

It wasn't her father who stood before her. It was Sir Harold.

"Why . . . Sir Harold. What are *you* doing here?"

"I wanted to make sure this exchange went off without a hitch."

She rushed to embrace him. "We've done it. Everything we've worked for all these months."

He broke from the embrace, looking her up and down. "Do you have the ruby?"

She reached into her pajama pockets and withdrew the immense stone.

Sir Harold gasped. "No wonder everyone wants the

cursed thing." He took it from her hand and held it to the light.

"This is a happy day for both of us," she said. "Sir Harold, you must brace yourself. I have some extraordinary news for you." She took a breath, wondering how best to tell him. Deciding there was no way to buffer such a revelation, she blurted out, "Cameron is alive."

"Cameron?" He couldn't seem to tear his gaze away from the Blood of India.

"Max Aveli *is* Cameron."

He slowly lowered the ruby and looked at her. "That's preposterous, child."

"I know it must seem so. But it's true. He survived the attack on Ngar's camp. He's been with Ngar for years. Ngar has been using him all this time to get his hands on the ruby. He's even convinced him that my father is guilty, so he could win him over to his cause. We'll have to help him. But it may take time."

He peered at her thoughtfully. "So you were right all along." He glanced out the window. "Where is he now?"

"In pursuit of me. It won't be long before he reaches the prison, if he hasn't already. I left instructions for him to be taken into protective custody."

"Don't worry. I'll take care of him. But first I'd better alert the warden."

"Don't let them hurt him."

"Of course not."

"And my father. When will they release him?"

"Just wait here. I'll take care of everything."

·   ·   ·

Kitty paced the office as she waited, thinking of the happy irony—on the day when she would reunite with her father, Sir Harold would also be rejoined with his son. They could all sail home together. . . .

After what seemed ages, the door opened and Sir Harold returned. "Your father's being held in the D Wing—maximum security. We can go there now."

Kitty followed him outside, where they joined three other men—a trio she recognized as former colonials who'd served with him in Rajasthan. Obviously, they'd made the journey with him. But why? she wondered.

They walked across a courtyard and into one of the six wings that radiated from the central tower. Every cell was overcrowded with Indian political prisoners. The smell of cramped bodies was overpowering. But all Kitty could think was that in a few moments more she would see her father again.

They came to a cell at the end of the corridor. The jailer unlocked the massive door and it opened with a clang. Sir Harold stepped aside and Kitty rushed in.

Max?

He was held to the wall in an upright position by leg and arm irons. Blood ran from his mouth and from cuts on his temple. But his eyes blazed with raw fury.

She rushed over to him. "What have they done to him? They promised they wouldn't hurt him!"

No one answered. Tenderly, she stroked his battered face. "I'm so sorry, my darling. This wasn't supposed to happen."

"Get out," Max ground out through his teeth. "Now. Before it's too late."

"Please forgive me. I couldn't let you take the ruby.

But you must believe me. Everything will be all right. Now that your father is here."

"You wanted to know why I never returned to my father." Max looked at Sir Harold with fury blazing in his eyes. "Tell her, *Father*. Tell her how you hated me. Tell her you're the one who shot me."

Utter silence followed his words. Shocked to the core, Kitty stared at Max with tears in her eyes. This was the most demented thing she'd ever heard in her life! "Your father loves you. Tell him, Sir Harold."

"Yes, Father," Max ground out through gritted teeth. "Tell us how you present a great face to the world. So affable, so sincere. But how underneath that façade you're a monster. Tell us how there's nothing in the world you hated more than me."

Sir Harold had been looking at his son quietly. Now he said, "*You* tell her."

"Why?" Kitty managed to mutter. "Why would he possibly hate you?"

"You never knew my mother. She was a dainty, beautiful, kind woman. Almost any man who came into contact with her half fell in love with her. My father was jealous from the start. And over the years his jealousy became a twisted obsession with keeping her away from other men. Imprisoning her, keeping her completely under his thumb."

"And tell her what happened next," Sir Harold said with a touch of anger in his voice. "Tell her how my fears were justified."

"You drove her to it," Max spat out. "When she met Jonathan Brace, she found a man who treated her with the respect, the dignity, the tenderness she deserved. When my father discovered the affair, he had Jonathan dishonorably discharged from the service and tightened the leash on my mother as never before."

"I was protecting what was mine," Sir Harold said.

Blood dripped into Max's eye. He wiped it against his shoulder, straining his bonds, before continuing in the same caustic tone. "When I was thirteen, Jonathan returned to India as a successful tea merchant. Wanting to get to my mother, he sought me out and had me deliver a message to her. When I saw her read that message, saw the light return to her eyes for the first time in years, I had no qualms about helping them. I became the go-between in their affair, delivering messages, helping her to sneak out of her room at night, making up lies and excuses to cover for her. Those were the only happy times I'd ever seen her have."

Kitty turned to look at Sir Harold. He was growing red in the face.

"About a month before our kidnapping, my father discovered what had been happening. I still remember it . . . remember him breaking down her door . . . storming into her room . . . beating her. When I tried to stop him, he turned on me, picking up a fireplace poker, lashing me with it, until I couldn't move. Then beating her with it. Again and again . . . and again . . ." His voice broke.

"And what was I supposed to do?" Sir Harold cried, impassioned now. "Stand by and let her—"

"She *died* that night," Max hissed. "But before she did, she made me take a vow. 'Promise me you won't seek revenge for this. Promise me you won't try to kill your father.' "

Tears were streaming down Kitty's face. One

thought kept echoing in her mind: *Sir Harold isn't even bothering to deny it!*

"After she died," Max continued, "he focused his rage on his 'turncoat son.' What you didn't know, Baji, was that the kidnapping was a relief to me. A lesser hell, to be sure. And when my father and the rescue party burst into our camp, his intention was to murder me. Knowing the bullet would be lost in the confusion, he aimed straight at my chest and fired."

"I only wish I'd been a better shot," Sir Harold growled.

"What are you saying?" Kitty cried, turning on him. "He's your *son!*"

"He was *never* my son!" Sir Harold raged. "He's the bastard issue of my whore of a wife."

Once again a throbbing silence filled the cell. Max's eyes hardened on Sir Harold's face. "*That's* why you hated me," he muttered through swollen lips.

"Bloody right. I suspected it, when I discovered her little affair. She denied it, of course. But a few lashes with the strap brought the truth to light. I took care of that rutting father of yours, too, never fear. You won't be seeing him again."

"And that's why you tried to kill me. You knew you weren't killing your own son. . . . I'm not your son." His voice carried a sense of wonder, relief, even joy.

"I would *never* harm a son of mine. But the bastard issue of a whore deserves to die. I'm only sorry I didn't succeed."

"And I," Max swore, "thank God I was never a son of yours!"

Suddenly, the world began to close in on Kitty. "Where . . . is . . . my . . . father?"

A faint smile came to Sir Harold's lips. "Poor blighter was killed while trying to escape just last night."

"But he was innocent! And they knew I was bringing the ruby—"

"Oh, he wasn't all that innocent. Actually, he was guilty as sin. But then who among the British in India isn't? Stealing from the wogs is what we do best."

"You were in on it all along," Max said.

"Of course I was. We'd have gotten away with it, too, if your friend Ngar hadn't found us out."

Reality hit Kitty with a rush. Her father was dead. He *had* been guilty. Quietly, she muttered, "Everything Max said is true."

"But then, what *is* truth? We all have different truths, don't we?"

In shock, she stammered, "But why are you . . . What do you stand to gain from all this?"

Max said, "No doubt he made a deal with the Crown. . . . He gives them the ruby and they give him . . . what? It must be something big."

Sir Harold smiled thinly. "I become the Viceroy of India. That's big enough, isn't it?"

"A position you'll use to loot all of India in the same way you looted Rajasthan."

"India won't remain British for very long in this new century. This may well be the last chance an enterprising man will have to seize the wealth of the subcontinent before the opportunity slips away forever."

Stunned, Kitty said, "There never was any pirate willing to free my father."

"Now you're catching on."

"You used me to get the ruby for you. And that day

at Scotland Yard—they knew we'd come. You told me how to get inside. You *arranged* for us to be captured." She looked at Max. At the cruel marks on the face she loved. At the hatred burning in his eyes. "What are you going to do with . . . with Max?"

"Oh, I think he can stay right here for the time being. Maybe—like your father—he'll try to escape." He chuckled wryly.

The horror of it all made Kitty nauseous. "My father never *did* try to escape. You had him killed. You couldn't afford to have your scapegoat go free to tell the world of your crimes. How much blood money did you pay the warden?"

"I didn't have to pay him anything." He looked over at his three henchmen. "Like my other friends here, he's a loyal follower. He knows I'll take care of him once I'm viceroy."

Max clenched bloody teeth and snarled. "So help me, God, I'll get out of here and I'll kill you. I swear it on my mother's grave."

Considering this threat, Sir Harold said mildly, "We'll just see about that."

Kitty looked at Max with new eyes. She'd never loved him more in her life, and yet she'd brought him to this. "You came here to protect me. And I—if I'd only known . . ." She threw herself on him, kissing his bloody cheek. "I'll get you out. I promise, my love."

"I shouldn't count on it, were I you," Sir Harold said calmly. "You'll be coming back to England with me. Charles still wants to marry you. His heart is set on it, I'm afraid. And, you see, Charles really *is* my son. As such, he deserves everything he desires." He moved closer to Max. "I want to make it up to the boy for having had a whore for a mother."

Sir Harold's men pulled Kitty kicking and screaming out of the Cellular Jail to a steamship anchored in the Port Blair harbor. She was locked in a rear cabin, which was already prepared for her arrival with fresh clothes and toilet articles. When the footsteps receded, she found the door was bolted from the outside. In frustration, she banged on the door, demanding release. But it soon became obvious that her jailers were oblivious to her calls.

Before long, from her porthole, she saw Sir Harold come aboard with the captain and two mates. As the anchor was raised and the engines roared to life, Sir Harold knocked on her cabin door and said, "As we come out of the harbor, we'll be making a swing by the Chatham Peninsula. It's quite an extraordinary sight. Be sure and have a look out your porthole."

"You're wasting your time with me," she cried. "I'll never marry Charles. The minute we get to England, I'll tell Scotland Yard everything I know."

"I might change your mind about that once we get safely home."

When I get to England, she told herself, *I will destroy you, if I have to do it with my bare hands. I'll come back here and I'll save Max, if it's the last thing I ever do.*

This thought was the only thing that kept her sane. It prevented her from tearing out her own heart from grief. She'd unknowingly betrayed the man she loved. She'd discovered her father was guilty after all, that these last months of toil and worry had been a sham.

She'd put her trust in England and had been stabbed in the back for her pains. Her hopes all dashed . . . her father dead . . . Max beaten and chained . . .

She couldn't think about that. She had to keep her head, escape, make amends.

Then, as she felt the ship make an abrupt swing toward the west, she thought of what Sir Harold had just told her. Chatham Peninsula. Why did that sound familiar? As she approached the porthole, she remembered. Chatham Peninsula was the public gallows of the Andaman Islands! A spot where passing ships could view the executions.

In a flash of horror, she saw two figures standing on the gallows. Max and another man. Below, surrounding them, was a squadron of British soldiers. The executioner slipped a black hood over Max's head, then placed a noose around his neck. He pulled a lever and the trapdoor fell from beneath Max's feet.

Max gave a mighty kick, desperately reaching for firm ground. With a scream, Kitty watched his hopeless struggle. The flailing legs kicked twice more, then dangled limply. Until he hung, deathly still, his head slumped grotesquely to the side.

19

itty's mind finally began to clear. She had no
idea how much time had passed. What recollec-
tions she had of the voyage were misty and
vague, brief snatches as she'd spun in and out of consciousness. The sound of the waves beating against the
bulkhead, the cry of seagulls, the interminable rocking
of the ship. Her head being lifted as cool liquid spilled
into her mouth, then nothing until the next such min-
istration. Then being carried off the ship in the cloak of
night on a stretcher, too weak to move, the faces of Sir
Harold's men swimming dizzily before her eyes. The
impression of being carried into a house. More cool
liquid.

Then nothing. She began to realize, fuzzily, that she

must have been drugged so as not to put up any fight or cause a scene.

All that time, in her brief moments of clarity, she'd sensed the heavy pressure of her heart. Some sensation of pain was struggling to surface, calling her to remember. But what was it? Every time she tried to grasp it, more cool liquid was poured down her throat and she lost the thought once again.

Now, as the effects of the drug slowly wore off, all that had happened came back in disjointed flashes. The ugly scene at the prison. Sir Harold's betrayal. Her father . . . guilty, after all . . .

And then the worst of it. The memory that had tried to surface through her enforced sleep. That had caused the heavy pain in her heart. The image of Max hanging from those gallows.

The rush of fresh pain hit her with such force that it seemed she relived it yet again. The horror of realizing what was happening. The helplessness of beating on her porthole, knowing there was nothing she could do. The emptiness of knowing it was too late. That he'd been ripped from her yet again in the most ghastly way possible.

Dead.

She'd lost him . . . how many times now? It seemed she was forever seeking and losing him. But this time it was final. There would be no miracle. Hot tears burned her eyes. She'd survived the loss of him once before. How, after such a brief and bittersweet reunion, could she possibly survive it again?

Her whole body was racked with pain. She shifted, wanting nothing more than to turn over and sob her grief into her arms. But she couldn't move.

She tried again. Reality crashed through her anguish as she became conscious that something was holding her down. She jerked her arms and then her legs. They wouldn't budge. She realized that she lay spread-eagle, her arms and legs fastened to posts.

Panicked, she began to struggle. But she was weak and it didn't take long to understand that her efforts were useless. She tried to calm herself, to determine where she was. Darkness enveloped her, but when she turned her head, she smelled fresh dirt. She was lying in some kind of pit. Yet she was inside a building. She spotted a window high above, covered with something that blotted out the light except for traces showing around the edges, like a promise of normalcy just out of reach.

Was her mind playing tricks on her? Was this some horrid dream?·

Just then she heard a door open, caught the spill of yellow light. She squinted against its unaccustomed glare. She saw a figure holding a lantern high.

"Hello, Sleeping Beauty. I see you're awake."

Sir Harold's voice. Cheerful, congenial, as he'd always been. Except that he was holding her prisoner.

"Where am I?" she asked, her voice sounding rusty from lack of use.

"In the root cellar of my home."

As Kitty's eyes adjusted to the light, she saw more clearly that a body-length pit had been dug in the earth of the cellar some three feet deep. Iron bars had been driven into the ground at the four corners, holding the ropes that bound her hands and feet.

"Would you like something to drink?" he asked, as if offering hospitality to a guest.

"So you can drug me again?"

He gave her an apologetic smile. "I'm sorry I had to do that. But it's over now. The time has come to make plans."

"After what you've done, do you have the audacity to think I'd be a part of anything you plan?"

"I realize you feel you've been deceived, my child. But there was a reason."

"I know the reason," she spat out. "Your greed and ambition has been behind everything you've ever done."

He had the grace to flush. "I'm not the monster you seem to think."

"You killed Max. You tricked me into stealing the ruby and then had my father killed. And you've staked me to your cellar like an animal. Monster? That's too kind a word for you."

He took a breath and squatted down beside her, setting the lantern on the floor so that it shone in her eyes. "You're only here because I knew the moment you regained consciousness, you'd try to escape. I had to find a way to make you listen so you'd understand. I'm going to tell you a story that might help you. It's a story I've told no one, and my telling it to you now is proof of my affection for you."

"You may save your breath and your affection, if this is how you show it."

He continued as if she hadn't spoken, clasping his hands before him and studying them as if reading the tale from within the pressed palms. "Even now I find it difficult to say the words. You see, my dear, though the world thinks of me as being a perfect English gentleman, I have a secret. I was born out of wedlock. I found out in the most painful and humiliating way imaginable. I was disinherited by the man I thought was my father and thrown out at a young age without a penny to my name. I swore to make sure no one ever knew of my shame. I changed my name, moved to the city, and told people I was the son of a respectable country squire. I learned to make my way in the world. I was determined to have money and position, all the things I'd been denied. So I went to India to seek my fortune. I scratched and clawed and attained the things I wanted by the sheer force of my will."

"And your deceit."

"I had no choice," he cried, his voice gaining momentum. "All the time, the knowledge of my secret haunted me. I lived in terror that someone would discover what I really was. The most important thing in my life was to build a wall of respectability about myself that could never be penetrated. So you can see how I felt when I learned that my firstborn son was *not* my son, but the bastard issue of a gutter whore and one of my disloyal subordinates. And you can imagine how I must have felt when this bastard child aided her in her flagrant adultery. . . . What was I to do? The boy was like a ghost sent back to haunt me. The thought that her bastard son would inherit everything I'd worked so hard for . . . I couldn't let that happen. Then he was kidnapped. It seemed the perfect solution. Those zealots would rid me of the constant thorn in my side. But when I found him alive and realized my opportunity— that my shot would be lost in the confusion—I had to take the chance. He deserved to die. He never should have been born in the first place." He paused. "Don't you see? It was the only way to rid myself of his evil."

Kitty stared at him incredulously. The man actually thought he was justified in his actions! His self-deception was chilling.

"I'm not a hard man, Kitty. I have a particularly soft spot in my heart for my real son, Charles. And I have a soft spot in my heart for you. I want you to be married and have the benefits of all I shall be able to do for you as viceroy of India. The two of you are perfect for each other. When I see you soaring through the air my heart swells in my chest. I say to myself, what a woman! She can be Charles's other half. Her strength can make up for his indecision and procrastination. What a team they'll make. Together, they're my future."

He reached for her hand but she summoned what strength she had left to twist it away. "You sick, demented beast. If it were up to me, you'd have no future."

"You don't know what you're saying. The drugs—"

"I know exactly what I'm saying. I detest you. I shall never marry your son. The only thing that keeps me alive right now is the faint hope that I might escape you and make you pay for everything you've done."

He rose with a lurch and stood towering above her. Suddenly the congenial old gentleman turned into the crazed figure at the prison in Port Blair. His whole physiognomy changed into something dark and loathsome.

"Then I was right to put you down here. I suspected your misguided loyalty to that bastard would cause you to be stubborn. I've tried to be reasonable with you. I even trusted you with my darkest secret. And how do you repay me? With insults. You *will* marry Charles. And if you think someone is going to come to your rescue, forget it. We've let it be known that you're in India, married to Charles even now. In one week I will be invested as viceroy and will leave for Calcutta. You will have agreed by then, or else—"

"Or else what? What else can you do to me?"

A hard gleam lit his eyes. "The maharajas of ancient times had a way of dealing with disloyal wives. They buried them alive. Slowly, so they could feel the terror of each spadeful of dirt. I've taken my inspiration from them. A fitting tribute, I'm sure you'll agree. You will pledge your loyalty to me and agree to become an obedient wife to my son or suffer a similar fate. Every hour I shall return and bury you that much deeper. You'll have plenty of time to ponder the consequences of your actions. In time, you will relent. And then all will be forgiven."

"You're wasting your time."

He stared at her for several moments. Then, without a word, he picked up a shovel, filled it with dirt, and tossed it into the pit. As it hit her, Kitty gave an involuntary jump of horror. He repeated the process three or four more times, enough to leave a thin smattering of dirt covering her. Some of it fell into her mouth and she spat it out, tasting the metallic tang on her tongue.

"Let us see how you feel in a few more hours," he said. Then he picked up the lantern and left her alone in the dark.

As he'd promised, Sir Harold returned every hour to repeat the awful process. "Are you ready to relent?" he'd ask. And when she refused to answer, he would toss another layer of dirt over her. After a few hours, the mound felt heavy upon her. Her mouth was so parched that she was constantly attempting to moisten it with her tongue. But she held on. Hatred for this villain who'd perpetrated this incalculable crime kept her going. Hatred and visions of revenge.

But after several hours more, she felt her reserves weaken. She was pinned down now by the ponderous weight of ever-increasing dirt. The lust for revenge gave way to despair when she thought again of Max. *I loved you so,* she told him, willing his spirit, wherever it was, to hear and understand. *You'll never know how much I loved you.*

Thinking of him, talking to him, was the only thing that kept the terror at bay when once again Sir Harold came in and tossed another spadeful onto the gathering pile.

"Have you reconsidered?"

She started awake, realizing that she'd dozed since his last visit. Wearily, she said, "I'll never do what you want. You might as well kill me now."

His face changed, settling once again into the mild demeanor she remembered well. "Speaking of death, I neglected to mention something that might interest you. A rather sad dispatch reached us this morning. Your friend Victoria is dead. It seems she took an accidental overdose of laudanum. Or so they say."

He'd saved this piece of information for just this time, when he judged that she was weakening under the strain.

Kitty turned her face away. She didn't even hear him leave. She knew it had been no accident. Victoria had

killed herself, choosing to be with Ramsey in death as
she couldn't be in life.

Her anger spent, all she could feel was sadness. For
Victoria. For her children. For Sir Harold, whom she'd
loved and trusted. She recalled how he'd abused his wife
for so long, just as Mortimer had abused Victoria.
Throwing her into the arms of another man. How both
women's lives had ended in tragedy. Just as her own
would end.

She began to wonder if she was losing her sanity in the
hours that followed. She drifted once again in and out of
consciousness. Sometimes she dreamed of Max. Sometimes she thought she saw him standing before her,
waiting. She remembered something Victoria had said.
What was it? Something about the soul mate's spirit
guiding his beloved even after death. *So we're never really
alone.* Ultimately, Victoria had felt too much alone. As
the grief settled in Kitty's heart she knew that she too
was losing her will to live. Better—so much better—to
join Max. Where there was no pain, no grief.

Again she heard the door open, again the footsteps,
the shovel spiking the earth, the dirt raining down on
her. He didn't speak now. There was no need. Then the
light left and again she was alone in the dark. Soon she
was up to her neck in dirt. The mound was so heavy,
she couldn't move. She began to pray. *Let it be soon. Let
me find the courage. A few minutes of suffocation and
then . . . come to me, Max. Help me.*

She heard the door open once again. Even in her
trancelike state, it seemed too soon. An hour hadn't yet
passed. This time she heard a voice.

"Kitty, oh my God!"

A lantern was brought close and Charles's face came into view as he crouched beside her. As she looked up at him, he burst into tears. "Kitty, please, for God's sake, don't go on with this."

She opened her mouth to respond, but the words wouldn't come. Her mouth was so parched that her tongue felt swollen.

"Father's told me everything. All you have to do is say you'll marry me and you'll be free."

Weakly, she shook her head.

"He wants so much for us. He says India will make us rich beyond our wildest dreams. It's all for us."

"He's mad," she managed to choke out.

"He's not mad. He's had a hard time of it. He's ambitious . . . ruthless, perhaps . . . but what great man isn't?"

"Charles, listen to me. He's out of his mind. And if you don't break with him, you're as doomed as I am."

"No. He's done all this for me, don't you see? Because I love you so much. Kitty . . ." He wiped away some of the tears that were streaming down his face. "Is it so awful to think of marrying me that you'd die instead? Can't you love me a little? I'd do everything to make you happy. Isn't that better than this?"

"That man you say wants us to be happy killed your brother. The brother you used to cry for when you were young."

"He wasn't my brother."

"He was your half brother."

"But Kitty, *Cameron* was the monster. Father explained it all to me. He was corrupted . . . twisted by India into something evil."

"You're wrong. He walked into a trap to try and save me. He sacrificed himself for me. He was more noble in reality than he was even in my girlhood fantasy. He . . . died for me."

He stared at her with wide eyes. "You love him," he said softly.

"More than my own life."

With her words, Charles collapsed completely, sobbing so his words were barely discernible. "I'm afraid. I'm so afraid. He's going to go through with this. Please, Kitty, even if you don't love me, agree to marry me to save your life. Don't let him kill you. I couldn't bear it. Please say you'll agree."

"I'd rather be dead," she told him softly. "At least then I'll be with the man I love."

Come, Baji. Fly with me.

20

By nightfall, Kitty was packed into her cold, clammy grave with only the oval of her face showing. The weight of earth pressing in on her was so heavy that it was difficult to breathe, as it was all but impossible for her to expand her lungs. Once again, as so many times before, she heard someone enter the room. Then the familiar sound of the shovel digging into the dirt, and then more dirt piled upon her, now covering her chin. Some of it landed on her face, but she was so tightly packed now that she couldn't move her head to brush it off.

Suddenly Sir Harold was standing over her. "You have one last chance," he told her, his voice sounding distant through the dirt covering her ears. "Agree to

marry Charles and you'll live. If not, I'll bury you alive
and let it be known that you died in India of fever.
What shall it be?"

It took all of Kitty's strength to part her lips and
rasp out one word: "Never!"

She saw a flicker of regret in his eyes. But he said,
"Very well. You have one last hour to reconsider your
decision. At the end of that hour, I will return and ask
you 'yes' or 'no'? If your answer is yes, you live. If
not . . ."

He left. The minutes passed, agonizingly slow. As
she lay there, immobile in her macabre encasement, she
realized that the next sound she heard would be the
opening of the door, heralding the approach of her tor-
mentor with the final deposit of dirt that would snuff
out her life. She couldn't think of that now. If she did,
the fear would surface once again. It wasn't death she
feared now. Death meant only that she would be with
Max again. It was the moment of dying that terrified
her. Knowing it was coming. Knowing she'd have to
endure the suffering of her lungs fighting for air before
her final respite and release. The seconds ticked by in
endless procession. Impatience seized her. Just let it be
over!

She reached out for Max's spirit, willing it to join
her, to help her across the threshold. As she sank deeper
into her meditative trance, she felt his presence fill her
with serenity and peace. Coming to save her from this
agony with the gift of ultimate escape.

The door creaked open. She heard his footsteps on
the hard-packed ground. The hour of her death was at
hand. She closed her mind to what was to come. Two
more minutes, maybe three, and it would be over. *Don't*

think about it now. Think about coming out on the other side.
Of opening your eyes and seeing Max standing there, his hand
held out, waiting.

"Baji."

It was Max's voice. Slowly, she opened her eyes. And
there, like a miracle, encased in a halo of light, was her
beloved. He shimmered before her blurry eyes like a
desert mirage. So beautiful. Standing there in his celes-
tial cloak, a guide to lead her through the darkness.

She smiled, all her tenderness welling up as tears of
relief bathed her eyes. "I knew you'd come."

"Be very quiet. I'm going to get you out."

"Yes, my love. I'm ready to go with you." Did she
say or think it? She couldn't tell.

He knelt down beside her and used his hands to
carefully shift the earth from around her neck.

"Don't bother with that," she told him. "I don't
need this body anymore. Just take *me* . . . my soul."

He was looking at her with an odd expression. "Baji,
I'm real."

"Yes, love. More real than you've ever been. Hurry.
Take me now."

He continued to look at her for a moment more.
Then he put his hands to her face. Gently, he said,
"Darling, listen to me. I'm going to take you with me.
Just hang on a while longer."

"Yes . . . I'm ready . . ." She felt herself sinking
into the ether. "I feel so peaceful," she told him dreamily. "As if I could just go to sleep."

"No, Baji, don't. Stay with me."

She looked at him and saw tears in his eyes. Did
spirits weep? "Don't cry, darling. It will be over soon."

Her eyes heavy, she felt herself drifting once again.

Some small part of her was conscious of his hands frantically digging, untying, lifting her from her bed of
earth. Powerful arms, so warm, so secure.

"Hold on, Baji. Please hold on."

The words floated to her through the mist. She laid
her cheek on his chest and whispered, "Thank you,"
before she gave in to the blackness that engulfed her.

Slowly, Kitty came to consciousness. Warmth enfolded
her. She heard the sound of water dripping into a pool.
Then she felt a cool cloth wipe her face. Where was she?
The scent of roses filled her senses along with something spicy. Sandalwood. She opened her eyes and saw
swimming before her the image of a woman's face. A
lovely Indian face—warm, honeyed skin, ebony hair,
dewy brown eyes. She was wearing a saffron sari, and a
red dot—a tika—adorned her forehead. An angel? Or
perhaps her grandmother, the legendary Rajput princess, welcoming her to the fold?

The woman smiled. "I see you are awake," she said in
Hindi.

And then she was gone. Kitty closed her eyes. She
felt someone settle beside her. Heard a soft, masculine
voice. "Baji."

When she opened her eyes again, she saw Max. His
handsome, chiseled face. Intense, caring eyes. "Thank
God," he said. "I thought I was going to lose you."

She looked around. She was lying in a bed in a simple
room. The walls were cracked, but clean. Incense
burned on a table by her side. Rose and sandalwood. A
basin of water sat beside it. The sounds of water dripping. Afternoon sun streamed in through the window.

The feeling of warmth. Looking at herself, she realized she was clean and wearing a soft cotton nightdress.

Max was sitting beside her on the bed. He took her hand in his. It was solid.

"Where am I?"

"In the East End. The poorest section of London, where Indian and Chinese immigrants live. You'll be safe. They won't think to look for you here."

It came to her that this was all too real. The sharp scent, the warmth of the sun, the pressure of Max's hand.

"I'm alive," she said in a precarious tone.

"Yes. Though we weren't sure for a while."

"Then that means—" She looked up at Max and saw his bold mouth form a smile.

"That's right."

"You're real. I didn't dream you. You aren't a spirit—"

"Touch me if you don't believe it."

She reached up with a shaky hand and touched his cheek. She could feel the bristle of a stubble on his jaw. And all at once she realized what it meant. Max was alive!

With a cry of joy, she surged up in the bed and took his face in her hands, smothering it with kisses. "You're really here! But—how?"

"Haven't you heard that cats have nine lives?" he teased.

"I saw you hang."

He pushed her back into the bed and bent to kiss her cheek. "What you saw was an old yoga technique that Ngar taught me. Simply put, you relax all the muscles in your neck and allow your body to go completely limp, controlling your respiration to give the impression of death. Once they were convinced I was dead, they wasted no time in tying rocks to my ankles and tossing me into the ocean. I waited until they'd left, then swam for the next ship out of Port Blair. I'm only sorry I didn't arrive sooner.''

She continued to stroke his face. "Oh, no, Max. You came after me, to try and protect me. And I nearly lost you. . . . Hold me, Max. I need to know you're real."

He lay down beside her and took her gently in his arms, holding her close. With her head on his chest, she could feel the steady beating of his heart. A wondrous sensation. The pulse of life.

"How long have I been here?"

"A few days. My friends have helped nurse you back to life."

"That woman—"

"Parveen."

"I thought she was my grandmother."

"You've been confused. You nearly died."

"And you've been here all this time?"

"Every second."

She snuggled close to him, feeling the security of his strong arms. But slowly, memory came back to her.

"Victoria's dead," she told him.

"I'm sorry to hear that. She was a good woman."

"She taught me something. That honoring the person we love is our most important obligation. More important than life or death or any petty struggle. She learned too late that it's everything. But we've been blessed with a miracle, Max. The chance to be together as we were intended."

His arm tightened about her and his head dropped

back against the wall. "I felt that in Khajuraho," he told her. "What I told you in Bombay was true. I hardly thought of you through the years, only as a child who'd befriended and helped me. But there was always something missing. I felt that I was searching for something—something I couldn't define. I thought I'd found it with Ngar and his cause. When I came to London and heard your name, I remembered you. I asked about you and learned how close you were to . . . the man I thought was my father. That you were trying to free your father, whom I knew to be guilty. I couldn't trust you, so I decided it was best that we never meet."

"Don't talk about that now."

"I have to. You have to understand. The time has come for truth between us. Growing up as I did, my entire life was a lie. I couldn't afford to trust anyone. But I trust you now. So there will be no more lies."

"Yes," she agreed. "Truth from now on. No more games."

"You trusted that man, and because you did, I thought you were a fool. I knew him to be evil, and the fact that he'd so completely fooled you made you an object of contempt in my eyes. But then, that first night at Timsley's, when I lifted your mask and realized who you were—I don't know how to explain it. Something inside me that had been dead sprang to life. I looked at you and it was like . . ." He paused, searching for the words.

"Like looking at your other self," she supplied.

"Yes. That's it exactly."

"I felt it, too."

"I mistook it for physical attraction. Your beauty,

your daring—I wouldn't be human if I didn't respond to it. But it angered me. I couldn't stop thinking about you. I told myself all the reasons to hate you. Your trust of Harold. Your embracing of the England I'd rejected."

"I *was* a fool. I saw that at Port Blair."

"None of it mattered. I wanted you as I've wanted nothing else. And then, when you asked if I was Cameron—when you brought back memories of a person who was dead and buried to me—I wanted to punish you. That day in the hangar, I told myself you were just a woman I despised. I wanted to seduce you and toss you aside, to show you what a sham your life was. And I did. But it shamed me. I felt as if I'd damaged something precious."

He paused and sighed. "I didn't want to love you. And when I knew I did, I hated myself for my weakness. But that night in Khajuraho something happened to me. I didn't feel like Max or Cameron or anyone I recognized. I felt like—I don't know."

She was quiet for a time. Finally, she asked, "Do you believe that people can have soul mates?"

He considered for a moment, then said, "I don't know. But I do know if I could choose a soul mate, it would be you."

"It almost makes me believe it's possible, the way we found each other again. If that isn't a miracle, I don't know what is."

"I just knew—in Khajuraho—that I'd always loved you."

"As I've always loved you." She turned in his arms and kissed his mouth, deeply, passionately. "This is all I need. I don't care about anything but you. England or India or politics or revenge. I just want to go away with you and live and be happy. Nothing else matters to me."

He was silent for a moment. "You asked me once if I had any life but my mission. Until that moment, I'd never thought about it before. But I realized you were right. I've never had the kind of life others do. I want that now. I want you for my wife. I want to kiss you last thing every night and wake up each morning with you beside me." She felt his muscles tense. "But there's one more thing I have to do first."

She stilled in his arms. "What's that?"

"I'm going to kill the villain who did this to you. To us."

Slowly, she pushed herself up and looked down into his face. It was hard again, resolute.

"The one good thing that's come out of this is that I'm free. He's not my father. That releases me from my promise to my mother."

"You don't need revenge, Max. It's not important now."

"It's important to me. Think what he's done to us. To my mother. To me. To you. To India. I can't turn my back on his evil."

"To India," she repeated, falling back into his arms. "I don't know how to feel about India. In Khajuraho, I had a transformation. I embraced India for the first time, felt her a part of me. But then—it's all confused. Growing up, I didn't know who I was. Was I Indian? Was I British? It seemed that I was all and nothing at the same time. I wanted to be one or the other. So I chose England. But then, at Port Blair, I saw what England had done to me. The lies, the deception . . . and I knew what a fool I'd been. But now . . ."

"Now?"

"If what we want is the right to live in harmony, as we were meant to, how can we do that if you kill Sir Harold?"

"How can I not?"

"I think there's another way. There's something he cares about more than life. His position. His respectability. His greed. If we could somehow take that from him—expose him for what he really is—it would be worse for him than death."

He considered her words. "And what of Charles?"

"I have to believe that once Charles realizes the extent of his father's villainy, he'll see that we're doing the right thing."

"I hope you're right."

"And India. We've unwittingly committed a great crime against her by stealing that ruby from her. Ashoka's prized jewel belongs in India. If we could steal it back and return it—"

"That's impossible," he said. "It's been put with the Crown Jewels in the Tower. The most guarded spot on earth. There's no way we could get it out of there."

"There must be. That's the only thing that will make up for the harm that we've done, make up for Sir Harold's villainy, and give us the peace of mind we need to start a new life. I'll need some time to regain my strength. But after that . . ."

Reluctantly, his lips curled in a smile. "It's almost too delicious."

He looked at her and they smiled into each other's eyes, sharing the same thought. What could be a more thrilling challenge for two cat burglars than the invasion of England's ultimate treasury?

.   .   .

The Tower of London complex consisted of twenty towers dotting the eighteen-acre site on the bank of the
Thames. For most of its nine hundred years it had been
an object of fear—a royal prison. But since the time of
Charles II, it had been London's foremost tourist attraction—the place where England's famed Crown Jewels
were kept on display for the public.

On this May afternoon, the mob of tourists included
Kitty and Max. In disguise, deliberately separating
from each other, they'd spent the last hour touring the
grounds and queuing up to enter Wakefield Tower
where the jewels were displayed behind heavy plate
glass.

It had been five days since Kitty's rescue. She would
have liked to have seen the look on Sir Harold's face as
he'd entered the root cellar to deposit the last spadefuls
of dirt and suffocate her, only to find that she'd vanished. Whom would he suspect? Charles? Likely he
would have been watching Charles carefully. Would he
be clever enough to figure out what had happened? Or
would he have thought she'd used some magical Rajput
means of escape at the last minute? Either way, she
posed a grave threat to him. He'd no doubt have his
henchmen combing London for her with instructions to
shoot on sight. Whatever he thought or knew, surely he
would never suspect that she'd be here, plotting such a
bold move. Or would he?

Casually, she strolled about the open Tower Green
toward her rendezvous with Max. He joined her with a
grim expression.

"What's wrong?" she asked.

"It looks impossible."

"Surely you're not intimidated by a mere fifty Beef-eaters and a whole company of the British Army," she said with a hint of sarcasm.

"Daunting as that may be, it's not the guards I'm concerned with. Have you taken a close look at the enclosure walls?"

She glanced about but could spot nothing out of the ordinary.

"Watch this."

Scanning the ground around his feet, he went to pick up a rock the size of a chestnut, which he hurled over the outside wall, missing it by inches. As it sailed over, a shrieking wail filled the air, startling everyone. Within seconds, a stream of armed men flooded out of the Waterloo Barracks. The gates slammed shut. Tourists were routed out of the buildings as an army major, Webley pistol in hand, shouted, "Everyone please stand still and remain calm."

They watched as a corporal of the guard scaled the wall and looked about. The corporal shouted down, "Nothing here, sir. Musta been another of those blasted ravens."

Similar reports were brought from every corner of the compound.

The major called out, "Sorry to inconvenience everyone. Please go about your business."

The gates were opened once again. The soldiers returned to their barracks. The tourists congratulated themselves on having quite a tale to tell.

"What was *that*?" Kitty asked.

"Something new. Something no Rajput warrior ever thought of. An electrical field has been placed all along the perimeter. There's no way anyone could possibly climb over it."

"Then it really is impossible."

His gaze was scanning the battlements. As she watched, he glanced up at the sky and his expression changed. The spark of an idea was bright in his eyes. "Baji . . ."

"What is it?"

He was looking up at the sky now as if he could actually see his plan in motion. "You remember your last exhibition? When your engine died and you glided in with barely a sound. Could you do that again? Purposely?"

"Where? Here?"

"Yes."

"At night?"

"There are lights on several of the towers."

"But even at night we'd be spotted."

"Maybe, but they're so sure of this new system that they don't even patrol the grounds at night. If we came in at, say, three in the morning . . . could you do it?"

"I might be able to land. But taking off is another matter. It would be dicey. We might make it. Or the engine might sputter and we'd go crashing right into the wall."

"But it is possible."

"Possible but insanely dangerous."

He turned to her with a twinkle in his eye. "If it wasn't dangerous . . ."

The lights of London were spread before them in all directions. An hour earlier, they'd roused Lawrey from his bed in his house near Hendon Field, gassed up the plane, and had taken off. From Hendon they cut over to the Thames, following it north toward the city. Suddenly, there it was before them: Tower Bridge and, just beyond, the Tower of London itself. As they hummed closer, the open field of the Tower Green appeared minuscule. It would be like landing in a shoebox.

The prospect sent a chill through Kitty. It would require split-second timing. If she were off even a fraction of an inch on her approach they'd surely crash. She'd have to touch down in a narrow path between a row of trees on the right and the west side of the White Tower on the left.

As if reading her mind, Max called from behind, "It's not too late to back out."

She shook her head and yelled back, "Just hang on."

A minute later she cut the engine. They were suddenly enveloped by a magnificent silence. She gently inched the throttle forward and they began their descent, swooping down like an eagle after a hare. Their target seemed to rush at them with the speed of a bullet. Over the top of the enclosing walls. Down into the snare of the open green. *Now, quickly,* she told herself, *level off. As soon as the wheels touch the ground, push down on the brake with all your might.*

In that instant they hit the ground with a shattering impact. As she pushed forward on the brake, the aircraft swerved to the right and skidded toward the wall at a rushing speed. The wall came closer . . . closer . . . then . . .

The plane mercifully stopped. They'd made it.

But the danger had only begun. They were now inside a prison with only one way out.

They sat for a minute, frozen in their seats, waiting for an alarm to sound. But the compound was quiet. Their silent entry hadn't disturbed the slumbering troops.

"Quickly," she whispered to him. "Let's turn the plane around and ready it for takeoff."

They hopped down. Each took a wing and they turned the plane around and backed it toward the wall with which they'd nearly collided. To take off from this impossibly narrow patch she'd have to rev the engine to full force. The noise would bring the entire complement of Waterloo Barracks rushing out at them. Every second would count.

They crept through the trees to Wakefield Tower, just behind Traitor's Gate, where prisoners were once brought in from the Thames. The locked doorway offered little challenge. They pushed the massive door open and entered the cool stone hallway. Climbing the flight of stairs to the entrance of the jewel room, Max lit a lantern. All at once they could see, on the other side of the plate glass, the treasure horde of the British Empire. A dazzling display of crowns, scepters, and jewel-studded royal regalia including the jeweled state sword, the most valuable in the world, and the Imperial State Crown made for Queen Victoria in 1837, weighed down by some two thousand eight hundred diamonds and other gems.

Max moved to the door at the side of the long display window. Here the lock was more intricate and gave him more trouble. He struggled for a full ten minutes before it finally clicked open. Kitty willed him to hurry, conscious that someone might venture out for a moonlight stroll and spot the plane.

They entered the domain of the Crown Jewels. As Kitty held the lantern, Max searched through the accumulated loot of centuries that glittered before them like gifts at the foot of a Christmas tree.

As the seconds ticked by, they rummaged through the contents, nearly blinded by the dazzle. The gems began to blur together, rubies, emeralds, diamonds of unimaginable proportions. And then, all at once, Max straightened and held out his palm. There, gleaming like a red star, was the Blood of India. So magnificent that even among this splendor it burned with a fire that put all the other gems to shame.

"Let's go," he said, pocketing the ruby.

They left, careful to relock the doors behind them. As they came outside, the night air seemed fresh and chill after the stuffiness of the keep. Still there was no movement about the courtyard. But as they climbed into the plane, Kitty's heart beat faster. This was the most dangerous part of all.

Max primed the propeller, then, as the engine roared to life, hurriedly climbed aboard. She glanced back at him and read his confidence in her in his eyes. He gave her a wink that said, "You can do it."

Taking a breath, she pushed the throttle to full power. The plane shook. The howl of the engine was deafening. From the corner of her eyes she could see lights coming on in the Waterloo Barracks . . . then half-dressed men rushing into the courtyard, guns in hand. She released the brake so they surged forward. A volley of shots rang out as they gathered speed. Barreling across the makeshift runway toward the towers and the fortress wall at the other end. Coming too fast.

Frantically she pushed on the aerilon. They rose a foot
in the air. Not enough. The wall was hard upon them.
Kitty braced herself for the impact. But all at once the
plane shot up, its wheels just skimming the top edge of
the wall, setting off the wail of the alarm. But it was too
late. The blare, the confusion, the volleyed shots, receded behind them as they soared into the safety of the
night sky.

Minutes later they landed at the Hendon airfield once
again. How long would it take for the authorities at the
Tower to discover that only one object was missing?
How long before they alerted the Secret Service, who
would put two and two together and realize that only
one person in England had both the motive to steal the
ruby and the plane with which to do it? They had to get
out of the country and get out fast. The first ship to
Calais.

Lawrey was waiting for them by the hangar. He
seemed agitated as they jumped down. "Scotland Yard
called," he said. "They wanted to know if a plane had
taken off tonight. I played dumb, but I don't think I
fooled them. I didn't know what to do, so I called your
friends."

"My friends?" Kitty asked.

Sir Harold and Charles stepped from out of the
shadow of the hangar behind Lawrey. Sir Harold had a
pistol in his hand. He stared at Max first with a flicker
of surprise, then with a look of growing anger and
hatred. "So a cat does have nine lives after all," he
greeted him. "How many bullets will I need to end
them all?"

21

Pointing the gun directly at Max's face, Sir Harold reached over and patted his leg, quickly finding the ruby in his pocket.

Disconcerted by this unexpected scene, Lawrey stepped forward. "I'm terribly sorry, Kitty. I had no idea. I thought—"

Before Lawrey could finish, Sir Harold calmly turned the gun from Max to the burly mechanic and pulled the trigger. The gun spurted fire and Lawrey, with a look of shock, fell dead to the ground.

"Father!" Charles cried.

Sir Harold snarled, "Shut up, boy." He turned back to Max and Kitty. "Scotland Yard will be here soon. Imagine their delight when I hand over the ruby along with the dead bodies of the thieves—the murderers of poor Lawrey, who tried his best to stop them. There's no Rajput trick that will save you from a bullet in the skull."

"Father, you're not going to kill Kitty!" Charles cried.

"She had her chance. She chose not to take it."

"But Father, I love her."

Sir Harold whirled on his son. "She hates your guts, boy. Can't you see? This vermin has twisted her so that she's as evil as he is. Come here. Take this." He put the gun in Charles's hand. "This is your chance to get even with her for what she did to you. This is your chance to be a man for once. My true son."

"I don't want to do this. I can't—"

"You can!" Sir Harold insisted. "You don't need that bitch. As my son, you can have the world at your feet. But not if they stop us. Kill them. Kill them for what they did to us."

Charles looked at Max. His hand on the gun was trembling. "When I think of all those years I spent missing you, thinking you were dead . . . idealizing you the way younger brothers do. The martyred Cameron. I even envied you because I knew Kitty loved you the way she could never love me. But I told myself it was all right, that you deserved her love after all that had happened to you. That even a portion of that love was all I deserved for having lived instead of you. Fool that I was."

Max looked at him with genuine regret coloring his eyes. "You were the one thing I missed all those years. When I went back to London—whenever I saw you—I felt the sadness of what he'd done to us. How he ripped us apart. He stole everything from me, even the chance to know my brother. You'll never know the emptiness I felt."

Kitty suddenly remembered the night she'd danced with Max at the French Embassy ball. The odd sadness that had crept into his eyes when he'd seen Charles approaching. His abrupt disappearance.

"Liar!" Charles cried. "You aren't my brother. You're a fraud. You helped my mother betray us. You made her hate us."

He sounded at the moment like a heartbroken child. "She didn't hate you, Charles," Max told him gently. "She adored you. She adored both of us. It was your father she hated. A man who beat her, tortured her, kept her prisoner. Just as he was doing to Kitty."

Sir Harold snarled, "She deserved everything she got. Like all women, she lived for deceit. And the only thing she understood was an iron hand."

"She was the kindest, most generous, most loving woman who ever lived," Max said, still holding Charles's gaze. "She didn't withdraw from us. He pushed her away. He took a delicate flower and crushed her beneath his boot."

"Delicate flower, my arse!" Sir Harold cried. "She was a whore bitch who deserved what she got. I should have killed her long before I did."

"You killed her?" Charles's voice was but a whimper.

Unhearing, Sir Harold wheeled on Kitty. "And you're just like her. You can never trust her, Charles, any more than I could trust that whore. Do it, boy. Pull the trigger. Now!"

"He's right, you know," Max said. "You pull the trigger now and you'll become him. That's what he wants. To mold you into another likeness of himself. A cold, cruel monster who cares about nothing and no one. Someone who would ill-use a woman to make himself feel like a man."

"You see!" Sir Harold cried, raving now. "You see his evil! His lies!"

"Think back, Charles. Think of our mother's face. The love in her eyes. See it. Hear her soft voice as she sang to you at night. On the nights when she wasn't crying in her bed because her brute of a husband had beaten her."

Trembling, Charles cast a panicked glance between his father and his brother, two poles pulling him in different directions.

"Pull the trigger, dammit. *Now!*"

Charles's lip quivered uncontrollably. He looked as if he might break down in tears at any moment. But suddenly he swiveled, turning the gun on his father. His finger jerked on the trigger and the gun discharged with a blast. Sir Harold fell to his knees, his eyes filled with disbelief. He gasped several times, the word "why" strangling in his throat.

For the first time in his life, Charles had taken an action completely on his own. His voice, a mere whine moments ago, was steady now. The voice of a man. "That bitch whore," he said slowly, enunciating every word, "was my mother, too."

Those were the last words Sir Harold ever heard. By the time he slumped to the ground, he was dead. Charles stood looking at him, the gun still in hand. Max went to him and put his hand on Charles's shoulder.

With his new assurance, Charles said, "Scotland Yard

will be here any minute. You needn't worry. I'm going to tell them everything."

Max reached down and pried the Blood of India from Sir Harold's hand. "Maybe. But they're still going to want this ruby."

"I'm afraid you'll never get out of England with it. Even if you get out of here, every port and train station will be blocked. Why don't you just give the ruby back? What difference does it make now?"

Kitty looked at Max. "No. The ruby belongs in India. We're taking it home."

Max's eyes softened on her face. "Then we've got to find someplace to hide," he said, "until we can get out of the country."

"Quickly," Kitty said. "Help me refuel the plane."

"Where are we going?" Max asked.

"We're going to France. We're going to fly the Channel."

"But that's crazy!" Charles protested. "Even the most foolhardy of France's greatest aviators are waiting until summer when the winds off the North Sea will be down. Even from Dover, it's farther than anyone has ever flown before. And you're starting miles from Dover. Kitty, you can't do it. It's insane."

"It's perfect," she insisted. "It won't occur to them that we'll attempt to fly the Channel, so they won't think to notify the French authorities. They'll assume we're hiding out somewhere in England."

She looked at Max. All this time he'd been studying her quietly. Now he asked, "Can you do it?"

"Just watch me. I'll prove to you that I can."

He stepped to her and took her face in his hands.

Softly, he said, "Baji, I love you. You don't have to prove anything to me."

She'd been trying to prove herself all of her life. The fact that she didn't need to prove anything to him made her feel as if the invisible shackles she'd worn had just dropped free. Liberated from expectations, free to do her best, knowing it would be enough. Tenderness and gratitude filled her heart. She reached up and kissed him and felt his confidence permeate her. With him, she could do anything.

They quickly fueled the plane. Just as they'd finished, Charles pointed toward the road in the distance. Half a mile or so up the way, they could see the lights of a line of police cars speeding toward the field. "You'd better hurry."

Kitty looked at the man she'd once planned to spend her life with. He seemed so changed. She kissed his cheek. "I'm so proud of you," she told him.

"Be happy, Kitty. And godspeed."

"You'll tell my aunt and uncle I'm all right?"

"Of course."

The two brothers turned to each other and embraced. "Take care of her," Charles said.

"I will."

The cars were coming closer. Kitty hurried into the hangar and came out with two long duster coats and goggles, which she and Max quickly donned before boarding the plane. As Charles primed the propeller, Kitty started the engine and they taxied onto the field.

The cars by now had caught up to them, chasing them down the strip. It was now a race to see if the plane could be cut off before it left the ground. As Kitty gathered speed, one car shot ahead, gunning its engine as it raced ahead of the plane. Then, as Kitty pulled back on the throttle, the car swerved into the plane's path. It would be close. Kitty held her breath.

The plane barreled closer. Policemen jumped out of the car, pointing guns. They were almost upon them when the plane surged upward, its wheels leaving the ground.

Some twenty minutes later, the first rays of the rising sun broke the horizon. It had been a smooth flight up to this point. But Kitty knew that as soon as they left the coastline, the Channel winds would toss them about like a matchstick in a storm drain.

"We'll be over Dover soon," she called back to Max. "Our best chance is to gain as high an altitude as we can before reaching the cliffs. I'm going to take the chance that we can get above the winds on this side. They'll still hit us on the French side, of course, but I'm hoping we'll escape the worst of them."

Max leaned forward and wrapped his arms about her shoulders. Her hair whipped back in his face but she felt the touch of his lips on her neck. Turning, she kissed him, steeling herself for the task ahead.

She pulled back on the throttle and the plane began to rise. As they ascended into the thin air above, Kitty felt a touch of dizziness flick through her. She shook her head and breathed in the crisp sea air. She was tired. They'd been up all night with no rest. The altitude would likely play tricks with her mind. She must stay alert. If any flight had ever counted, this was it.

As the sun rose higher, slanting its rays in the eastern sky, she looked down and saw the white cliffs of Dover come into view, stark and magnificent as they jutted up against the sea. Twenty-one miles across the Channel lay Calais.

She glanced back at Max and called, "We're higher than anyone has ever been in a plane before."

"We're on top of the world, Baji!" he called back. "We own the sky."

He sounded so much like the old Cameron, glorying in the excitement of it all, that she felt a rush of tenderness. To him this was a grand adventure. But she knew how dangerous it really was. Though flying the Channel had been her dream, though she'd planned and worked toward this goal, there was still no guarantee. She hardened her resolve. Somehow, she would get them there safely.

She'd guessed right. As the cliffs of Dover receded behind them, the air this high above was relatively calm. But as she looked at the gas gauge she realized the strain of reaching such an altitude was depleting their fuel faster than she'd anticipated. Even with the new larger fuel tank, they could well run out before reaching the other side.

As the minutes passed, they found themselves out of sight of any land, surrounded by nothing but the variegated blues of sea and sky. Far below, the water was choppy, giving testament to the winds that raged, winds they would have to battle on their descent. She felt Max's breath against her ear. "It's glorious!"

"Enjoy it now. It will be rough going ahead."

As the miles slowly crept by, the clear weather began to change a bit at a time. First a few white clouds that they passed through like a dream. A few miles distant, the clouds darkened, heavy with the tinge of rain. Mist rose from the sea, clouding their view. Soon they were flying in a dense fog that was slowly crawling toward England. Kitty wiped her goggles constantly, straining for some sign of clearing. If this continued they could easily lose their direction.

It was time to go down. From up here, she would never spot land. Pushing the throttle forward, she called back to Max, "Hang on!"

They began their descent through the ever-thickening clouds. The rain began to fall, a little at first, increasing steadily until soon they were drenched. Water puddled at Kitty's feet. Her head felt light, her shoulders tense from the strain of trying to hold the plane steady as they headed into the crosscut of wind. The plane was lurching now, tossed in the gale. Her hands burned as she gripped the controls. But as the clouds whipped past, she spotted a brief glimpse of land. The coastline of France was coming into view.

She glanced at the fuel gauge to find the needle hovering at empty. Just a few minutes more, she willed.

Her goggles were fogging up. She wiped them again, but the mist was gathering inside. Impatiently, she pushed them up onto her head and once again caught a brief glimmer of land.

Suddenly the wind changed, whirling about them like a whirlpool. She jerked the throttle and as she did, the plane began to spin out of control.

She heard Max's voice behind her. "Are you all right?"

The plane was falling fast, buffeted back and forth by the fierce, conflicting winds. She nodded, struggling to right the plane, but her head was reeling.

Desperately clutching the throttle, she fought for

control. Rain and wind whipped at them. They plunged through the layer of clouds.

"I can see the coast," he told her. "It's coming fast."

His voice was calm, giving her courage. She had to concentrate on the task at hand and forget the possible consequences.

"What does the fuel gauge read?" he called.

After a brief hesitation, she answered, "Empty."

Just as she said it, the engine began to sputter and the plane dropped. Holding tight to the throttle, she struggled to ride the wind.

The muscles of her arms ached mercilessly as she fought the controls. They were plunging fast. The coast of France loomed dizzily before her. But they were falling too rapidly. At this rate, they'd crash into the rocks below.

She pulled back on the throttle as hard as she could. The engine still sputtered but the plane began to level off.

"It's not enough," he called. "We need more height."

She tried, but the throttle was pulled full tilt. They were rushing on a downward course straight for the rocks below. They were going to crash.

But all at once the erratic wind shifted. A violent gust tossed them high. Kitty caught sight of the coastline spinning before her just before the plane surged upward. They cleared the rocks, then fell again as the draft altered its course once more, sending them crashing to the ground.

The impact knocked Max forward into her, crushing her lungs so she couldn't breathe. The plane skidded and spun, the right wing scraping the ground and carrying brush in its path. They bounced high then crashed as the plane tipped and broke in two, hurling them out. Kitty landed with a heavy thud and blacked out.

The next thing she knew, she was being lifted in powerful arms. She came to consciousness slowly, her mind fuzzy and fighting for the surface. She swabbed her eyes with her sleeve and saw the blur of Max's face before her, carrying her to safety.

"Are you badly hurt?" he asked.

"I'm fine," she assured him, although her body felt battered. Blood seeped into her eye from a cut she'd received in the crash.

He brushed it away with a tender hand. "My brave darling. You did it. You flew the Channel."

She suddenly realized it was true. "*We* did it," she smiled. "Together."

He looked back at the shattered plane, burning now. "A pity no one can ever know it."

"It's all right," she said, resting her cheek against his chest. "We'll know."

She felt his arms tighten about her as the blackness came to claim her once again.

They recuperated in an inn outside of Calais for a few days, then boarded a steamer for Bombay. The first night after dinner, they walked on deck in the brisk breeze to anticipate the journey ahead. Long nights at sea to talk and make love, to discover each other anew. A temporary island of safety and serenity, suspended between the two poles—England and India—where trouble and uncertainty awaited. A singular luxury, after all they'd been through.

Back in their cabin, Kitty caught sight of herself in the dresser mirror and went to the glass to examine the small scar above her eye where she'd been cut in the crash. "Will you still love me if this scar doesn't go away?" she asked idly.

Max came up behind her and turned her to face him. "You're ravishing," he said, kissing the scar. "Every time I look at you, I think you're the most stunning woman I've ever seen."

She flushed. "And what about when I'm old and grey?"

"Then I'll love you even more, for all the years of happiness you'll have given me."

He kissed her tenderly. At the touch of his lips, all thought of missions and danger and betrayals melted away. She felt the responsibility of the task ahead evaporate. In its place was a woman who existed merely for the pleasure of the moment.

Slowly, he undressed her, kissing her flesh as the clothes slipped free beneath his hands. Her body began to quiver, feeling each touch as if for the first time. Coming alive beneath a moist and feasting mouth, beneath hands that caressed and cherished every inch of her.

When they were naked and lying on the narrow bed, her mouth and hands explored his body with a leisure she'd never been afforded. His sun-darkened face and strong, bristled jaw. The column of his neck where his pulse beat like a drum. Broad shoulders and firmly muscled chest—where she found the merest trace of the bullet scar beneath the crisp dark hair, and kissed it as if to relieve remembered pain. His nipples, which she sucked until his breath was raw and ragged in his throat. The rampant, corded column of his erection, jutting proud. She ran her fingertips over it, marveling at the juxtaposition of steellike strength encased in a velvety sheath. Ruggedly powerful in its chiseled beauty, yet secretly vulnerable to pain.

"Take it in your mouth," he urged.

She looked at him and saw the smoldering fire in his half-hooded eyes. Her mouth hungered to obey, but she felt foolishly unprepared. "I don't know how," she confessed.

"You learn by doing." He put his hand to the back of her head and guided it close. Hesitantly, she kissed the swollen head. Then her mouth closed over him. Shuddering excitement, sublime fulfillment. So hungry to please that before long it felt like the most natural communion in the world. She lost herself in what she was doing, worshiping him with a warm and succulent mouth, feeling him burgeon and throb—supreme compliment to her shy attempts. Using her hands, her lips, her tongue in synchronized movements that spurred him on.

Before long his breath filled the room. Groans of pleasure as he grasped her head and conducted her deeper, deeper . . . Loving the feel of power as she sensed he was ready to explode.

He pulled her up and rolled with her until she was on her back, lying beneath him, his weight heavy on her limbs. Glorying in their newfound intimacy as he kissed her with rough passion, kissed the mouth that had tasted him, his hands exploring her sensitive flesh. "You're a fast learner," he said into her ear, his voice an appreciative growl.

"There's so much I want you to teach me. Things we saw at Khajuraho. Things I never—"

He cut her off with a blinding kiss. "Later," he said. "I'm going to fuck you now."

Her heart slammed against her breast in eager anticipation. He entered her like the shot of an arrow and she gasped aloud. Lust carried her on the crest of a wave that rose higher with each powerful thrust. She felt helpless beneath him, her mouth slack with pleasure, her body screaming in ecstasy. Higher . . . higher . . . and then she was crying out before his mouth clamped down on hers, muffling her screams as he plundered her. As she shook and clawed him in unbelievable and unimagined bliss.

She felt limp afterward, her head falling to the side, her body all but singing. But he didn't stop. He found her breast with his mouth and sucked, arousing her anew, keeping up a steady rhythm that soon had her gasping and clutching at his hair. "Again," he told her, and she obeyed, shattering beneath him like broken glass.

And later still, "Again," he said, kissing her madly, his stamina astounding, their bodies slick and hungry, coming together with an eruption that seemed to set the cabin aflame.

Finally, they rested, their bodies entwined. He held her tight, cherishing the closeness, the feel of her in his arms. Wanting never to let her go.

"I never knew what it was to be happy," he told her, kissing her hair. "I can't remember ever being anything but . . . lonely. I don't know that I ever had a happy moment. Until now. You've brought me that. Someone to share myself with. Come what may."

"That's the loveliest thing anyone has ever said to me."

"It's true. But—"

She raised herself up on an elbow and looked down on him. "What, love?"

She saw in his eyes a stark vulnerability. "You were looking for Cameron, yet you found Max. Is it enough?"

Tenderness and love spilled over in her smile. "More than enough. More than I ever dared dream possible. I thought you were cold and ruthless. Yet I see now that it was a mask you wore to hide your past. And your pain. You don't have to hide from me ever again. I want to heal that pain, with so much love that you overflow with it. I want to erase every lonely moment you've ever had with hours, days, months, and years—a lifetime of knowing that I love you just as you are. That I'll always love you, no matter what."

A shadow passed over his eyes. "No matter what," he repeated, thinking of the future.

She put a fingertip to his lips. "Let's not think of what might happen now. I just want to enjoy this respite. Think of this cabin as an island—a sanctuary where no one can touch us. I want to stay in this bed and love you until you're too exhausted to move. And then love you some more."

He gave her a wicked grin. Rolling over on top of her, he flattened her into the rumpled bed. "Be careful what you wish for," he warned before kissing her again.

He was already hard.

22

The horses loped over the dusty Rajasthani hills that stretched north of Mount Abu. All morning the peak had loomed before them, drawing them like a magnet. The site of their childhood ordeal. The place where Kitty had lost her first and only love. And where she feared she might lose it yet again.

This feeling of dread had gripped her the moment they'd stepped from the ship in Bombay. Up to that instant, the journey across Europe and through the Suez Canal had seemed like a honeymoon. Now, as they neared their destination, her uneasiness intensified, bordering on panic.

As they neared the base of the mountain, the terrain was suddenly familiar. Memories flooded through her.

A band of terrified children. The young girl she'd been, dangled by her ankles, a taunt to the open jaws of a crocodile. Little Sarah, her scared face illuminated by the moonlight, whimpering, "I want to go home." Just ahead the river curled in front of them. The spot where Ngar had brought her and Cameron for their first lesson in the Rajput arts.

Ngar.

She drew rein. The horse, smelling water, bobbed its head and nickered in protest. Max turned in the saddle and asked, "What is it?"

Kitty was trembling inside, the dread welling up like a fist. "Let's give the horses some water," she suggested, stalling for time.

They let their mounts drink at the edge of the river while Max studied her curiously. "We're almost there. Don't be afraid, Baji."

She sighed and turned to him. "Maybe it's foolish. I know now that all you told me was true. But I can't help wondering. Can we really trust Ngar? Say they succeed in using the ruby as a rallying symbol to free themselves from Britain. What then? Will there be a place for you—for us—in that new India? And will Ngar feel he can completely trust you? You *are* British, after all."

"I may be British by birth, but my heart is with India. It always has been."

"I suppose that's a part of my anxiety. I don't understand why you feel so bonded with India. Enough that you've given your life to her."

"Baji, come here." He took her hand and led her to a flat rock where he sat, pulling her down beside him. Holding her hand, he said quietly, "India is a nation in bondage. Just as my mother was a woman in bondage. I saw what being held captive did to her. And I've seen what it's done to the people of India. Losing your freedom to choose, being dictated to even by a benevolent captor, changes people. It crushes their spirits, takes away their initiative and their hope."

"As it did to Victoria," Kitty murmured.

"I couldn't help my mother break free. But maybe I can help the India I love. Its people may be poorer when Britain leaves. They may well fight among themselves. But at least they'll be free of a foreign master who has no right to be here. That in itself would be reward enough. And when it's done . . . well, India isn't just one kind of people. It's many races, many religions, many tribes. There's room for everyone here. Even you and me."

She sat quietly for a time, thinking of all he'd said. "It makes some sense to me now," she said at last. "I admire your sentiments. It's a lovely thought, everyone living in harmony. But are you sure they'll see things as you do? Will they ever be able to view you as anything but a reminder of their former oppressors? And will you really be able to turn your back on your own people? I've tried, you know, and I can't. Not completely. We are who we are."

"All I can do is follow what I know to be right."

"Still, I can't help worrying. Something warns me that this isn't what you think it is. That Ngar—"

He squeezed her hand. "We can trust Ngar. I told you. He's like a father to me."

"We haven't had much luck with fathers, you and I."

Smiling, he kissed the tip of her nose. "Our luck's about to change."

They heard horse's hooves and looked up to see a rider approaching. Max recognized him and went to greet him. "Our leader eagerly awaits your return," the horseman told him, then galloped off in a cloud of dust to herald the couple's arrival.

Max and Kitty mounted and followed him into the encampment. Men lined the way, staring at them as they passed, armed with rifles and swords. Dozens of men. The numbers grew as they proceeded, until they came into the clearing surrounded by boulders. There, hundreds of men awaited them, all similarly armed. Men from every corner of India. Pathans, Assamese, dark-skinned Kerelans from South India, light-skinned Aryans from the north, and scattered throughout, the bushy mustaches of the Rajput warriors. More men, and more and more, spilling over from the ledges of rock, pressing in against them, forming a solid wall along the path leading to Ngar's tent. The sheer volume of the crowd alarmed Kitty. The handful of men who'd kidnapped them fourteen years before had grown into an army—a well-oiled military machine.

As they came to a halt, the tent flap opened and Ngar stepped out. His mustache had gone grey and lines creased his face. But Kitty would recognize him anywhere. The proud bearing and keen eyes were unmistakable.

They dismounted and Max went forward to embrace his old friend. Breaking the embrace, Ngar asked Max, "Have you brought it?"

Max stepped to the horse, took the ruby from the saddlebag, then held it forth. Carefully, with due reverence, Ngar took it and caressed it in his fingers. To himself he murmured, "How long I have waited for this." Then, looking at Max, he added, "You have performed your task well, my son. Now nothing can stop us."

Spotting a boulder at the side of the tent, he jumped atop it. Standing tall above the crowd, he cried, "Behold, my brethren. The indisputable blessing of Shiva, the Destroyer. The hallowed ruby of the great Ashoka, our forefather. The Blood of India!"

With a mighty thrust, he held it high in the air.

The ruby caught the sun and split its beam into a circle of dazzling scarlet shafts, the refracted rays sweeping over the assembly as if emanating from the fingers of God. A startled gasp reverberated through the crowd. As one, the men dropped to their knees, bowing before the miraculous manifestation.

It was only then, hearing the whispered prayers of awe rippling through the throng, that Kitty realized the full power and magic of the stone. The mythic symbolism that could mobilize these men—all so different—into a single united cause.

"This, my brothers," cried Ngar, "is the final ingredient of our great crusade. The source of eternal energy that will empower us and propel us to glory. With this sanction of the gods, we cannot fail."

Kitty had never seen him so dynamic and charismatic. His whole face seemed different, his body taut and trembling with the force of his conviction. He looked like some medieval artist's conception of Moses, shouting the Commandments from his holy mountain perch. The cheer of a thousand voices rose like the triumph of a trumpet's blare. Tears of emotion sparkled in Ngar's eyes, mirrored throughout the crowd.

Ngar stood for many moments, eyes closed, face

tipped to heaven, savoring the moment, the chanting of the crowd.

But some, a faction off to the side, began a different chant. It blended at first with the others, but eventually the power of it began to drown out the rest. As Kitty strained to hear, she began to pick out the words "Death to the conquerors!"

One man, about the age of Ngar, raised his hand for silence. He stood taller than most, and was darker than some, without the Rajput mustache, the glow of conviction gleaming in his eyes as he addressed all his brothers as one. "I, Kadamba of Goa, say to you now, the time has come!" he called so all could hear. "We will rise up as one. In Bombay, Delhi, Calcutta . . . in the cantonments of Mysore, Umballa, and Dehra Dun . . . in the hill stations of Simla and Darjeeling and Srinagar . . . we will slay every British man, woman, and child who is desecrating our land. We will line the Grand Trunk Road from one end of India to another with a display of their heads. What the English tyrants refer to as the Mutiny of '57 will seem but a pale prelude. Our beloved Ganges will run red with their blood. The Blood of India!"

Cheers from his own faction rose to a fever pitch. Men raised rifles and swords and shouted chants in a dozen different tongues, while the rest of the men looked to Ngar with questions in their eyes. Max stared at it all, at the zealous faces, the twisted lips, the weapons raised high in gluttony for revenge. He ran to the center of the gathering and held up his hand for silence, turning round to face every faction of the crowd, until the clamor died down.

Max turned to Kadamba. "The Blood of India is a symbol of peace. Not war."

"Peace!" Kadamba spat out. "The British idea of peace is the servitude of all dark-skinned peoples. Those of us who toil and love this land."

"Nothing was ever said about slaughter!" Max cried.

Ngar regarded him thoughtfully as the men watched, silent now. "Indeed it was not," he agreed. The air was charged with tension.

"Then the time has come," Kadamba proclaimed.

"You dare defy me?" Ngar demanded of the man.

"It is this Englishman who defies you!"

Max called to him, "I defy the insanity that has turned you to this. Slaughter was never part of our dream."

But Kadamba wasn't listening. "Seize him!"

The men around him hesitated. Ngar glared at Kadamba. "By what right do you issue such commands?" he demanded. "This man you call English is my heir. Our brother."

Max grabbed the opportunity to address the crowd. "Friends, listen to me. This massacre will prompt an even more brutal reaction from the British—it will set back our cause a hundred years. The civilized world will rise up against us. They will brand us savages, say we're too barbaric to govern ourselves. This is not the way."

"Enough!" shrieked Kadamba. "Take the British dog away so that we will be subjected to no more of his whining."

With an angry sweep of his hand, he impelled them to action. His men charged through the crowd and overpowered Max.

But Max fought them, calling, "Wait!" They paused.

"I demand my ancient right to settle our differences in combat."

Not a sound was heard. Kadamba said through gritted teeth, "*You* claim the right? You have forfeited your rights!"

"Was I not trained as a Rajput warrior, named as Babu's heir? Have I not brought the Ashoka ruby at great peril to fulfill the prophecy? I have the right."

The men looked to Ngar, uncertain now. "He has the right," Ngar agreed.

Kadamba's nostrils flared. "Very well," he ground out. "As the challenged one, I make the choice of weapons. I choose the *wagh nakh*—the tiger's claws."

A rumble passed through the crowd. "What is it?" Kitty asked the man closest to her.

"It is the preferred weapon of Kadamba," he explained. "No one is more proficient at its use."

The weapons were brought and laid on a cloth on the ground before them. They were wicked-looking devices, similar to brass knuckles. Five razor-sharp, pointed blades protruded from an elaborately carved metal band that was grasped by the fist.

As was the Rajput custom, each contender bowed low over the weapons. Then they fitted the claws to their hands and faced one another.

Max made the first swipe, but Kadamba easily sidestepped it. "I really do not want to kill you."

"Then call off this talk of massacre."

"You . . . fool!"

It seemed a barbarous dance they performed, lunging and parrying as in swordplay, but forced to brave injury in order to get close enough to strike. Max had the advantage of youth, but Kadamba possessed experience and a breathtaking technique. As Max thrust again, Kadamba met his weapon with his own, halting him so it appeared that they stood locked together, fingers entwined.

Max broke free and lunged again. Kadamba whirled and danced effortlessly out of his path.

Max thrust again, in anger now, slashing Kadamba's sleeve. Five ribbons of blood showed on the older man's arm.

"Traitor!" Kadamba spat out contemptuously just before he clawed Max's shoulder, drawing blood.

Wincing from the pain, Max said, "You are the traitor, Kadamba. To Babu, to us. To India."

Their weapons locked together once again. They stood staring into each other's eyes, breathing hard. "I love India," Kadamba told him. "As you say you do."

"That's the love of a zealot. A love without compassion or mercy or forgiveness. That twisted love has turned you into a fanatic."

He ducked, twirled around, and rose up to slash Kadamba's face, leaving streaks of blood on his cheek.

In a sudden lightning movement, Kadamba dropped to the ground. But halfway down, he broke his fall with an extended arm and, using his whole body as a flying wedge, he swung and kicked Max's feet out from under him. Swiftly, he leapt onto Max, holding the tiger's claw to his throat.

"You and Babu have betrayed us all. Destiny has decreed that your two heads will lead the parade of India's vengeance on the Grand Trunk Road."

From this position, Max glanced at Kitty.

Watching this barbaric scene, she knew she had to do something. Glancing around, she spotted the ruby, lying on the boulder where Ngar had placed it in the confusion. Grabbing it, she called, "Max!"

Kadamba turned her way. As he did, the tiger's claw slipped and drew blood.

She held the ruby for them to see. Then she threw it to Max. His free hand reached up and caught it.

As Ngar had done earlier, he thrust the ruby upward in his palm. It caught the sun and once again, the clearing exploded in the radiance of bloodred beams. In a strained voice, he called, "The power of Ashoka is mine!"

As they had before, the men dropped to the ground. But this time they trembled in fear. Kadamba, who believed in the power of the ruby as much as the men, stared at his former comrade with a horrified gaze. Max felt the blades at his throat slip as Kadamba reached in a desperate effort to snatch the ruby from him.

With a tremendous lunge, Max brought his claw up and plunged its razor-sharp blades directly into Kadamba's heart. The older man glared at him, one last look of the defeated, before the life left him and he slumped to the side.

Pushing him off, Max rose and held the ruby high. Before him, many of the crowd were cowering. Others were rising to their feet, unsure of what had happened, or what they now must do. Ngar passed through them to stand by Max's side. Max cast him a quick look of gratitude. Then, breathing hard, he called, "No one disputes that India must and will be free. The British themselves know they can't hold on to it much longer. The question is, what kind of India will replace the Raj? Two thousand years ago, Ashoka, the great emperor, used this talisman to create a golden age of peace and unity. Return to your homes. Sheathe your weapons. Let Ashoka's spirit fill you. And I swear to you that I will give this ruby to those who deserve it, who will pledge themselves to re-creating Ashoka's dream in this new century."

A week later, Max and Kitty stepped from a tonga and gazed up at the soaring towers and cupolas of the City Palace in Udaipur. Glancing at each other, they took a breath, steeling themselves.

"Are you ready for this?" Kitty asked.

"It's the only way."

They crossed the outer courtyard where, months before, they'd made a daring escape. As they did, a tall Englishman came up to greet them. It was Carrington of the Indian Secret Service.

He glanced at his pocket watch and said, "I was beginning to think you wouldn't show. They're waiting inside."

He led them through a contingent of Rajput guards up a staircase and through a series of narrow hallways. As they walked, Max asked him, "You've contacted Inspector Worthington in London?"

"He has agreed that all charges against the two of you will be dropped. All of Sir Harold's coconspirators have been rounded up."

"What about his son, Charles?" Kitty asked.

"He's told the authorities all he knows. That, on top of your explanation for his father's shooting, will set him free, as well."

With the death of Kadamba, the threat of a massive mutiny in India had ended for now. But that still left

Max and Kitty with a dilemma: what to do with the ruby?

They came out into what was called the Peacock Courtyard—a small open space within the palace walls where the Maharana of Udaipur held court. The walls were exquisitely decorated with mosaics of colorful peacocks. Inside, the maharana stood waiting for them with a stern countenance. Looking at Kitty, he said, "You have disappointed me greatly. You really should not be so distrustful of people. Had you told me what you wanted—"

"You would have given us the ruby?" she asked.

"Of course not. But we could have talked about it. I am, after all, a reasonable man."

"I see. Then you had no intention of cutting off my hand?"

He considered. "No, I would most assuredly have cut it off."

She smiled wryly. "You call that reasonable?"

"That, as you English say, is all water under the bridge now. Besides which, you had your revenge. They are still picking up the pieces of my beautiful flying machine along the rail line to Chatarpur."

"Are the others all here?" Carrington asked in his most official tone.

"They are all here and awaiting us inside. Where no servant might overhear."

They followed the maharana through the courtyard and into the living quarters to a small room brightly festive with frescoes and glass mosaics. There, three men awaited them. The great Parsi industrialist Sir Jamsethji Tata, who'd built the Taj Mahal Hotel to avenge the snub of being excluded from the "whites only" hotels of Bombay. G. K. Gokhale, the noted politician and leader of the Indian Congress Party, who was advocating a gradual and peaceful independence from England. And a third man, a frail, London-trained lawyer whom Gokhale had asked to be part of the transaction.

They sat at an elaborately inlaid table. The maharana asked, "Where is the jewel?"

Kitty took it from her bag and carefully laid it on the table. Even in the dim light it seemed to glow with a fire all its own.

"And where is my apology?" the maharana persisted.

"I have it here," Carrington said, withdrawing an envelope with the king's seal. "An official letter signed by His Majesty King Edward formally apologizing for the part played by the British government in the theft of the stone. And relinquishing any claim to its ownership."

Max stretched forward and shoved the stone across the table so that it landed at its edge, just before the maharana.

The maharana picked up the gem, looking at it wistfully. Shaking his head, he looked at Gokhale and said, "As much as it pains me, I hereby turn over the stone to you and relinquish all legal claim to it."

Gokhale took it and said, "The stone will be taken to Geneva, Switzerland, where it will be placed in the account of the Republic of India, to be retrieved at such a time as that free and independent republic comes into existence. Thus ensuring that Ashoka's ruby will never again become the political tool of ruthless and self-serving men."

Kitty found herself staring at the thin lawyer who sat

humbly, his hands clasped before him. Something about the look in his eyes—so serene and gentle, yet so charismatic—captivated her. She'd never felt such a sense of quiet spirituality in a man before.

As they were leaving the room, she said to Carrington, "I know Tata and Gokhale, but who was the third man?"

"Some fellow who's been rabble-rousing among the Indian community in South Africa for the past few years. A bit of a nuisance, really, but Gokhale supports him and insisted he be part of this. I believe his name is Gandhi." He glanced at his notebook. "Mohandas K. Gandhi."

EPILOGUE

Kitty and Max stepped through the outer archway. There, stretching before them, at the end of a long, fountained walk, was the Taj Mahal. It glistened in the midst of a peacock sky like a shimmering white jewel. Fluid, graceful, as soft and rounded as a woman's body. A dream in white marble. It seemed impossible that anything so exquisite could be fashioned from cold stone.

Max took Kitty's hand. Together they descended the front stair to the pathway below. The monument—the tomb the Mughal emperor, Shah Jahan, had built for his beloved wife Mumtaz—drew them toward it with a pull that seemed to offer the promise of eternal love.

They walked through the crowds of tourists, oblivious to them. The spirit of love was palpable. Over-whelming. Kitty felt it fill her heart. The privilege of being here with the man she loved enveloped her with a sense of magnificence. Of awe and wonder and joy.

They'd been married in a church in Udaipur the week before with the maharana and Carrington in at-tendance. Kitty's only sorrow was that Victoria couldn't be there to share her happiness. On the way to Agra for their honeymoon, they'd discovered that yesterday was a particularly auspicious day for weddings. Marriage parties abounded, and the villages were decked out in garlands of flowers, as the brides and grooms paraded through the streets. Impulsively, they'd joined in the festivities and had renewed their vows in a Hindu cere-mony, making their union complete.

Now Max turned to his bride with a loving look. "They say Shah Jahan couldn't forget Mumtaz because she was the most gifted of all women in the art of love."

A thrill rushed through Kitty, thinking of the night to come. When she would lie in his arms and love him in the shadow of the Taj Mahal. She wrapped her arms around his neck and kissed him. "Maybe she learned a thing or two in Khajuraho," she teased. "Which re-minds me. You promised to teach me a thing or two."

He swept her with a scalding look.

"I promise to be an apt pupil." She added. "In fact, I'm hungry to learn!"

"Then how can I resist?" he grinned.

As they proceeded toward the fountains, arm in arm, they came upon a group of men huddled excitedly over a newspaper. Max steered them toward the group and asked in Hindi, "May we have a look?"

When they handed him the paper, he and Kitty read

the headline. A Frenchman named Blériot had just the day before flown the English Channel in thirty-six minutes, astonishing the world and winning the prize offered by the *Daily Mail*. The international press was heralding the flight as a triumph in aviation. England, her unassailable borders no longer secure, was scrambling to catch up in the race to rule the skies.

Max handed the paper back and turned to Kitty. "It should have been you."

But Kitty found to her surprise that she felt no hint of jealousy that a Frenchman was taking credit for her feat. "We shall always know I did it first." Pressing her cheek to his shoulder, she added, "Besides, I'd much rather be here with you."

"We could always tell them."

She shook her head. "They'd never believe us. But it's more than that. I wanted to be the first in order to prove myself to the world. To a world where I didn't belong. I know that now. Just as I know that I no longer have to prove anything to anyone."

"You never did."

"I didn't know that until you made me feel it."

As the sun continued to set, the Taj Mahal took on an iridescent glow, like an opal flashing in the sun. They found a marble bench away from the crowd and sat watching, their arms wrapped about each other.

They stayed and watched long after the crowds had left. Until the pink glow turned lavender, then deepened to violet. Until the sky grew dark and the stars appeared. Diamonds in a velvet sky. Until the moon cast its mystical light on the monument and it took on the aspect of a palace fashioned from fairy dust.

Alone together, they felt the spirit of the great ruler's

love and longing for his wife—an intimate reflection of
their own experiences along the way.

"I've just made a remarkable discovery," she told
him.

"What's that?"

"I love India!"

He looked at her and smiled, as if he'd known it
would come to this all along.

"Ever since Ngar proved your faith in him, the bad
memories have lost their hold on me. I look at everything—the people, the contradictions, the wonders and
mysticism—and none of it threatens me. Instead, it
seems that I'm being embraced by all of it. Welcomed.
But particularly here." She sighed. "I suppose all lovers
feel that the Taj was put here just for them. To show us
all how precious love is."

"There's a hill over there," Max said, pointing,
"where Shah Jahan was imprisoned by his son. He
stayed there for years, gazing into the distance at this
tomb where his wife was buried. Waiting to die."

"So he could join her." She sat quietly for a moment.
"I know what it's like to be without you. And, when I
thought you were dead, I wanted to die to be with
you."

"I wonder," he mused.

"What?"

"If we all have to learn that the hard way."

"I suppose the point is that we *do* learn. And speaking of learning . . . wasn't there something you
promised to teach me?"

He grinned, his teeth looking wolfishly white in the
moonlight. "Come along, then."

He led her to the right of the Taj Mahal and down a

flight of stone steps, where a smaller replica of the tomb stood in the shadows. Removing a key from his pocket, he inserted it into the lock.

"What are you doing?" she asked, looking over her shoulder to make sure no night guard spotted them.

"It's all right. The British government uses this as a guest house for important officials. Carrington arranged for us to have it for the night."

"You mean we're going to sleep here?"

He arched a brow. "I wouldn't plan on getting much sleep, if I were you."

His veiled promise had lit a fire in her. She couldn't wait to see what amorous play he might have in mind.

Throwing open the huge arched doorways, they found a large bedroom inside. Max lit a candle and they saw a large bed facing the doorway. Kitty fell onto it and, propping herself up into the pillows, gasped. The archway formed a perfect frame for the view beyond— the Taj Mahal gleaming softly in the rising moon.

Leaving the doors open, Max settled down beside her, stretching out on the bed and pulling her into his arms. They lay quietly for some time, watching as the moonlight shifted on the graceful monument beyond. Feeling once again the romance and mystery seep into their souls.

"I hate for this to end," she said. "I want to stay here, just like this, forever."

"It hasn't ended yet. In fact, we've hardly begun."

"But when it does end . . . what then?"

He was silent for a few moments. "I'd like to stay in India," he said at last. "Some of Ngar's men went about it in the wrong way, but I still believe in the same cause I always did. I'd like for us to work for the peaceful independence of India—toward the day when the Blood of India will be returned to its rightful place once again. An India that's open to everyone." He paused. "Would you mind so much?"

"Not anymore. Being in India again has changed me somehow. I'm not sure I realized it until now. I'm not certain I can explain *how* it's changed me. When I lost you the first time, it was as if I lost a part of myself. But I've found her again. The child I was. A sense of innocence, and with it a realization of what's really important. I made my way alone—and yet, I was only half of what I could be. What I am with you. I've found the answer to my eternal quest. That nagging feeling that I was searching for something I couldn't find. I was confused for so long about where I belonged and who I was. But now I know. I belong with you. India gave me that. India is home. So, yes. We'll stay." After a brief pause, she added, "Besides, I'd like to do what I can for Victoria's children."

"As I'd like to make it up to Charles for all he's lost."

"Perhaps you could ask him to come and join us. That way, the two of you could get to know one another again. Be true brothers, as you should have all along."

His arm tightened about her. "I love you more than it's possible to say."

"I waited so long to hear you say it. But now . . . all I want is for you to show me."

He turned to her with a grin. "I should warn you. It's a dangerous path you're treading. Once you've embarked, there's no turning back."

"I don't know," she said, her lips nuzzling his. "It seems to me the real danger is opening your heart to love. But then, if it wasn't dangerous, it wouldn't be any fun."

He captured her lips with his and tumbled her back into the bed to show her just how much fun the danger of true love could be.

ACKNOWLEDGMENTS

My heartfelt appreciation goes to the following special people: my husband, Bill, without whom this book wouldn't exist; my daughter, Janie, for being the best daughter anyone could wish for; my editors: Beth de Guzman for all her support and encouragement, and Wendy Chen for all her hard work, and with warm wishes for a happy new life; my ever-wonderful and effervescent agent, Meg Ruley; Mike Kalm and Janet Mann for their delightful company in India; and Robin Karis for sending me the poem at the beginning of the book, and for all her kind assistance. Finally, to the one who helped me to see India with new eyes and who shared with me the golden enchantment of the Taj Mahal.

ABOUT THE AUTHOR

KATHERINE O'NEAL is the daughter of a U.S. Air Force pilot and a fiercely British artist who met in India in the fifties. The family traveled extensively and lived for many years in Asia. Katherine is married to William Arnold, a noted film critic and author of the bestselling books *Shadowland* and *China Gate*—a man she feels makes her heroes pale in comparison. They make their home in Seattle, but continue the tradition of travel whenever possible. Their daughter, Janie, spent a year in France as an exchange student.

Katherine loves to hear from readers. Please write to her at:

P.O. Box 2452
Seattle, WA 98111-2452

and enclose a self-addressed stamped envelope for a response and news of forthcoming books.